A NECESSARY KILL

JAMES P. SUMNER

A NECESSARY KILL

THIRD EDITION PUBLISHED IN 2021 BY BOTH BARRELS PUBLISHING
COPYRIGHT © JAMES P. SUMNER 2017

EDITING AND COVER DESIGN BY: BOTHBARRELSAUTHORSERVICES.COM

ISBNS:
978-1-914191-18-3 (PAPERBACK)

VISIT THE AUTHOR'S WEBSITE: JAMESPSUMNER.COM

Where we go international...

A NECESSARY KILL

ADRIAN HELL: BOOK 5

1

ADRIAN HELL

The world's gone to shit, and all I did was stand there and watch. Do you have any idea what it feels like to believe you could've stopped something bad but didn't? It's the worst feeling there is, and I wouldn't wish it on anyone.

That was almost a fortnight ago. Since then, I've been doing the whole *Kung Fu* thing—walking the earth on my own, thinking about shit. Oh, and looking over my shoulder every two minutes. My paranoia's working overtime on account of the biggest intelligence agency in the world wanting me dead.

I put my hand to the collar of my shirt and reach inside to touch the flash drive I have around my neck, checking for the billionth time that it's still there. It contains all the evidence GlobaTech obtained from the NSA's and CIA's servers. It has proof that the CIA doctored intelligence reports to frame both GlobaTech and me, implicating us in the terrorist attack.

Bastards.

And not only were the terrorists CIA pawns used to orchestrate the devastating attack, but the trail of information and money all leads back to one man.

Charles Cunningham.

The sixth, if you want to be fancy. And yes, it's the same Charles Cunningham currently sitting in the Oval Office of the White House. I'm still not one hundred percent clear why he wanted to blow up half the world, but I intend to ask the sonofabitch before I kill him.

He's got the whole world fooled into believing he's everyone's savior, but secretly, he still has control of the Cerberus satellite. He told everyone he had personally decommissioned it because of a *vulnerability* that allowed it to be hacked by the bad guys and used to launch all the nukes that caused this shitstorm.

He's still holding us all to ransom, and everyone thinks he's the goddamn hero.

I have had some good news, however. And God knows I've been due some. GlobaTech has some documents that prove Cunningham is behind all this. Ryan Schultz, my favorite ex-secretary of defense, is running things over there now, and the lucky bastard has Josh by his side. My former partner in crime is doing the heavy lifting for GlobaTech, in terms of its logistics and resources. His most recent pet project was to put together an elite unit that can help me in my fight against Cunningham.

Apparently, some engineer who worked on Cerberus unknowingly had classified paperwork that detailed the requests for the hidden extras that allowed this tragedy to happen. And the president signed them. Now we can prove he knew about the so-called vulnerability inside the satellite all along, which immediately brings into question the speech he gave twenty-four hours after the attack, publicly claiming ignorance of it all. And if people starting questioning *that*, they're more likely to pay attention to the evidence around my neck.

Then, slowly but surely, the walls will tumble down.

The president knows I have this information, but my threat of releasing it to the media should, in theory, stop them from trying to kill me. I just need to stay alive long enough to take out Cunningham and undo whatever plans he's put in motion. I can't exactly *un*-detonate a nuke, but at least I can stop him from doing anything else.

Well, that's the plan, anyway. But things like this take time, patience, and diplomacy—none of which I've had the good fortune to be blessed with.

I'm probably the last person qualified to raise an argument on morality, but Cunningham's a piece of shit. He painted me as the enemy. He was behind hurting the people I care about. And he masterminded the largest terrorist attack in history.

There are two Berettas at my back that have something to say to him about all of that.

But, as I'm sure you can appreciate, this isn't exactly a standard hit. He's the president. He's so well protected, he's the metaphor people use when they're describing something that's incredibly well protected. And with Josh working his way up the corporate ladder at GlobaTech, he's too visible to risk being seen helping me. He can't afford to be linked to what's about to happen.

I'm on my own. And without his expertise and guidance, I'm free to do this however the hell I want.

What could possibly go wrong?

I've had to drop off the grid, as they say, while I put together a plan. Being at the top of the CIA's hit list isn't nearly as glamourous as it sounds, and the last thing I need is those assholes breathing down my neck every five minutes. So, that means minimal contact with Josh and absolutely no contact with Tori.

I really miss her.

After that meeting last week at GlobaTech's headquarters, I said my goodbyes and disappeared. Even Josh doesn't know where I am. I've communicated with him once since then, and that was just so he could tell me about the new information he's uncovered.

Sheriff Raynor took Tori back to Devil's Spring. I asked her to get The Ferryman back up and running for me while I was gone. She has all the money she needs to do it, and she practically ran the place anyway, so it shouldn't be much of a stretch for her. Plus, it'll keep her occupied, so she doesn't drive herself crazy thinking about me and what I'm doing.

She was sad when I left. I tried to comfort her by saying it would all be okay, and I'd be back before she knew it.

I hate lying to her.

I'm about to kill the president of the United States. The leader of the free world. That isn't the kind of job you come back from. I know it. Josh knows it. Hell, I reckon even *Tori* knows it, deep down. But my words of comfort were what she needed to hear, and I left her safe in the knowledge we wouldn't be apart for long, which was what I wanted.

As for me, I've worked my way slowly across the country, and I'm currently basking in the somewhat uncharacteristic heat of Bangor, Maine. Apart from my Berettas and my necklace of evidence, I have only my shoulder bag with me, which contains my favorite leather jacket, some ammo, and a burner phone.

I came to Maine because even *I* know going after the president on my own is stupid. Usually, Josh and I would take on anyone and everyone together, without hesitation. But Josh isn't here. Not this time. And this contract is big. It'll be my magnum opus. I guess it could also be my swan song. If working with Josh all these years has taught me one thing, it's not to let pride get in the way of a good kill.

So, I'm here looking for help.

As time passes, you get to know the people in your line of work. Josh has an entire network of facilitators, all of whom manage contracts for people like me. But while he knows the guys *behind* the guys with guns, I know a few of the guys with guns. I don't mean to sound elitist, but I've made a point over the years to establish and maintain a courteous relationship with a few assassins who, either by my own reckoning or their justified reputation, will be around for a while. I'm not the only one who thinks I'm the best of the best. I guess you could say my little black book contains the best of the rest.

One guy in particular lives here in Bangor. Last I heard, he was working exclusively for a local mob boss. Like me, this guy would probably be classed as an old-timer. In our line of work, you get that title one of two ways—by being good or by being smart. You rarely get both. Look at me. I'm not smart. That's what Josh was for. This guy's a decent professional but has purposefully kept himself low-key. He's never really had his skills tested, so he's never had cause to evolve or hone his craft.

But... the guy is smart. He's never taken risks or splashed any cash. Where possible, he's opted for exclusivity, which gives him security and protection.

No, I don't expect this guy to help me. But I reckon he's a good place to start if I want to find someone who will.

2

ADRIAN HELL

I'm walking down Broadway. It's pushing seventy degrees, despite the noticeable wind. The sun's navigating the gaps between the scattered clouds overhead. I'm comfortable without my jacket. I picked up some clothes from a discount store back in Indiana. I know I could probably buy the entire store, but I'm living off the cash in my pocket, and I survived off a limited budget for years.

I'm wearing a red and blue flannel shirt, with the sleeves rolled up to just above my elbows and a couple of buttons unfastened at the top. It's not what I would normally wear, but I'm on the run. I don't want to look like I normally do.

My hair's grown a little too. I have more beard than stubble now, which is irritating the shit out of me. My hair's grown thicker than it has in years. I guess I should seek comfort in knowing I can still actually grow it.

I walk past a furniture store and glance in the window at my reflection. I'm unrecognizable, even to myself.

And now I have *Streets of Philadelphia* by Bruce Springsteen in my head...

The last known address of the guy I'm here to see is a restaurant he used to work at between contracts. Now he works for the local mob. I don't know if he'll still be here, but it's the only starting point I have.

After a few minutes, I see the place across the street. The parking lot out front looks empty. I cross over and head for the main entrance, push the door open, and step inside.

It's a Chinese bar and restaurant. The interior looks like someone has watched a bunch of movies set in China and tried to copy the culture here. There's a large sculpture of a red and gold dragon in front of me and detailed lanterns hanging overhead to conceal the actual light fixtures. The entrance is on the left of the building, and the interior stretches away both in front of me and to the right, with the dining area in the former area and the bar in the latter.

I catch the eye of a waitress behind the counter and walk over. I see booths lining both the side by the window and the opposite wall, which is red and has hand-drawn images of dragons and swords hanging on it. There are seven people seated—a young couple on my left, one guy sitting alone in the middle, and a group of four men in one of the booths by the window.

I take a seat at the bar and rest my bag against the stool by my feet. The waitress comes over and smiles. She's Caucasian and can't be older than twenty-five, with shoulder-length dark hair and a nice smile.

"Will you be eating with us today, sir?" she asks.

I smile. "No, thanks. I'm actually looking for an old friend. He used to work here. I don't know if he still does."

"I can ask around in the back for you. What's your friend's name?"

7

"Ashton Case."

The split-second flash of concern on her face tells me everything I need to know. She momentarily glances over at the table of four men, which I notice but ignore for now. She recovers quickly.

"Oh, Ashton? Yeah, he... ah... he doesn't work here anymore," she says. "I'm sorry."

Yeah, right.

"Uh-huh. When did he leave?"

"Oh, it was a while ago now... I *think*."

I can only assume she's being vague because she doesn't know how much contact I've had with him, nor how recently. I've said I'm an old friend, which suggests we *do* speak, but she doesn't want to commit to a time frame in case I realize she's lying. I'll play it cool for now. I don't want to push things.

"Okay, not to worry. D'you think I could get a drink while I'm here?"

She smiles again, relaxing. "Sure thing. What would you like?"

I glance behind her and spot a row of Bud in one of the fridges. I gesture to them with a nod. "I'll have a bottle, please."

She turns and crouches, grabbing a beer. I smile at the welcome hiss as she unscrews the top and drops it in a metal container beside the cash register.

She slides it across the counter to me. "That'll be three-fifty."

I take out a five-dollar bill and hand it to her. "Keep the change."

She smiles, and I take a much-needed swig of the drink. I catch her gaze flick over to the table of four again. I'm leaning against the bar, facing the seating area with the window booths away to my right. I see the hushed mutterings among the men and the discreet looks I'm getting, which aren't actually as discreet as they might think.

They're getting ready to make their move. I should probably address this issue now, to see if I can stop it from getting out of hand.

I look at the waitress and smile, trying to appear sympathetic. "Look, I'm not here to cause trouble, I promise. I know who Ashton works for, and I know what he does for a living. I also know he worked here on occasion. I'm genuinely an old acquaintance, and if he *is* here, I just wanna talk to him. No fuss."

The waitress sighs and shifts uncomfortably on the spot, looking unsure. I understand her dilemma. On the one hand, she probably believes me, which she has every reason to do. I'm not lying. On the other hand, she's probably been told to deny all knowledge if anyone asks about Case and to inform him or his boss of any inquiries.

I see movement to my right. I turn my head slightly and watch the men stand, organize themselves, straighten their clothes, and walk slowly toward me. They fan into a line as they approach the bar.

The waitress looks afraid, which gives me yet more unspoken information. She knows Case is probably in the back, watching this on a security feed. My guess is she alerted him to my presence by pressing a silent alarm hidden behind the bar.

The four guys now in front of me are a laughable attempt at contract muscle—further proof this place is owned by the mob. I'm guessing the waitress is reasonably new because she looks scared. She probably knows what this place is like but hasn't worked here long enough to see it with her own eyes. She doesn't have the tired confidence people exposed to this life usually have—that almost reluctant feeling of security. The belief you're untouchable because of who you work for.

I look at the line of ass-clowns, deciphering the silent messages their bodies are sending me. The guy on the far right, for example, is slightly favoring his right leg. Judging by the size of his waist, which is far from thin, I'm guessing... a weak knee.

Then there's the second guy from the left—the tallest of the group but no bigger than me. He's practically laughing. He thinks he's the big dick around here. The leader of the pack. Maybe he thinks his height makes him more important than the others. He's the prick I'm going to hit first.

And hardest.

I look back at the waitress. "All right, this was obviously a bad idea. You should probably take yourself someplace else for a moment or two. I promise I'll keep the damage to a minimum. I don't want you getting in trouble with your boss."

She furrows her brow with confusion, wondering why I'm talking like *I'll* be causing damage when I'm outnumbered four to one.

Bless her.

I pick up my bottle and take another sip of beer as I plan my first five moves.

I doubt I'll need more than five.

Fighting is like chess. Plan ahead and you've won before you even start.

The tall one inches forward. "You need to leave. You're in the wrong place, asshole."

"Actually, Princess, the fact you four are threatening me kinda says I'm in the *right* place, and you just *want* me to leave. That isn't happening. Just save yourselves a lot of time and suffering and get Ashton Case for me. I'm here as a friend—got my little white flag and everything. There's no need for this. I've got enough on my plate without having to waste my energy on the Four Horsemen of the Apothecary."

The guy frowns.

I sigh. "Apothecary. It's like a drug store."

I pause to give him chance to work it out, but he's not getting it.

I shake my head, like I'm addressing a child who doesn't understand why he's being told off. "I'm insinuating you're not threatening..."

He continues to stare at me with a vacant expression on his face.

I sigh again. "Okay, never mind."

I push myself off my stool and thrust my forehead into the nose of the guy in front of me, shattering the cartilage. The crack and subsequent squelch of exploding blood are audible and a little gross.

First move.

As he's falling backward, I bring my leg up slightly, then whip it straight out, hitting the man on my far right on the side of his knee. He drops to the floor and rolls around, clutching at it.

Second move.

I grab my beer bottle by the neck and flip it in my hand, spilling its contents on the floor. I look at the guy second from the right and quickly smash it down like a hammer on the top of his head. The glass shatters on impact, and he drops to the floor.

It's not like in the movies, either, where they use that thin, fake shit. This is thick, heavy, real glass, and it requires a ridiculous amount of force to break it. And doing so over his skull will leave him feeling unhappy for a while.

Third move.

I spin counterclockwise, raising my arm in anticipation of the remaining guy on the far left engaging his brain and deciding he should do something. I block his inevitable punch, deflecting it with my forearm. As I spin, my right arm is already coming around, fist clenched. It flies through the gap caused by the deflection and connects firmly with his jaw. He falls away, bouncing off the surface of the bar and hitting the floor.

Fourth move.

Using my momentum to keep the turn going, I bring my left elbow up and whip it backward, connecting with the first guy, who's just getting to his feet and thinking about doing something silly. It catches him on the cheekbone and puts him back down, hard.

Fifth move.

Job done.

"I thought it was you," I hear a voice say behind me.

I turn around to see Ashton Case standing at the side of the bar, near the entrance, with the waitress next to him. He's a tall man with broad shoulders. A little chubbier than I remember, but then again, I haven't seen him in a long time. He's clean-shaven, with a rough face and dark eyes. His voice is gravelly in the way only smoking forty a day can achieve.

"Didn't recognize you with the beard at first," he continues, gesturing to his own face. "How have you been, Adrian?"

"Been better," I say with a shrug. I gesture to the pile of bodies on the floor with my thumb. "These guys with you?"

He waves his hand dismissively. "Nah. We all work for the same man, but those assholes have nothin' to do with me."

I walk over to him and we shake hands.

"Whatever it is must be bad if you've come here," he says. "Drink?"

"Please. I dropped my last one."

He smiles. "Yeah, I saw. Come on. We'll go in the back." He looks at the waitress. "Naomi, sweetheart, would you mind bringing me and my friend a couple of cold ones? I'll be in my office."

Naomi smiles. "Sure thing, Ash." She looks at me apologetically. "Sorry about before. I wasn't sure—"

I hold my hand up, cutting her off. "No need to apologize. You did well."

She heads back behind the bar. I retrieve my bag from over by my stool, then follow Case through a door beside the restaurant's seating area.

We walk up some stairs and through another door, which leads to a studio apartment. It has a basic layout but is exquisitely furnished. There's a large leather sofa with its back to the door, facing a flat screen TV mounted on the opposite wall. Over to the left is a four-poster bed with closets on either side. Across from that, by the window, is an office area filled with computer equipment and smaller screens. Next to the door, on the near wall, is a bathroom.

"Nice place," I say, impressed.

Case shrugs. "It's minimal but effective. I eat downstairs when I'm hungry. When I'm here, I either sleep or shit. What more do you need, right?"

"Fair point."

We walk across the room and both sit on the sofa.

"So, what brings you here, Adrian?"

I fix him with a look with my tired eyes. I take a deep breath, scratch the hair on my throat, and proceed to tell him everything that's happened in the last couple of weeks.

3

ADRIAN HELL

My story took a while and three beers apiece, but he's all caught up now.

"So, that's about it," I say. "What do you think?"

Case is sitting in front of me, staring at the wall, his jaw slack and eyes wide. I watch him for a moment, waiting for some kind of response, but nothing is forthcoming.

I know *that* feeling.

I smile. "Yeah, welcome to *my* life."

He looks at me. "How the fuck did you wind up in the middle of all *that*?"

I shrug. "A whole lot of bad luck, mostly. End of the day, we might try to leave the life, but the life rarely leaves us, Ash."

"No kiddin'. So, all of what you just said is on the level?"

I nod. "I'm afraid so. I had a front row seat for the apocalypse. The media are simply calling it 4/17."

Case shrugs his shoulders. "You know it's bad when people refer to a tragedy by its date."

"Exactly. But the damage the attacks caused isn't limited to the physical fallout. The half of the world *not* decimated is still in danger of being corrupted and... *cleansed* by Cunningham's master plan."

Case shakes his head slowly with disbelief. "And you're *sure* the president is behind this?"

I pull the flash drive from inside my shirt and show it to him. "Got it all here. My next move is to stop him, so the guys over at GlobaTech Industries can focus on fixing the world and getting things back to the way they were. Or better. You never know..."

Case stands and paces across the room, staring at the floor with his hands in his pockets.

"And how do you intend to do that?" he asks. "I mean, it's the president of the United fucking States, Adrian. What're you gonna do?" He scoffs. "*Kill* him?"

I fix him with an unblinking stare but say nothing.

"Holy shit. You're gonna try to kill him, aren't you?"

I nod. "There's no other way. He's too powerful. He's got the CIA running interference for him, and he's got all three branches of the military at his disposal, should another country get any ideas. Not to mention he still has control of Cerberus. No, the only way to end this is to put him down."

"But Adrian... I mean... that's an impossible shot, even for you!"

I shrug. "Booth and Oswald managed it."

"Yeah, but they didn't have the obstacles we face today—the security, the technology. You won't get within fifty miles of the guy if you have a weapon. Christ, in your situation, you'll be lucky if you get within a hundred miles!"

I take a deep breath and sip my beer. "I know. You're right. That's why I'm here. I need help, Ash."

He shakes his head and sits back down. "Uh-uh. No way are you dragging me into this shit, you crazy bastard!"

"Heh, relax—I'm not here for that. I figured you were either too smart or too much of a pussy to sign on for this."

He shakes his head and smiles. "Hey, fuck you, all right?"

I hold my hands up. "Okay, so you're too smart. But I did *kinda* hope you'd know a few people who maybe aren't as smart and might be interested?"

He strokes his chin thoughtfully. "Hmm. What kind of payday are we talkin' here?"

I shrug. "Honestly? I hadn't thought about it. But if we pull it off... let's say twenty million for whoever survives."

"Jesus! Where are you gonna get *that* kind of money?"

"You let me worry about that. I had a pretty big payday a couple of years back. I'm good for it. Can you point me in the right direction, Ash?"

He falls silent, and I give him time to think. It's a lot to ask. I know that. I stand, beer in hand, and pace around the apartment, occasionally glancing out the windows.

"You got any ideas as to how you intend to do it?" he asks me.

I look back at him from across the room. "You're probably best off not knowing that much about it. Plausible deniability an' all that. But Ash, you gotta know that if I do this, at some point, somebody's gonna trace it all back to this conversation. The less you know, the better. I just need a few names, then you'll never see me again."

Case nods. "All right. I reckon I know a couple of people who might be interested..." He moves over to the desk, opens a drawer, and takes out a pad and pen. He leans over and scribbles down some information. After a minute, he tears off the page, walks over, and hands it to me. "There you go. Four names."

I look at the list. I've heard of one of them.

I glance up at him and frown. "Are these newbies? I don't recognize any of these names, except The European—and he's a bit of a prick, if I'm honest."

He chuckles. "Yeah, he can be. But he's a damn good killer with very few morals. As for the other three, no, they're not new to the game. They're exceptionally talented in their own... *unique* way. But I should warn you, Adrian. Some of these folks are a little... *eccentric*, shall we say. That last name, especially. Maybe use 'em as plan B, okay?"

I stare at the list. "Jesus, they even *sound* a little crazy."

"Ha! A little? Adrian, they haven't just roamed off the reservation. They've left the goddamn planet! But I figured you might find use for someone who thinks outside the box, y'know."

He smiles and I laugh with him. "Yeah, it might come in handy. Listen, thanks for this, Ash. If I make it through this, I'll owe you."

"Hey, you owe me whether you make it through or not. I ain't gonna forget this."

We shake hands, and I fold the paper up and tuck it into my pocket.

Well, this is a step forward. I have a few names of people who might be up for helping me out. The next step is to—

There's an urgent knocking on the door. We exchange a glance. I instinctively move my hand behind me, feeling the cold reassurance of my Beretta on my fingertips.

"Who is it?" asks Case.

"I-it's Naomi," comes the flustered reply.

He moves quickly to the door, opening it wide. The waitress from downstairs is standing there, looking concerned.

"What is it?"

She glances at me before replying. "There are some men downstairs, asking for him." She points at me.

I frown. "What do they look like?"

She shrugs. "Just normal guys. Black suits, sunglasses. Three of them. Big, black SUV parked out front too."

Shit.

"Ash, that's the CIA." I fight to keep any panic from my voice. "I don't know how they've found me, but I need a way out of here, now!"

After what I've just told him, I can see he understands how bad this is. He turns, quickly looking around his apartment. His eyes settle on the far corner by the computers.

"The window." He points. "Directly below it is the canopy over the entrance."

I move over to the window and glance down. The canopy is maybe seven feet below, and it's a good eight feet from the ground.

This is going to hurt, isn't it?

Well, never mind that. Focus, Adrian. Come on!

Right, I'm going to need a ride...

I look back over my shoulder, intending to ask, and see a set of keys flying toward me. I react fast, flinching slightly as I catch them. I stare at them, then back at Case.

"It's a black Audi , parked around back," he says. "Scratch it and I'll shoot you. Return it first chance you get."

I smile. "Thanks, Ash. For everything."

He nods. "Now get the hell out of here, you crazy sonofabitch."

I stuff the keys in my pocket, hook my bag over both shoulders, and slide the window up. The warm breeze hits me as I poke my head outside. I grab the frame and climb out, one leg at a time, resting my weight on the wall. With one last look at Case, I drop down. I land on the canopy, which is made of a thick plastic sheet, and bounce off it as if it were a trampoline. I spin around as I fall and hit the ground face-down, like I'm doing a push-up.

I grunt from the impact, but I can't allow myself time to recover. I spring to my feet and dash around the side of the restaurant to the parking lot. There're only a handful of cars here, so it's not hard to find Case's Audi. It's a convertible TT, and the top's already down.

I run over as I'm unhooking my bag from my shoulders. I throw it onto the back seat as I jump over the door and land hard behind the wheel. I scramble in my pocket for the key and fire up the engine. I gun the gas and speed off, the tires screeching and leaving their marks on the blacktop behind me. I draw level with the entrance just as the three G-men burst out onto the street, guns drawn.

I duck as low as I can while turning right, narrowly missing an oncoming car. The needle's pushing eighty as the first shots ring out. The high-pitched ping of the bullets ricochet around me. One cracks the door mirror next to me.

I wince. Ash is gonna kill me—assuming these assholes don't.

The gunfire stops as quickly as it started, and I sit up again, focusing on the road. I glance in my rearview and see the black SUV swing into view behind me, quickly gathering speed and closing the gap between us.

Up ahead, I see a junction. The sign tells me I can take a left and join I-95, which I'm pretty sure takes me west toward Massachusetts. That works out well. The first name on my list has a last known address of Manchester, New Hampshire, which is over that way.

Unfortunately, I need to shake off these shit-kickers following me first.

Ahead of me, the lights are turning red.

There's not much traffic. Screw it.

I navigate the lanes and approach the intersection with the needle pushing a hundred. I weave between two cars and slam on the brakes, making a hard left. The tires screech loudly again, and smoke builds up behind the car. I level it out and step back on the gas, merging onto I-95 at speed.

Behind me, the SUV is keeping pace, relentless in its pursuit.

I need to get rid of these guys—and fast. It won't be long before they get their friends to join them, and even I know I can't take on the entire CIA all at once.

The road ahead is as straight as an arrow and reasonably clear, so I ease off the gas a little and allow them to close the gap. I can see the look of grim determination on the driver's face in my rearview.

The lane next to me is empty...

I whip the wheel to the right and stamp hard on the brakes, causing the Audi to spin clockwise, off to the side. The SUV shoots past me. I quickly turn the wheel the opposite way, fighting to regain control of the vehicle, which I manage to do as I'm completing a full circle. The back end fishtails, but I straighten up and position myself directly behind the CIA agents.

Phew!

I lean forward and reach behind me, taking out one of my Berettas. I rest my hand on the top of the windshield and fire five rounds in quick succession. At this speed, aiming is tricky, but all bar one hit the mark.

The SUV swerves uncontrollably as the bullets impact the back of it, cracking the rear windshield. The driver didn't expect me to shoot at them.

Seriously, I figured they would've done *some* research on me. I'm a little insulted!

They regain control and move to the left, slowing to draw level with me. I think they're going to try ramming me. Given I'm doing a hundred and ten miles per hour, and they're in a much larger, heavier vehicle, that isn't likely to end well for me.

I move alongside them and smile at the agent riding shotgun. He rolls down his window and leans out, slowly bringing his weapon into view. Checking that the road immediately ahead is clear, I whip my own gun up and stare at him. I see in his eyes the exact moment he realizes he wasn't quick enough to beat me.

I aim just to the right of where I want to hit, to compensate for the speed I'm traveling, and pull the trigger once.

The noise is drowned out by the roaring wind, but the effects are just as devastating. The agent's head snaps back violently as the bullet strikes him between the eyes. Again, the vehicle swerves. The driver struggles to maintain control as the dead agent's body lurches backward from the impact, hitting him.

I know they'll be distracted for a few more seconds, so this is my chance...

I slam on the brakes and push myself up slightly in my seat. I keep one hand on the wheel, so I stay straight while I aim. As the SUV carries on ahead, I fire twice, hitting the front tire with the second round.

The rubber disintegrates almost immediately. The SUV jolts violently, then slides sideways and flips over, rolling away from me. It smashes into three other vehicles. The sound of metal tearing and colliding with more metal is ferociously loud, grating through me like nails on a chalkboard.

I speed up, navigating the minefield of debris scattering across the interstate until I draw level with the SUV. It's come to a stop, spinning on its roof, away from the other cars. I bring my gun up as I move past, trying to time my shot with the revolution of the SUV...

BANG!

I fire once as the exposed gas tank presents itself. The resulting explosion shakes the ground around me, filling my rearview with smoke and flames. I drop the gun on the passenger seat again as I refocus on the road. The acrid smell of burning fuel is strong in the air.

In the distance, the faint sound of sirens drifts across the interstate.

Time for me to be somewhere else, I think...

Traffic is slowing to a crawl as people on both sides of the road stop to look at the remains of the SUV, barely visible among the flames. I weave through and take the first exit.

I need to ditch this car and swap it for something less conspicuous. Aside from a few bullet holes, it's still in good condition. I'll call Case once I reach New Hampshire and tell him where his wheels are.

I just hope the assholes who were chasing me didn't call back to the mothership with my whereabouts before they blew up.

How the hell did they even find me? I've been so careful.

Well, no sense worrying about that now. I've bought myself a few hours, at least. I need to get another car and track down the first name on this list. I don't have time to waste.

4

MEANWHILE...

President Cunningham was sitting at the head of a long, polished table in the Situation Room, underneath the West Wing of the White House, meeting with members of his National Security Council. Opposite him, mounted on the wall, was a large display screen, currently switched off. He leaned back in his chair, listening to the discussion as he took a sip from his bottle of water.

On his immediate left was Elaine Phillips, the secretary of state. She was a strong woman in her early fifties with graying blonde hair. She was known for being forthright and direct. Cunningham held her in high regard. She was strong-willed, frightfully intelligent, and widely respected by both parties. He knew he couldn't simply replace her the way he had many of the others. Consequently, he exercised caution whenever she was present at meetings because she wasn't privy to his ongoing agenda.

To her left was General Matthews, sitting straight, hands

clasped on the table in front of him, wearing a mixed expression on his face that was difficult to read.

Sitting across from him was Gerald Heskith, Cunningham's chief of staff. He was a loyal and long-standing friend who had been instrumental not only in getting him elected but also in helping him shape his vision for a new future. He was a little overweight, with the excess sitting primarily on his gut. He was a highly intelligent man, and many within the administration believed him to be a natural successor to Cunningham when the time came.

On Heskith's right was the secretary of defense, Bruce Fielding. He was also committed to helping President Cunningham usher in a new era of peace. He had been brought in to replace Ryan Schultz, whom Cunningham had felt wasn't the right fit.

Fielding was currently deep in conversation with General Pat Green, Chairman of the Joint Chiefs of Staff, who was sitting at the opposite end of the table, facing the president.

"I understand what you're saying, Pat. I do," said Fielding, his voice deep and authoritative. "But there's no sense in sending troops overseas at this stage. GlobaTech Industries has it covered, and I believe our priority should be the ongoing safety of our own citizens."

General Green was used to clashing with Fielding over issues regarding the armed forces. He often felt his advice was redundant or unwanted, despite his position and military history. But in light of recent events, he was struggling to exercise his usual level of diplomacy.

He shook his head. "I can't fathom why you would disagree with me on this. Why sit and wait for any problems to come to us? If we take responsibility and get involved *now*, we can help the countries that need it and directly contribute to the prevention of further conflict."

Both men fell silent, sensing the stalemate.

Cunningham sat forward in his chair, taking a deep breath as he contemplated both viewpoints. Despite completely agreeing with Secretary Fielding—primarily because he had *told* Fielding what to say before the meeting —he knew the importance of keeping up appearances.

He looked to his left. "Elaine, what do you think?"

Secretary Phillips was slightly taken aback. "Mr. President, it's not really my place to comment on matters relating to our country's armed forces. I—"

Cunningham held up his hand. "As my secretary of state, I'm asking for an informed opinion on the current state of foreign diplomacy. Will sending our troops overseas make any significant difference, in your opinion?"

She nodded and took a breath. "At the moment, I think GlobaTech is doing a fantastic job. Aside from the foreign aid and security it's providing, it's the PR equivalent of celebrities visiting an orphanage on Christmas. With both China and Russia so drastically affected by 4/17, the UN peacekeeping force has been crippled. Forgive my frankness, Mr. President, but the way things are right now, we might as well privatize the entire United Nations and give GlobaTech the contract. I don't know what kind of threats our country might face in the future, but I don't think that our immediate involvement would make enough difference to justify it, sir."

Fielding smiled. Phillips cast a quick, apologetic glance to General Green, who looked even more deflated now that his point of view had been debunked by another member of the council.

Cunningham nodded slowly. Secretly, he was happy that

his gamble had paid off and that someone independent to his cause had agreed with his most recent move.

"General Green, I appreciate your concerns and your advice," he said, looking across the group. "But I will not send any of our armed forces overseas at this time. Globa-Tech Industries has the full backing of the White House, and I personally have every confidence it can provide the necessary assistance needed by the affected nations while using its significant security forces to maintain peace."

Green went to say something but stopped himself. The president had spoken, and everyone knew that was the end of the matter. He sat back in his chair and nodded. "Yes, Mr. President."

"Thank you." He paused, then looked over at General Matthews. "Tom, I'd like you to stay for a few minutes to discuss some intelligence reports."

Matthews nodded. "Of course, Mr. President."

"The rest of you, thank you for your time. We're done here."

Heskith remained seated, but the others stood, thanked the president for his time, and left the room.

When the door closed, General Matthews leaned forward in his chair, resting his elbows on the desk. "Mr. President, I—"

"Tom, let me stop you there," said Heskith. "Now isn't the time for excuses or apologies. Do you understand? The president has given you one task, and that's all we're interested in."

Matthews went to reply but refrained. He knew Heskith spoke for the president. Despite feeling undermined, he accepted the fact that he was out of favor right now, which was likely why President Cunningham wanted to keep any direct communication to a minimum.

"Of course," he replied. "Mr. President, for the last forty-eight hours, my team has been using the Cerberus network to locate and track Adrian Hell. A unit intercepted him in Bangor, Maine less than an hour ago."

Cunningham sat up straight in his chair, suddenly interested in the words coming out of the CIA director's mouth. He exchanged a glance with Heskith. "You have him?"

Matthews shifted uncomfortably in his seat. He slid a finger between the collar of his shirt and throat—a subconscious effort to get more oxygen. "Ah... not exactly, sir. No. He managed to escape, but we're confident we'll relocate him. There's only so far he could've—"

Cunningham held up his hand for silence, then rested his head in it and massaged the bridge of his nose between his index finger and thumb. He took a couple of deep breaths, trying to summon a hidden reserve of patience. "So, let me see if I understand this. After that clusterfuck in Prague a few days ago, I—against my better judgment, I might add—gave you full control of the Cerberus satellite with the sole purpose of finding one man and killing him. You found him and sent a team to take him out. Not only did he manage to escape, you're now telling me you can't find him again? Is that right?"

Matthews sighed and nodded. "At the moment, that's where we're at, sir."

Cunningham looked at Heskith, who silently raised an eyebrow. He took another sip of water, then turned back to Matthews. "Okay, here's what's going to happen. Get a unit over to his last known location. Remove any traces of the CIA's involvement in whatever the hell happened that led to him escaping. Then find him again. The next time we speak, Tom, you're going to tell me Adrian Hell is dead. Are we clear?"

Matthews nodded again.

"Good. You don't need me to tell you how close we are to the next phase, Tom. Adrian Hell is the only thing that could potentially stop it from happening, and I can't allow that."

"Of course, Mr. President."

"Okay, we're done here." He looked at his chief of staff. "Gerry, I want you to sit in on this conference call, okay?"

"Yes, Mr. President," he replied.

Matthews stood. "Thank you, Mr. President." He left the room, and the door was closed again behind him.

Heskith got to his feet and walked to the end of the table. He picked up a remote and turned on the large screen facing them.

"Are we good to go?" asked Cunningham.

Heskith pressed a few buttons, looked at the president, and nodded. "We're good, sir."

He sat back down in his seat. After a moment, the screen flickered into life. A man sitting behind a desk appeared on the screen. He was wearing a brown military suit, with medals adorning the left breast. Behind him was a North Korean flag.

"Mr. President," said the man in broken English. "It's been too long... my friend."

5

ADRIAN HELL

19:48 EDT

I left Case's Audi in the parking lot outside a grocery store and *borrowed* an old brown truck that was sitting next to it. I made it to Manchester without further incident and found a no-name, low-rent motel for the night.

The sun's beginning its descent, and the deep orange glow is lighting up the early evening sky. I'm standing on the street corner near the motel, trying to get my bearings. The last known location of the first name on my list is a hospital close to the Notre Dame Bridge, not far from the banks of the Merrimack River. According to a local, whom I asked for directions, it should be on the opposite side of Lafayette Park from where I am now.

Bit strange, though—a hitman working in a hospital.

My spider sense is all over the place. I don't doubt the information Case gave me. Maybe I'm just a little shaken from the unexpected run-in with the CIA? Still, it's not as if I have any alternative options, so I guess I'm going to see the doctor...

I set off walking, make my way through the park, and come out the other side in front of a Dunkin' Donuts. Seriously, I saw, like, eight of these things as I drove through town earlier. I'm astounded there aren't more fat people in New Hampshire!

I see the hospital up ahead on the other side of the street. I sit on a bench and study the building. There's a semicircular driveway in front of the entrance, designed for ambulances to get close to the doors in an emergency. To the left is the parking lot, which looks full. I see some staff loitering outside, having a quick cigarette on their break.

The driveway is under cover where it meets the main doors. I can just about see the curve of a black dome fixed to the brickwork, which houses the security cameras. They'll have a full three-sixty-degree view. No way am I getting inside without being caught on camera. It's not worth the risk to just play it cool and stroll through. I can guarantee every security feed west of Maine will now be monitored around the clock by the CIA—and probably the NSA and Homeland too—following my altercation on the interstate earlier.

No, I need to be discreet if I want to get in there. And how do I find the guy once I do? I doubt he'll be wearing a nametag. I sigh, wishing that I could call Josh and ask him for help. I'm useless on my own when it comes to shit like this.

Ah, screw it.

I cross the street at a casual pace and head through the main entrance. I try to make it look natural as I turn away from the camera so that my face isn't totally visible. If they're running any kind of recognition software, a partial scan will take longer to get any hits, which buys me some time.

Inside, I come to a reception area. The vanilla tiling on the floor stinks of disinfectant. I think every hospital in the world must use the same brand, so they get that same stench. They must've recently cleaned the floor too; the odor is strong and stings my nostrils.

My footfalls are amplified by the heels of my boots as I walk up to the front desk, which runs along most of the left side. Opposite, rows of interlinking chairs form the waiting area, which is currently half-occupied. It's the usual collection of people with visible lacerations, people who look like shit, and people who look fine—which makes me wonder what they're actually here for.

The desk is staffed by two nurses. Both are wearing navy blue uniforms, with name badges clipped above their left breast. One of them is talking calmly into a phone; the other is tapping away at a computer.

"Excuse me," I say.

The one at the computer looks up with weary disinterest.

I smile. "Hi. I was hoping you could help me. I was told an old friend of mine works here. Jonas Briggs? Do you know where I could find him?"

She frowns and shakes her head. "No, sorry. Don't know anyone by that name who works here. Although, I work the day shift. He might work nights." She looks at the computer and presses a few buttons on the keyboard. "No, nothing showing on the staff directory, either..." She spins around in her chair and looks at her colleague, who has just come off the phone. "You know a Jonas Briggs?" she asks her. "Works here, apparently..."

The other nurse, a portly woman in her late forties,

shakes her head. "No... nobody here by that name. Certainly not on my shift, anyway."

I sigh, unable to hide the frustration. Falling at the first hurdle like this isn't a good sign. Maybe Briggs uses a fake name while he's working... or maybe *Briggs* is a fake name. I don't know. But regardless of what he calls himself, being here's a bust.

"Okay, thanks for your time, ladies." I turn and head back out the main entrance. I stand on the sidewalk next to the driveway, glancing both ways along the street.

I pause, then look up and stare straight into the black dome of security cameras. I wait a moment, then walk off across the street, back through the park, and into my motel room.

Just playing a hunch.

April 27, 2017 — 01:51 EDT

My eyes snap open as I'm ripped from my sleep by the quietest of noises. The slightest disturbance in the air around me, and my subconscious takes control. Years of training honed my mind to be as much a weapon as the guns I carry with me.

I feel a sharp pressure on my neck, pushing against the skin without breaking it. I glance to my left and see a dark figure looming over me, holding a hypodermic needle to the side of my throat. In the darkness, I can't make out his features. I can just see the whites of his eyes staring at me.

It's a little freaky, like something out of a horror film.

But it looks like my hunch paid off. I figured if this guy was smart enough to use a fake identity for his day job, to protect himself from anyone in *my* world finding him, chances are he probably had some way of finding out if anyone came looking too. To do that, I thought he either managed to hack into the security feeds at the hospital, or he had some kind of flag in place so he could tell when somebody searched for his name in the system.

It's why I looked at the camera before I left, so he could see me if I happened to be right. I know it was risky, but it's more important right now to get people on my side. Even if I'm right about security feeds being monitored by the CIA, I'll be long gone by the time anyone tracks me here. Plus, there's no way they would think anything of me being in a hospital besides possibly being injured. They won't know I'm recruiting.

It was a calculated gamble, which apparently paid off.

I tilt my head back and to the side, trying to alleviate some of the pressure from the needle. "Jonas Briggs, I presume?"

"Who the fuck's asking?" he replies. "And before you think about lying to me, pay close attention to the needle. It contains a little cocktail of my own design. Completely undetectable in any blood tests and extremely lethal."

I smile. "Well, at least I know I've found the right person..."

"Who are you?"

"Jonas—assuming that's your name? Needle or not, it doesn't matter. I'm not here to lie to you. But for the sake of full disclosure, I want you to go ahead and lift up the blanket next to your leg."

He's silent, but after a moment of hesitation, he does. Even in the gloom, he can see my hand holding a Beretta, which is aiming accurately at the left side of his stomach.

I feel the needle move away from my skin.

"You stick me with that thing, I'll make sure you bleed out in an agony you can't imagine. But that's just me being honest with you. I'm not here as an enemy."

Slowly, he moves away to stand over by the table at the end of the bed. I reach across and flick the light on beside me, bathing the room in a bright glow that forces me to squint.

Once my eyes adjust, I take a good look at him. He's a short guy, maybe five-nine. He has a thick neck and looks well put together, treading the fine line between muscular and fat. He's bald and his head is round. The skin around his cheekbones is tough and pockmarked.

I sit up in bed and lean against the headboard, resting my gun on my lap, allowing him to get a good look at me as well.

"Are you Jonas Briggs?" I ask.

He says nothing and doesn't move, neither confirming nor denying the fact.

"Okay, I can understand your hesitation. Usually, I'd be just as skeptical, but in the interest of time—or lack thereof—I'll go first. My name is Adrian Hell, and I'm here to ask for your help."

His eyes betray his surprise. He rests on the edge of the desk and places the needle carefully down next to him.

"Adrian Hell?" he says with a hint of disbelief in his voice. "Jesus... how did you find me?"

"I got your name, along with a few others, from Ashton Case."

"You know Ash, huh?"

I shrug. "I wouldn't say we're best friends, but he's an acquaintance I've come to respect."

Briggs nods slowly. "Yeah, I'm Jonas. What do you want?"

I smile. "In my experience, the answer to that question usually requires a couple of beers..."

Briggs checks his watch. "Fine. Get dressed. I know a place."

"At this time?"

He stands and makes for the door. "Yup... open all night."

02:51 EDT

It turns out the place he knows is a strip club. Should have guessed, really. What else would be open at this time?

We're sitting on either side of a small, round table just in front of a low stage, with a pole connected to the ceiling in the middle. We're both sipping a whiskey, straight up on the rocks. The chairs are a cream-colored leather and deceptively comfortable.

The girl strutting around on the stage is naked apart from a barely-there thong and heels. The place is pretty busy, despite the hour, and the men sitting nearby are transfixed by the dancer, looking like a pack of hungry wolves circling their prey.

The place isn't far from my motel, and we've been here about fifteen minutes. I'm getting pretty good at condensing the shit I'm caught up in, so I gave Briggs the lowdown as we drank.

"Well, I can't say I'm surprised," he says, his voice rough. "I've never liked the CIA. And Cunningham? Well... credit where it's due—it's one helluva stunt he's pulled."

I flick my eyebrows up in silent acknowledgement. "Yeah, that's one way of looking at it. But I'm not letting it stand. He needs to be taken down, and I'm hoping you'll agree to help me do it."

He stares at the dancer momentarily, but I don't think he's paying attention to her. His eyes are too glazed over. "That's a big ask. What's in it for me?"

"What? Besides literally saving the world?"

He shrugs. "I ain't here for the glory, unlike *some* people."

I frown. "And what's that supposed to mean?"

"Well... look at you. You've carved yourself out a nice little corner of this game, haven't you? Adrian Hell, living legend, et cetera. You're practically a household name. You trying to tell me you're not doing this, on some level, to further your image?"

I finish my drink and put the glass down a little harder than was necessary. I'm starting to dislike Mr. Briggs.

I fight to keep my voice calm and courteous. "I didn't create this image for my own benefit, all right? Other people created it for me, simply because I'm so fucking good at what I do. My reputation is justified, unlike most in our line of work. But I don't do this for the thrill or to satisfy some sick perversion. I do it because I'm good at it, and it pays well. And, on this occasion, it's the right fucking thing to do."

Briggs is silent for a moment. "Whatever. Like I said... what's in it for me?"

I sigh. "Twenty million dollars."

He chokes on the mouthful of whiskey he's just taken, dribbling some down his chin. He wipes his mouth with the back of his hand and puts his glass down, his eyes wide.

"Are you shitting me? Twenty *million*?"

I nod.

"Who's funding your little war on the White House?"

"Does it matter?"

"Hey, if I do this, I want to know everything."

That's a fair enough request.

I shrug. "Okay. I am."

"You?"

"Yup."

"How the hell can you afford that?"

"Because I'm a wealthy man. And because I'm not doing this to make money. Like I said, I'm doing this mostly because it's the right thing to do."

"Mostly?"

"There's a small part of me looking for revenge, I'll admit. I had to watch someone I knew and respected die as the president executed his grand plan to reset the world. *And* the sonofabitch he hired to be the front man for it all killed my dog."

Briggs rolls his eyes. "The bastard..."

The sarcasm wasn't hard to miss—a result of years of Josh's training.

"Hey, I loved that dog, Jonas. You have no idea."

He sighs, looking at the dancer again as she hangs upside-down on the pole, gyrating. He turns back to me, holding my gaze. "So, for twenty million dollars, you want my help to kill the president?"

I nod. "That pretty much sums it up, yeah."

"Have you given any thought as to *how* you want to go after the impossible shot?"

"Honestly? Not really. I had one idea, but I don't think it'll work. I want to get the team together first and then look at how we're going to pull this off."

"Team? So, wait... I've gotta share my payout?"

I shake my head. "No, it's twenty million *each*. Don't worry."

"Fuck me... how rich *are* you, man?"

I smile. "I get by. So, are you in?"

He sighs and, after a moment, shrugs. "Why not? I'd be crazy to turn down that kinda money, whatever the job. But if you try to screw me on this, I'll put you to sleep. We clear?"

I nod. Usually, I wouldn't respond well to threats like that, but these are desperate times, and I can understand where he's coming from.

"This is on the level, Jonas. No strings. We pull it off, you get your money. If anyone needs to take the fall for it, I'll make sure it's me."

"Huh... that's mighty noble of you."

"Well, I've got a lot I need to answer for, I guess. As long as Cunningham is stopped and the people I care about stay safe, I'm not that bothered what happens to me."

"Fair enough. So, what now?"

"Now? Make your peace with whomever you've got to make your peace with. It's gonna be a long road, and it's a journey we might not come back from. Understand the moment you're seen with me, the CIA will target you with everything they have."

Briggs smiles. "Sounds kinda fun."

"And *that's* why I came to you. We'll meet in the bar at Caesar's in Atlantic City three days from now. You don't show, you're out. You breathe a word of this to anyone, you're dead. Clear?"

I see him trying to suppress a smile. "Clear."

"You got a smartphone and an e-mail address?"

He frowns. "Yeah, why?"

"Calls and texts can be traced, but if we both log into the same e-mail account, we can save messages as drafts, so we both see them without transmitting the data."

I know, I know—that's technical for me, right? Well, I can't take all the credit. It's something Josh told me about once. Despite what he thinks, I'm not a complete caveman when it comes to all things high-tech, and I always listened when he started telling me things that sounded smart.

Briggs raises an eyebrow. "Very covert. Okay." He grabs a napkin and borrows a pen from a passing waitress. He writes down his log-in details and passes the napkin to me.

I fold it up and tuck it into my jacket pocket. "Check it regularly. I'll keep in touch."

I stand, throw a twenty onto the table to pay for the drinks, and nod a silent goodbye to my new colleague. I walk out of the club without looking back.

That's one name off my list. Now for the other three.

6

ADRIAN HELL

I managed another couple of hours of rest after leaving the strip club, then hit the road shortly after five. I made the six-hour drive to Baltimore without incident. I drove sensibly, taking side roads where possible, and kept to the speed limits at all times.

I say that, but in this piece-of-shit truck, it's not as if I could go any faster even if I wanted to.

The weather has slowly deteriorated. I hit the city limits about ten minutes ago, and this rain looks like it's settling in for the long haul. It started out as one of those persistent light showers that looks worse than it is, but it's been getting heavier with each minute that passes, and right now it's a full-blown downpour.

The next name on my list is the one Case said to use as plan B. The crazy-sounding one. Only reason I'm here is because it's the closest one to me, so I figure I might as well stop by as I'm passing.

I came in on I-95 and took the bridge over the Patapsco River. I followed the road east, navigating the busy, wet streets until I reached Druid Lake and my destination. It's a large, gothic-looking building, almost like a castle, surrounded by forest on the banks of the lake.

The Stonebanks Institute for the Criminally Insane. Named for some guy who apparently revolutionized electroshock therapy treatment in the 1920s. Well, that's what the plaque on the wall out front says, anyway.

I'm sitting in the car outside the tall, locked, cast-iron gates, staring out the window. The building is made from old brick and covered in moss. It looks like something from an Anne Rice novel. This storm isn't exactly helping, either. The clouds are thick and gray, making it look like evening time outside. Plus, in addition to the rain, I can hear the rumbling of distant thunder overhead. All we need now is some random lightning and we've got ourselves our very own *House on Haunted Hill*.

The sky lights up with a flash of lightning, accompanied a few moments later by a loud blast of thunder.

I sigh.

Wonderful.

I turn my jacket collar up and get out of the car. I hunch against the weather and walk at a brisk pace through the entrance archway to the right of the gates. The driveway is long and forms a circle at the end in front of the main doors. In the center is a large water feature. It's a circular stone basin, large and low, with a fountain built into a marble plinth in the middle. The streams of water shoot up and arc down into the basin, which is close to overflowing thanks to the rain.

I stop at the foot of the steps. I look skyward, watching the rain fall against the backdrop of the building. High above, stone gargoyles, probably carved hundreds of years ago into the corners of the building, stare across the grounds, no doubt relishing the storm.

Yeah... this place gives me the creeps.

I climb the steps and walk through the first set of doors. I wipe my feet on the rough floor in the vestibule. I run my hands quickly over my hair, brushing my new fringe away from my face and preventing any rain from dripping into my eyes.

I never used to have this problem. I really need a haircut!

I push open the inner doors and walk through, feeling a blast of warm air from the heater above. I'm standing in a holding area. To my left, behind thick glass, is the front desk. A nurse is behind it, sitting upright and stiff, professional to a fault. Ahead of me is a line of four men wearing navy blue uniforms and armed with nightsticks and mace canisters. They were idly chatting among themselves, but that's stopped now that I've appeared.

"Name?" asks the nurse unceremoniously.

I'm distracted by the level of security and have to shake my head to refocus. I move over to the glass. "Hi, ah... I was hoping to visit with Ruby DeSouza."

An almost imperceptible twitch of her eyebrow tells me she's more than familiar with the name. She flashes a quick glance over to the line of guards. "And you are?"

"I'm a member of the family."

I'm not. That's a lie.

Her lips form a thin line. She glares at me the way a teacher would glare at a pupil when they tell her for the hundredth time that their dog ate their homework.

"Miss DeSouza has no family," she replies challengingly.

I frown but don't hesitate. "I'm her cousin... on her mother's side. I know she has no *immediate* family, and that's

42

why I feel so bad for not visiting her sooner. I'm really all she has, and I just want to see how she's doing. Please... I've traveled a long way."

She sighs heavily and opens a compartment on her side of the counter. She slides a clipboard through it, which I take, briefly skimming over the attached paperwork.

"Fill that out, and we'll escort you through the facility to her cell."

I shrug and nod. "Yeah, no problem."

I lean on the part of the desk not covered by the glass and quickly fill the forms out, using as much fake yet believable information as I can come up with on the spot. They might check it in detail later, but that'll take a while, and I intend to be long gone by the time they realize it's all bullshit.

I pass the clipboard back through to her a few moments later. She quickly checks over the details, then nods at the guards.

I turn, and one of them steps to meet me. "Hold your arms out to the sides for me."

I do and smile. "I'm unarmed, officer."

"I'm sure you are, but this is for your protection."

Well, that doesn't sound overly reassuring...

"*My* protection?" I ask.

"The inmates here are extremely dangerous. Every one of them. We need to make sure there's nothing on you that they could potentially take and use against you. Part of what you just signed is a disclaimer saying you understand the risk to your person while on these premises, and you won't hold either the Stonebanks Institution or the state of Maryland responsible for anything that may happen to you."

Ah. Well... that's just peachy! I don't really know what to say to that.

"Huh…" is about all I can manage.

The guard finishes patting me down. "Okay, you're clear. You'll have an escort at all times, and you won't be allowed more than five minutes alone with the prisoner."

"Is that standard procedure?"

He shakes his head. "No, standard procedure is thirty minutes. With your… *cousin*, you get five."

Oh.

I nod and follow him through another set of doors. We enter a large reception area. Inside, it's actually a beautiful place. The floor's circular, with black and white tiling polished to a shine. Straight ahead is a staircase covered by a deep red carpet, with wide, stained-wood handrails running up either side. It stops on a small landing, beneath a tall window that takes up most of the wall, then stretches away to the left and right, continuing up to the next floor.

On either side of me are corridors lit by flickering light fixtures that cast long, haunting shadows across the walls.

I bet there's some serious *crazy* in this place.

The guard steps to one side, and one of his colleagues follows us through to take the lead. "He'll show you to her cell." He turns and disappears back through the door, closing it firmly behind him. I hear the locks turn from the other side.

I look at the guard. He seems young but has an air of fearlessness about him. "You worked here long?"

He nods. "Eighteen months, give or take."

"Like it?"

He shrugs. "Not particularly."

I smile uncomfortably and follow him as he walks across the corridor and up the stairs. We climb up, go left, and come out on the floor above. There's no carpet here—just cold, hard tile. Facing the stairs is another desk. It's a makeshift security station. Two guards sit behind it, monitoring video feeds on their small screens.

The guard heads down the corridor. I move alongside him. My footsteps sound loud in the unnerving silence that surrounds us.

"How come it's so quiet?" I ask. "I figured this place would be alive with the sound of madness or something."

"All the cells are partially soundproof. They have to be. Otherwise, it'd be like a goddamn zoo in here."

"Huh. Makes sense."

There's no natural light along the corridor. The fixtures overhead are motion activated, so in front and behind us is pitch-black. Only the lights directly above us are lit up as we walk.

I snap my head sideways.

I swear I just heard something from the door nearest to me...

I frown, slowing as I take a cautious step toward it.

I think this place is starting to get to me. He *just* finished telling me the rooms are soundproof...

But I definitely heard—

"I'd keep away from the doors if I were you," the guard says, distracting me.

I turn my head to meet his gaze. See, now that he's told me to keep away, I have an overwhelming urge to move closer and look through the letterbox window at eye level. It's an almost spiteful curiosity.

Spiteful... stupid—same difference.

It's in my nature to do the opposite of what people who think they're in charge tell me to do. It's an illness, I know. But especially given the way everyone's acting around here, I feel compelled to look inside one of these cells, just to get a glimpse of what I might be dealing with when I meet Ruby.

I move over to the door, listening closely. There's a privacy cover fastened over the small window. I move my hand slowly toward it and turn the catch as quietly as possible, holding my breath. I lower it gently, grimacing as the metal hinge squeaks. I put my face close to the window and peer inside. It's completely black. I can't see anything. A bit of an anti-climax, I admit. I guess I was thinking I'd—

A pair of eyes opens right against the glass.

I jump back, raising my arms instinctively. "Jesus fucking Christ!"

My heart's racing. That scared the shit out of me!

The eyes stare at me. The pupils are gray as old stone and the whites are stained with red streaks. They don't move or blink. They just... watch me.

The guard appears and moves to the door. Without hesitating or looking at the eyes, he bangs his nightstick against the glass, then closes the flap.

He presses a button on the intercom, which is mounted on the wall to the side of the door. "Back away from the door! Now!" He turns to me. "I *did* warn you..."

I laugh only to hide the embarrassment, not because I thought any part of that was fucking funny.

"Heh... yeah, I won't be doing that again. Don't worry."

We continue on. About halfway down, a metal gate is blocking the way. The guard takes a key and opens it. He allows me to go through, then follows me and locks it behind us. We soon approach the end of the corridor. There's a door in front of us. The guard stops next to it.

"Your cousin's in that room," he says, nodding to the door on my right. "But we don't open it up without a full team. Instead, we keep her in this particular cell because, along with the one opposite, it's linked to an observation room, where you can see her and communicate with her without having to step inside."

I'm *really* tempted to look through the window...

No. Don't do it, Adrian.

"Is that not overkill?" I ask. "Even for *this* place?"

The guard unlocks the door, then looks back at me, frowning. "You don't know what she's in here for, do you?"

I shake my head. I have a feeling I'm not going to like this...

"She set fire to a care home," he continues. "Killed everyone in there. All sixty-two of the old bastards. Courts ruled she was certifiable, so they sent her here instead of giving her the chair. She's... tormented, to say the least."

Holy...

"Shit. Well, like I said, I'm just... y'know... doing right by the family..."

I thought she was in the business? That's pretty out there, even for an assassin. I wonder if Case made a mistake. Saying that, he *did* say she was a plan B.

Christ, can you imagine what she would do if I let her loose in the White House? I smile to myself at the thought. It would certainly be *one* way of stopping Cunningham— burn the building to the ground!

Hmm...

The guard opens the door and steps to the side. "You've got five minutes with her. Any longer than that, and she tends to get a little... agitated."

I smile and walk through. The door closes behind me. The room is long and has two temporary walls dividing it with cheap doors cut into the plasterboard. I open the one on the right. There are two chairs side by side, facing a window that's currently hidden behind closed curtains. Other than that, the room is empty.

I move over to the window. I feel myself hesitate before reaching for the curtains. There could be anything behind these. I'm not entirely sure I want to know.

No—man up, Adrian!

I pull them back to reveal Ruby DeSouza's cell.

Huh.

It's well-lit by the fluorescent lighting overhead. The walls are gray brick, and the floor is tiled. Everywhere is spotless; there's not a mark to be found on any surface. At the far end is a single bed, neatly made. The door is in the other corner. Nearest me, next to the window, is a toilet and sink with a desk opposite.

In the center of the room, there's a woman sitting quietly on a chair, facing the window. Facing me. She's... well, she's stunning, if I'm honest. But she's staring right at me, which is freaking me out a little.

And now she's tilting her head slowly at an angle, not blinking.

Okay, I don't like it.

I sit in one of the chairs and compose myself, taking a deep breath. This place is doing a number on me, and I need to get my shit together.

I take another breath.

She's still staring at me.

Her hair is jet-black and cut short into a bob that finishes level with her chin. Her eyes are green, with long, black lashes. She's wearing—and don't ask me how she got the outfit—a short black dress. The kind of dress women wear to a nightclub. Her long, toned legs are crossed, and her hands are clasped on her lap. She has no shoes on, and she's bouncing her foot like she's sitting in a doctor's waiting room, idly passing the time.

What the...

"Ruby?"

The foot stops bouncing. She uncrosses and recrosses her legs the opposite way.

I get a brief image of *Basic Instinct* in my head and thank God she's not Sharon Stone right now.

She moves her head slowly to a different angle, never taking her eyes off me.

"You're not... *him*," she says. Her voice is faint, like a whisper. "Where is he?"

I frown. "Where's who?"

"The nice man in the hat and the suit and the power tie, which has four different pastel colors merging into each other. He comes here once a day, about this time, with his newspaper and his tea. Oh, he likes his tea. Same cup, every day. The *same* cup. I hope he washes it after each use. It will become stained. Yes, it will. Stained. Like blood. Bloodstains. They don't wash out. No, no, no, they don't. They don't wash out."

Wow.

That's... ah... that's some kind of crazy!

She hasn't moved. She's still sitting all prim and proper. But those eyes... man, I can see the demons in those eyes.

They're impressive.

I know a thing or two about dealing with demons and about letting them out. Ruby here seems to let them roam free around the clock.

Her emerald orbs are darting in all directions now, like she's trying to track a fly that's buzzing around her. But still she sits, all delicate.

"Well, I don't know about that," I say. "But *I'm* here. I came to see you. To make sure you're okay."

Her eyes snap to me in an instant. Her brow furrows with an immediate, unjustified hatred. "And who the fuck are *you*? Heretic! What the *fuck* are you doing here?" She spits out the words with venom, saliva forming on her lips.

I'm starting to think this maybe wasn't such a good idea.

So, I'm assuming the patience and understanding route probably isn't going to get me anywhere. I'll try another approach.

"Okay, Ruby, tone down the psycho. I'm better at it than you and a helluva lot better at hiding it. I'm here to offer you a job. Do you know what I mean by that? When I say *job*?"

Her face relaxes, but the frown stays. I think it's more from confusion than anger, though. She tilts her head alternatively left and right, like a dog trying to understand its master's command.

I sigh. "Look, I've only got a few minutes with you. For some reason, the guards here seem to be scared of you. Why is that, do you think?"

A smile slowly creeps across her face and reaches her eyes, which light up with a fiendish glee. She stands, not bothering to shimmy her dress down. It's ridden up a little, revealing most of her thighs. She walks casually toward me, up on her toes, placing one foot exaggeratedly in front of the other until she's mere inches from the window.

She strokes her hand up and down the glass playfully, then turns around and reaches behind her. She grabs the zipper near the base of her neck and pulls it down all the way to the top of her ass.

I shift in my seat, feeling uncomfortable all of a sudden. "Hey, what are you doing? Don't be doing that now. Come on."

She slips the dress off one shoulder, then the other... slowly, like she's putting on a show. She shakes her hips as she ushers it down her body.

She's naked underneath.

I quickly look to the floor, putting my head in my hand. "Oh, sweet Jesus..."

I'm a man, like any other—in *some* ways, at least. Ruby is an attractive woman, and she's now naked in front of me. I don't want to see her like that, but there's really nowhere else to look. The window runs the full width of the wall and almost floor to ceiling.

This is weird. Really, *really* weird.

Josh would be loving this—not only for the gratuitous nudity but also for my obvious discomfort.

Ruby steps out of the dress and walks back toward her chair, stopping just in front of it. She puts her arms out to the sides, moving them slowly up and over her head. She bends her knees and arches her back, stretching. She stands up straight and turns around.

I jump in my seat. "Fuck me!"

Her frankly incredible body is covered from throat to groin in a network of scars. Self-inflicted wounds in the shape of pentagrams tattoo her chest and stomach. The freshly healed cuts are a deep red.

"This is how I keep my demons locked inside," she says seductively. "It stops them coming out to play. Do you like my demons?"

I shrug, squirming in my seat. "Ah... not really, no. It's a little bizarre, if I'm honest."

She frowns. "You do not like me? You do not *want* me? Why are you here? The people who come here always like me... always want me. They cheer for me, beg me for more. And they visit me. Late at night, when they think I'm asleep, they visit. They try to unlock my door with their key. Try to let my demons out. But I don't let them come out. No, no, no. They stay locked behind my door. Yes, they do." She pauses to giggle like a little girl, putting one hand to her mouth.

"Their keys aren't big enough to open *my* door. But I don't tell them they're wasting their time. It's fun watching them try."

I shake my head and smile, which gradually gives way to a laugh.

Sonofabitch.

It's the eyes. They never lie. And Ruby DeSouza's eyes are no different. I'm not saying she isn't a little... out there... but this—it's an act. An elaborate, clever act. I don't know the reason behind it. But I know it's all for show. She had me—hook, line, and sinker—right until the double entendre about the guards interfering with her at night. I saw her struggling to keep a straight face. Her eyes betrayed her.

I stand and applaud.

She stops, frozen in place and naked, staring at me, genuinely confused.

"Very good," I say. "You should be an actress. Now put your fucking clothes on, sit your ass down, and listen to what I have to say."

She doesn't move for a moment, frowning at me. Eventually, she gives in, moving quickly over to her dress and putting it back on. "Who are you?"

Her voice sounds drastically different now. More down to earth. More... *sane*.

"I'm Adrian Hell."

Her mouth drops open with shock. "Get the fuck outta here! Really?"

I smile and nod.

"No shit! What are *you* doing here? And hey, how did you know I was faking it?"

I shrug. "You're good. Don't get me wrong. And the whole naked thing—nice touch. *Very* nice touch. But I saw it in your eyes. You were trying not to laugh. You couldn't quite stay in character."

"Damn it..." She sighs as she zips her dress back up. "So, what do you want?"

I must admit, I feel much better about potentially having her on board. I think her natural talent for deception probably makes her a formidable killer. And she's definitely crazy enough to want in.

"I'm here to offer you a job. But thanks to your little striptease, I only have about thirty seconds left to give you my sales pitch before the guard comes back."

She shrugs. "So, make it quick."

"Okay... how would you feel about earning twenty million dollars to help me assassinate the president of the United States?"

She raises an eyebrow. "Are you serious?"

"Deadly."

"Huh. Okay, I'm in. Sounds kinda fun."

I shake my head and smile. She didn't even hesitate.

"There's just one thing. I'm *kinda* incarcerated here for —" She pauses to look at her wrist, even though she's not wearing a watch. "—oh, the rest of my life! It was a nice idea at the time, but I didn't think it through, I'll admit. If you want my help, you'll have to bust me out of *here* first."

I hear the door open outside the room. I don't have much time.

"I'm guessing that's not going to be as easy as it sounds?"

She shakes her head.

Damn it.

"Okay, sit tight. I'll think of something."

Great. Now I just need to think of something!

The door to the room opens, and the guard appears. "Okay, time's up. Let's go."

"Can I not just have a couple more minutes with her?"

"I'm afraid not. Too much excitement sets her off."

I glance sideways at her, suppressing a smile. She winks at me.

"Yeah... I can imagine."

I walk over to the door, pausing in front of the guard. He's about my height—similar build and shape. A bit younger than me. He's on edge, and his body language is tense.

I look over his shoulder at Ruby, who's sitting patiently in her chair, watching me.

I've never been one to really plan things. And if I were being brutally honest with myself, my track record of improvising in the heat of the moment is poor at best.

But when in doubt, stick with what you know...

I whip my body to the right, slamming my elbow into the guard's temple. No warning, minimal movement, maximum effect. He drops to the floor in a heap.

Ruby stands and runs to the window, slamming her hand on it. "Are you *crazy*?"

I gesture to the surroundings. "Really? You're asking me if *I'm* crazy after what I just had to sit through?"

I crouch down and take the nightstick and keychain. I dash into the corridor, fumbling around with the keys, trying to find the right one. I strike gold on the sixth and pull the door open. She's standing in front of it, arms crossed over her chest.

She pokes her head out and quickly looks left and right. "Are you an idiot? I mean, I was acting... but you—you're *genuinely* this fucking stupid, aren't you?"

I frown. "Hey, hold on a minute, lady! I'm doing you a favor, busting you out of here!"

"And I'm eternally grateful. But my door, like the one

opposite, is alarmed. It's not linked to the main system like everyone else's, so it can't be opened centrally. There are extra security measures for high-risk inmates, should they have a system failure, hence the alarm. No one can open my cell without everyone finding out."

"Oh."

"Plus, that guard you just laid out has a panic button that's electronically linked to a heart rate monitor. So, if anything happens to him, it sends an alert to the central system, also telling everyone."

"Ah."

"So, Adrian, while I'm glad you're getting me out, tell me —what do you intend to do about *them*?"

She points to her left. Through the darkness, I see the lights flickering into life above the metal gate separating us from the stairs. I see the two guards from the desk standing with five of their friends. They're armed with cattle prods. I can see the blue line of electricity crackling at the end.

I look back at Ruby and shrug. "Good question."

7

ADRIAN HELL

"Well?" she asks.

"Shush!" I hiss. "I'm thinking."

We're at the end of a corridor. The only way out is directly ahead of us, through a locked metal gate and a team of armed security guards. I have a nightstick of the non-electrified variety and a half-dressed woman, whom I'm trying to bust out of an insane asylum.

I'll be honest. Nothing's jumping out at me...

Ruby sighs. "Oh, for crying out loud—move!"

I feel a little bewildered. I step to the side, allowing her out of her room. As she passes me, I see her sink back into character once more. The madness fills her eyes, and her body language changes as she morphs back into the psychotic bitch I saw a few minutes ago. She disappears inside the observation room, then comes out a moment later, dragging the unconscious guard behind her by his collar.

"What the hell are you doing?" I whisper.

She stays in character, tilting her head slowly and staring at me with insane eyes.

She says nothing.

"Oh, right... I see."

It's probably best I let her do her thing.

She drags the guard into the middle of the corridor and stands over him, a leg on either side of his body. She hitches her dress up, then slowly crouches down, straddling his waist. She leans forward and rests her hands on his shoulders. Then she looks down the long corridor, through the gates, into the eyes and souls of each security guard in turn.

"Oh, he's mine!" she shouts. "A lovely gift—oh, yes he is! Daughter needs a new dress..."

Jesus Christ, it's Gollum!

She starts unbuttoning his shirt. "Daughter will make herself a new one, so she's pretty for when the man with the tea comes back. Pretty in her own flesh... pretty in *his*!"

She rips the guard's shirt open and digs her nails into his chest, drawing blood. She snaps her head around, stares straight at me, and lets out a scream that would make a banshee piss.

"Let's see how good you really are, heretic!"

Oh, boy...

I look down the corridor at the team of security personnel. They're running toward us, approaching the metal gate. The one in front is already reaching for the keys. They'll be coming to save their colleague and restrain the crazy lady.

This is not a drill, they'll be thinking.

Now what do I do?

Hang on...

I have a nightstick. And I'm Adrian Hell. I know *exactly* what to do.

She's not the only one with demons to let out.

Holding the nightstick in my right hand, I walk purposefully to meet the guards as they file through the gate. They'll have to come through one at a time, so if I'm quick, I might be able to pick one or two off before I'm overrun. That will even things up a little bit.

I reach them as the first guard is pushing the gate open. I swing fast from the hip. He's slow to react, unprepared for any resistance. The nightstick connects with his temple. He goes down, slides across the floor, and hits the wall to my left. His cattle prod slides away behind me, spinning.

That might come in handy...

The next one through has time to adjust, but it won't do him any good. I jab him hard in the stomach. He keels over, the wind knocked out of him. I smash the stick over the back of his head. He face-plants to the floor, out before he hits the tiles.

The remaining five pile through as fast as they can. Their faces are a mixture of anger and panic. I launch my nightstick at them, then turn to run back toward Ruby. I pause only for a split-second to scoop up the electrified baton on my way past.

I make it back to her, skid to a stop, and spin around to make my last stand against the oncoming guards. They stop maybe ten feet away and fan out to cover the full width of the corridor.

"Give it up," says one of them, over on the right. "What you're doing is a federal crime. We *will* detain you by any means necessary until the FBI arrive."

Federal?

FBI?

I glance at Ruby, who's on her feet, standing over the unconscious guard with half his chest shredded. Her arms are out to the sides, and she's hunched forward in a feral stance. Her eyes are almost demonic.

Fuck me—she looks like Wolverine!

They say the most believable actors treat the characters they portray as extensions of themselves—who they are but with the volume turned up. If that's the case, Ruby DeSouza deserves a fucking Oscar! And possibly some psychiatric support.

"Look, I know what it looks like," I say to the guards. "But she shouldn't be here. There's a situation that requires her attention, and I don't have time to go through the motions and officially appeal for her release. Just step aside, and no one else has to get hurt."

As one, they step toward us. What training they've had must have focused on working as a team to quickly and effectively take down crazy people.

And right now, it doesn't get much crazier than this.

I shrug. "Okay... maybe a few more people need to get hurt. But answer me this: what *exactly* did you mean when you said *federal*?"

One of the guards takes another step forward, raising his cattle prod. "This is a federally funded facility. That means when we sound the alarm, an FBI tactical unit comes running."

"Ah... well, I'm glad we cleared that up. So, listen—I'm going to have to ask you real nice *not* to press that alarm, okay? Under any circumstances."

The guard smiles. "Too late, asshole."

Shit.

"They're maybe three minutes out."

Double shit.

I cast another glance at Ruby, whose mental act is visibly giving way to concern.

Any advance on double shit?

"We've also sent them your picture, taken from our security feed," says another guard, probably the oldest of the five. "Turns out, they're really interested in *you*, boy! They're sending two units to make sure you play nice."

There it is.

Triple shit.

"Yeah... I don't know what it is you've done, but they couldn't believe their luck when we told 'em about you!"

He smiles, which pisses me off. I take a deep breath, in and out, to focus my mind. Being in this place has really thrown me off my game, but shit just got serious. If the FBI are coming, then I'm shit out of luck because the CIA won't be far behind.

"Gimme the keys," I say to Ruby without taking my eyes off the guards. I reach to the side, and she places them in my hand. To the guards, I say, "Right, listen up. My friend here isn't crazy. She's extremely dangerous and a damn fine actress, but she ain't crazy. She's here to hide out because she's actually an assassin. You boys have been doing her a favor all this time, which I'm sure she's grateful for."

They shuffle uncomfortably on the spot and exchange glances of uncertainty and concern. It's all in the eyes, you see. Even though what I'm saying sounds ridiculous, the practiced intensity in the stare I'm fixing them with makes them believe me.

"I, on the other hand... well, I'm *definitely* dangerous and arguably a little crazy as well. The FBI are gonna waltz in here and try to arrest me, and they're gonna need to climb over your unconscious bodies to do it. And they're gonna fail. Wanna know why?"

No one answers. No one moves.

I lunge forward, jabbing the business end of the cattle

prod into the stomach of the guy nearest to me. It buzzes quickly and loudly, like when a fly hits one of those Insect-O-Cutor devices you see in restaurant kitchens. The guard screams and shakes, then drops to the floor, out cold and twitching.

I step over him swinging the stick around, catching another guard on the jaw. As he starts to drop, I spin around and thrust the stick forward, hitting the next guard I see in the groin. His eyes go wide. He opens his mouth to scream, but no sound comes out. I'm guessing the pain is too much to process...

I feel a little bad about that one.

That's three down in as many seconds. The two left are the farthest away from me on either side. I step toward the one on my left as I throw the cattle prod, shiny end first like a spear, at the guy on the right. It hits him squarely in the chest, taking him out of the equation.

I raise my arm, blocking the swing of the remaining guard's weapon with ease. With his head and chest exposed, I hit him hard in the jaw with my fist. He staggers back, dropping his stick as he hits the wall. He's groggy but awake. I whip my leg up, kicking him hard in the gut. He wheezes, doubles over, and sinks slowly to the floor. Another swift kick to the side of the head puts him down for good.

"*That's* why."

I look back at Ruby.

She's standing, out of character, staring at me with a disbelieving smile on her face. "Well, aren't you a pleasant surprise! You live up to your reputation. I'll give you that."

"Thanks. Now come on."

We run to the metal gate, which I open for us and lock again once we're through. We stop at the desk at the top of the stairs, which is now deserted. I point down the opposite wing of the building. "What's down there?"

"More cells. Why?"

I move around the desk and sit at the computer. "We need a distraction."

I'm thinking about what Ruby said before. All the cells apart from hers and the one opposite are controlled centrally. That means this computer must be able to open them. I just need to figure out how.

I tap away at the keyboard, navigating my way through the various menus and submenus, using what knowledge I've picked up from Josh over the years to quickly work out how to open all the doors.

I hope the FBI is prepared for a riot.

I press a button, and the loud click of every cell opening in unison echoes down the corridors.

Ruby's eyes go wide, and she punches my arm. "Are you fucking kidding me? Do you have any idea how dangerous these inmates are?"

I shrug. "Are they any worse than the FBI? Worse than me?"

She's breathing heavily, probably from adrenaline. She doesn't respond.

"I'm sure we'll be able to blend in and sneak out before the FBI can regain control. It'll be fine."

She glances past me for a split-second, looking at the corridor we came from, then refocuses on me. "That's a good plan, Adrian. A brilliant plan. But we might be safer leaving with a couple of SWAT teams."

I frown. "What do you mean?"

She points behind me. "I am *far* from the worst thing in here. There are people in here who make me look like someone from *Desperate Housewives*."

I turn and look over my shoulder. There are nine people walking toward us. I shit you not... it's like a scene from *Dawn of the Dead*. They're staggering slowly down the corridor with glazed, medicated expressions on their faces, looking around absently as they come to terms with their unexpected freedom.

I turn to look down the opposite corridor and see much the same.

I feel Ruby tapping my shoulder. "Ah... Adrian..."

I follow her gaze and see one of them at the back of the pack, fumbling inside a guard's pocket. I can just about see them take a set of keys and head to the far end, toward the door opposite Ruby's cell.

The only other room not linked to the central system.

They stand in front of the door for a few moments, then step back as it opens. The guy who walks out has messy, graying hair. He shuffles barefoot into the middle of the corridor. His robe is open, showing a stained white vest and striped boxer shorts.

"Adrian, we... we should probably go."

I can't take my eyes off this guy. He looks so strange. He's —Jesus, he's foaming at the goddamn mouth! His shuffling is speeding up too. He draws level with another patient. I see his hand disappear into the pocket of his robe as he moves to her side. He takes out what looks to be a homemade shank of some kind.

Like lightning, he grabs the inmate—a woman in her fifties—by her hair and yanks her head back, exposing her throat. He whips his hand up and pierces the flesh underneath her chin. Once... twice... too many times—holy shit!

He pauses only to let the blood flow over his hand for a moment. He moves the shank to his own forehead and slowly slices across it, creating a thin, dark line that starts to pour down his face. As his skin is painted by the blood, his eyes seem to glow. The whites shine through the crimson mask and stare straight through me.

That was... that was some pretty dark shit.

The rest of the zombie horde stop and turn, staring at him with looks of bewilderment. He lets out a guttural scream, which prompts the rest of them to do the same. They turn back around. Some groan, some yell, and others stay worryingly silent. But they start walking toward us, this time with more purpose.

The one with the keys makes his way to the front of the pack, re-opening the metal security gate halfway along the corridor. I'm actually a little relieved they've ignored the guards I left on the floor...

"Adrian, we need to go. Right now," urges Ruby.

"Yeah... I think you might be right."

The crazy man charges forward, shoving other inmates out the way. They regain what little focus they had to begin with and chase after him.

"Oh, shit!" I grab Ruby's hand, and we set off running down the stairs, narrowly avoiding being crushed by the two rampaging gangs of maniacs as they meet in the middle.

We quickly come to the circular hub. Ahead of us, the door to the reception area is closed. I see another large group of guards assembled behind it. I have a key, but it won't do us much good if we're mobbed the moment we open the damn thing.

I hear a noise behind us and look over my shoulder. My new stalker is standing at the top of the stairs with a smile on his face and the shank in his hand, which is dripping blood all over the carpet.

Ruby takes the lead, dragging me off to our right. "Come on—this way."

"Where are we going?"

"Anywhere that isn't here!"

We run down the corridor, frantically glancing at either side for an open door, but every one we try is locked.

This is bad. Five security guards, I can handle. They're slow, predictable, and poorly trained. But close to twenty crazed inmates loose in an asylum who have no issue with self-harming or killing—that's a different thing altogether. I know a lost cause when I see one, and we absolutely would *not* win that fight.

So, we run.

But unfortunately, we seem to have headed down another dead end.

Shit.

I look over my shoulder and see the inmates stop about halfway down the corridor. They shift back into their slow, demented shuffle. Blood is still dripping on the floor from my stalker's blade and from his head wound.

"This is the dumbest thing you've ever done," says Ruby.

I shrug. "You gotta admit, given you've only known me twenty minutes and I've only done two things, for *both* of them to be the dumbest thing you've seen me do is pretty impressive."

I feel her turn to look at me. "You're crazier than anyone in here. You know that?"

I smile, not taking my eyes off the inmates. "Thanks."

"Not a compliment..."

"So *you* say..."

I step back, drawing level with a door on my right. I glance through the porthole window and see it's a therapy room. I reach for the handle and try it.

The door opens.

I grab Ruby's arm and drag her sideways into the room

after me. I slam the door, turn the lock, and pull the table immediately to my right in front of it.

"Okay, that should buy us some time. We need to—"

She hits my arm, interrupting me. She's standing at my side, facing the room. I look at her and see she's staring blankly behind me, transfixed by something.

I close my eyes and sigh. "What now?"

I turn around and look at the room. It's a perfect square, maybe fifteen by fifteen. The wall opposite the door has two windows behind metal bars, stretching up from waist height to the ceiling. There are plastic chairs positioned in a circle on one side, and opposite is a row of cupboards running the full width of the room. I'm guessing they have activity equipment stored in them.

In the far corner, staring at us with a vacant expression, is a man standing awkwardly and clutching a teddy bear. He's wearing white coveralls and has to be close to seven feet tall. He's an absolute fucking mountain.

"Oh, you've gotta be kidding me..."

12:07 EDT

If he were my height, he'd be incredibly overweight, but because he's so tall, the fat is spread over a larger area, so he just looks big and bulky. His jowls are dark with stubble, and his thick lips glisten with saliva.

He turns his head slowly to look at me and smiles. "Hi."

His voice is low and simple.

I wave silently, trying to remain as calm as I can.

Ruby steps forward, her hands on her face in fake surprise. "My God, it's you! It's really you! You're here to save me, aren't you? They told me you would come. The man who drinks tea and his friends—they said you'd rescue me."

Christ, she's off again...

The big guy looks at her.

"I'm George," he announces slowly. "Hi!"

"George... George... you are the chosen one, are you not?"

"Uh... Hi!"

The mob outside starts banging on the door, urgently trying to break through. George looks oblivious and a little confused.

"We're going to have some fun," continues Ruby. "We're going to play a game of peekaboo with our new friends outside." She moves in close to him and leans against his chest the way a daughter would with her father, her hand flat next to her face. "Behind that door, the demons come. No, don't look! Don't look at their eyes. We must put them to sleep. Let them rest."

George is completely unaware that she's next to him. He's just staring at the door. There's no emotion on his face. There's... nothing. Just a *Vacant* sign hanging between his ears. But he's a monster of a man. Maybe a gentle giant. Maybe a sleeping bear. Whatever he is, I hope Ruby knows what she's doing.

"De... mon?" he mutters.

Ruby smiles. "Yes! Yes! Demon! Right outside the door. They need to sleep. They need to rest. Help me, Chosen One. Help me!"

He looks down at her slowly. "Sleep..."

He pushes her away and walks toward the door. I hastily step aside, not wishing to anger ol' *Sloth* here anymore than I want to piss off the crazy gang outside.

I move to the back of the room and stand beside Ruby. "Good work."

"Thanks. Be ready to run."

With considerable ease, George moves the table using one hand. He yanks the door open, not bothering to unlock it first. The frame cracks and splinters as the lock breaks.

Our view is mostly obscured by his hulking frame, but I hear the commotion outside cease almost immediately.

"De... mon?" he says again.

He's met with silence. Ignoring everything else, he strides into the corridor, smashing his enormous shovel-like fists into the first couple of lunatics he sees. I can just about see them hit the floor. The jaw of the one nearest to the door is hanging loose, and their eyes are open and blank. I'm guessing they're dead.

The noise restarts as everyone's attention turns to George.

I grab Ruby's wrist. "Come on. We're leaving." We move to the door, waiting for a gap in the crowd. "Okay, now!"

We slip out and set off back down the corridor, running as fast as we can. I have my hand around Ruby's wrist. She's doing her best to keep up with me.

We make it back to the door that leads to the reception area. I glance quickly through the window and see the group of guards still standing there. A few of them are facing the main doors, talking among themselves.

The FBI must be almost here, if they're not already.

"Is there any other way out of here?" I ask her.

"I'm not sure. There's a basement level, but I don't know if there's a back door."

"Damn it. Well, we need to try. The front door's not an option, and this place will be swarming with Feds any second."

"Okay, this way."

We set off down the corridor to the right. Halfway along is a metal door. I take the keys and start trying them in the lock.

Ruby looks back the way we came, keeping watch. "Will you hurry up?"

I try another key. "I'm going as fast as I—" The door unlocks. "Okay, I'm in."

I pull it open, holding it so that she can go through. I follow her and lock it behind me.

We're in a maintenance area, which is dimly lit by fading lights affixed to the walls on either side. The ground is plain concrete with patches of water all around. Overhead, exposed piping wrapped in silver duct tape runs along the ceiling.

The corridor is narrow, and after a few hundred yards, a metal staircase descends into more darkness.

"Well, this isn't creepy at all…"

She ignores me and makes her way down. After a few steps, lights flicker into life above us.

"You happy now?" she calls back over her shoulder.

"I am. Thanks."

We reach the bottom and follow the corridor around. It opens into a central space with corridors stretching out on every compass point, presumably running underneath the entire building.

It's damp and dark, and the air is stale.

"Which way?" I ask her.

"I don't know," she replies abruptly. "You've been down here as many times as I have."

"Okay, let's think about this and—"

"You two all right?"

The voice startles us, and we jump, spinning around to

find the source of the question. Over in the doorway of a small room is a man wearing maintenance coveralls and a baseball cap. He's skinny, probably in his late fifties, with a thick, gray beard.

"Who are you?" I ask urgently, taking a step toward him.

He holds his hands up defensively. "Hey, I'm just the janitor. I didn't do nothing."

His voice is raspy, and his hands are trembling.

Ruby moves in front of me. "We need to get out of here. The inmates are loose and running riot upstairs. Is there another way out of the building down here?"

He looks both of us up and down. "Sure. There's the back door I use."

He nods over to his right, down the corridor opposite us.

"That's great!"

She takes a step toward it, but I grab her arm to stop her. "Hang on. If it's a main door, it'll be covered by the Fed—" I look at the janitor. "...the other guys. Any other ways?"

He shakes his head. "No. Well, except..."

I raise an eyebrow. "Except? We like *except*. Except what?"

"There's a service tunnel contractors use when they clean the sewers." He points down the next corridor directly ahead of him. "There's an access point that leads into the main sewer network beneath the city. It runs for miles."

"Sounds perfect. Thanks. And if anyone comes down here asking, you didn't see us, okay?"

The guy shrugs. "I don't see nothing. I'm just the janitor."

"Good man."

I jog over to the corridor. Lights flicker on as I approach. It's short and a dead end. On the left is a small room containing cleaning supplies with the door open. Against the wall at the end is a large machine for buffing the floor tiles.

In one wall is a hatch. I move over to it and spin the circular handle in the middle, unlocking it. I pull it open to reveal a tunnel, maybe three feet high and the same across.

Oh.

"No way," says Ruby next to me. She leans forward and sniffs. "I'm not going in there. The place stinks!"

"Oh, well, that's fair enough. Tell you what... you head back upstairs and distract the crazy people until the FBI arrives, so I can get out of here."

She flips me the middle finger but says nothing.

"Look, I don't really want to crawl on my hands and knees through shit, either, but it's that or leave in the back of a van surrounded by two SWAT teams. It's your call, sweetheart, but I know what's getting my vote."

She briefly looks down at herself. "I'm wearing nothing but this dress..."

I shrug. "So you'll have less laundry to do afterward. Bonus. You wanna go first?"

She shakes her head and sighs heavily, then steps aside, gesturing to the entrance. "Age before beauty."

I roll my eyes. "Whatever."

I climb inside. I'm struggling to fit comfortably, even on all fours. It's as if the tunnel itself is smaller than the entrance. And it really does stink in here! The sides are greasy and covered in a combination of mold, some kind of weird slime, and cobwebs.

I get maybe fifteen feet in and begin to feel an involuntary anxiety. It's only natural, being in such an enclosed space, even if you're not claustrophobic. I take a moment to compose myself and calm down before pressing on, clearing my mind of any concerns it has.

I hear Ruby climb in behind me. "Oh my God... this sucks."

"Will you quit moaning?" I shout back. "I don't like it, either, but we have no other choice."

We shuffle on in silence and soon reach a junction, where we can go either left or right. I move slightly to one side, making more space beside me for Ruby.

I look back at her. "What do you think?"

She's cursing under her breath as she moves next to me. "I don't know. Ugh—I hate this! It was nicer in my cell. But you *had* to come along and ruin things for me, didn't you! Oh, whatever..."

"I'll remember that when it's time to pay you twenty million dollars..."

She sighs and looks down each direction, then shrugs. "I dunno... right?"

I smile. "Okay, right it is."

She sets off and I follow. I try to avert my eyes while still looking where I'm going because all I can see in front of me is Ruby's ass. And she's in a short dress without underwear...

"You better not be looking at anything back there!" she says a little too playfully.

"I'm trying my best not to..."

The air's becoming stagnant, and the smell of sewage is strong.

I just had an awful thought.

I hope the way in and out through these tunnels is marked in some way. Otherwise, we could be in here for days...

My hand rests in something warm and sticky.

I look down and sigh.

Shit.

8

ADRIAN HELL

We've been in the tunnels for a half-hour, maybe more. The entrance under the asylum feeds into the main network that runs beneath the city, which, thankfully, is much larger. There's shallow water running along the middle of the tunnels, with walkways along both sides and connecting footbridges periodically along the way.

Unfortunately, lighting is sporadic at best, and signs don't appear regularly enough to be useful, unless you work down here for a living and understand how to navigate this labyrinth.

Yeah... we're a little lost.

We stop at another junction.

"I hate you," says Ruby.

I nod. "Fair enough. I hate myself most days too. You get used to it."

"Do you have any idea where we're going?"

"Yeah, because I often traverse the Baltimore sewer system." I sigh, immediately angry with myself for being unnecessarily flippant. "Sorry. That was a little uncalled for."

She shakes her head. "No, it's me. I stink and I'm frustrated and I'm filthy. But I'm grateful for you getting me out of there... and for the work."

"It's all right. Let's just focus on getting out of *here*. The good news is that if we're lost, the chances of anyone finding us are pretty slim."

She shrugs. "True, but the streets above are gonna be crawling with Baltimore PD and, presumably, FBI agents too—all searching for us."

"Well, let's see where we end up. No sense in getting ahead of ourselves. Come on."

We make our way across another bridge, moving over to the other side of the waterway. Up ahead, I see a sign on the near wall, which I point to. "That street name mean anything to you?"

She squints in the gloom. "West 39th? Yeah... it's a couple miles northeast of the asylum." She laughs. "Oh my God—we must've traveled directly beneath the university! That's great!"

I smile. "I think we've been fortunate to go in a consistently straight direction under the circumstances, so I'm not complaining."

We speed up and turn the corner. It's a dead end with a ladder ascending the wall. I follow it up with my gaze and see the pinprick of light shining down through the manhole cover.

I put a hand and foot on the ladder. "Come on. I'll go first. Watch your step, okay? It's a good twenty feet top to bottom."

I set off, climbing the ladder carefully. The steps are slippery from a combination of grime and moisture. I hear Ruby follow a few moments later.

It takes less than a minute to reach the top. I stop in a hunch, leaning my head forward so that my shoulders and neck rest against the cover above me. I adjust my grip and set my footing, making myself as sturdy as possible. With some considerable effort, I use my legs, back, and shoulders to push up against the cover.

It moves but barely.

I try again. Same routine... same result.

"What's the hold up?" Ruby shouts.

I grimace as I try a third time to no avail. "It won't budge."

"Do you want *me* to try?" she asks, with no attempt to hide her sarcasm.

I look down and glare at her. I clench my jaw muscles and grip the sides of the ladder tightly until my knuckles turn white. I take a breath. Through gritted teeth, I growl a muffled roar of anger and frustration as I push up one more time, with every ounce of strength I can muster.

It gives way and goes flying off like a Frisbee. I almost lose my footing, unprepared for how easily it moved. My head breaches the hole, and the fresh air hits my nostrils. I take a deep lungful, as if welcoming an old friend I haven't seen in years.

The rain hasn't relented its onslaught. It's still gray and cold because of the low cloud cover. I move my head to look around, trying to get a feel for where we are, and—

"Oh, shit!"

I duck back inside the hole, narrowly avoiding the front tire of a car. I close my eyes, breathing heavily, and rest my head against the ladder.

"What is it?" asks Ruby.

"We're in the middle of the goddamn street! I'm guessing there was a car stopped on the cover, which is why it wouldn't move before."

She starts laughing. "Well, try not to lose your head about it..."

I look down and narrow my eyes at her. I don't like not being the funny one.

I ignore her. "Come on. We'll need to be quick."

I move up again, more cautiously this time. I peek my head out and scan up and down the street. A car's approaching. I quickly duck and wait for it to pass, then look out again. Beyond it, the lights are on red. Cars are slowing all around.

It's now or never...

"Let's go." I climb out and hold up a grateful hand to the car that brakes early to avoid hitting me. I kneel down and reach for Ruby, who grabs my forearm. "Got you."

I help her out, and we quickly run over to the sidewalk. There's some grass and trees beside a parking lot behind a school. We take cover from the steady rain under one of the trees, catching our breath and letting the adrenaline subside.

I look around and see nothing worth worrying about, although I can hear sirens in the distance. "It won't be long before they set up roadblocks around the city. We need to move."

Ruby laughs. "Roadblocks? I'm not *that* dangerous, y'know..."

I smile. "They'd be for me, sweetheart."

"And what makes *you* so special?"

"I just broke you out of an insane asylum to help me kill the president. Have you not stopped to wonder why?"

She shrugs. "Been a little busy. So... go on—why *are* we killing him?"

"I'll tell you on the way."

"On the way where?"

"We need to head back to the institute. I'm not bothered about the car I stole, but I need my bag out of it—if it's not been taken already."

"Are you kidding me? Why?"

"For my guns."

"There are plenty of places for us to get weapons."

"I know, but these ones are special."

"Oh, wait. Don't you have those—what are they? Matching... Berettas?"

I nod and smile weakly, feeling a little embarrassed that my reputation continues to precede me.

"Adrian, I get the whole *boys and their toys* thing, okay? I do. But if we go back there after what we've just done... shit, *you* should be locked inside there!"

I sigh heavily. She's right. I mean, *obviously,* it's a stupid idea. But I really like my guns. I have little consistency in my life nowadays. I lost my original Berettas in San Francisco a few years back. These replacements were a gift from Robert Clark—a man who became the closest thing to a friend someone like me could have. And I watched him die trying to stop the CIA director from nuking half the planet. They're a legacy.

On the other hand, logically, they're just guns. And Ruby's right. I can get weapons anywhere... I guess.

I move my hand to my chest, absently feeling for the flash drive around my neck underneath my shirt. It's still there, reassuringly.

Fuck it. I'll get new guns. Bob wouldn't have minded.

"Okay. First, we find a car."

Ruby nods and gestures behind us with her thumb at the almost full parking lot. "No issues there."

"Second, we get you some clothes. Then, third, we need to get the fuck out of Baltimore."

"Where are you thinking of going?"

I pause, then smile as a brilliant idea hits me. "I know a place about three hours from here. You'll love it."

16:41 EDT

I boosted a dark green sedan, and we stopped off to borrow a change of clothes for both of us from a nearby store. I ditched the flannel shirt look in favor of a more comfortable and familiar plain T-shirt and jeans. My old leather jacket was in my shoulder bag, which is now lost forever, so I had to settle for a regular brown jacket with a hood attached to it. Probably for the best, given the weather.

We cautiously navigated the streets, avoiding any sirens, and eventually made it onto I-95. We turned onto I-476 just before Philly and headed north.

Overall, it took a little under three hours to reach Allentown.

On the way, I brought Ruby up to speed on everything. Being incarcerated, she didn't have access to TV or newspapers, so she was genuinely unaware of everything that had happened.

She reacted the way most people do.

It's interesting that regardless of whom I tell and what they do for a living, they're all affected the same way. She's a contract killer and arguably certifiable, yet she started crying when I told her about the attacks and who was behind them. She then fell asleep after an hour or so, leaving me to drive on in silence.

It feels... weird. So many flashbacks and memories rush into my mind. I made this exact journey almost three years ago. Josh was driving his Winnebago, and I was heading into battle.

Christ... that feels like a lifetime ago.

But that man, the one who tore the corrupted fabric of this city down piece by piece, is long dead. I'm coming here now to see what was left in his wake.

Last time I was here, I did some business with a man named Oscar Brown, owner of the first—and as far as I know, *only*—superstore for black market weapons. I'm going to need hardware for me *and* my new team. Oscar's come through for me more than once in the past, and I trust him not to advertise my latest visit.

I pull up outside the warehouse complex and kill the engine. It still looks like I remember. It's even raining, like last time. I look at the first of the three units facing the entrance and smile fondly.

I wonder if he still has that chopper in there...

I nudge Ruby's arm, and she snorts as she wakes up. "We're here."

She blinks hard, clearing the grit from her eyes, and looks around. "Where's *here*, exactly?"

I smile. "Candyland."

I get out and pull the hood on my jacket up to protect me against the rain. I walk around the front of the car and meet her as she steps out. She's wearing black leggings with low-heeled brown ankle boots. She has a white tank top on underneath a brown fitted jacket. Her hair's tied up. She looks nice—certainly different from the first time I saw her.

She stares at me challengingly. "Hey, you want a picture? It'll last longer."

I shake my head, snapping myself out of it. "Sorry. I wasn't staring. I was—"

"Yeah, you were..." She smiles. "Come on. I'm getting soaked."

I feel my cheeks flush a little. We jog across the street into the complex and head toward the warehouse, which is standing alone on the right. We make it to the steps leading up to the entrance when the door opens.

A man appears in front of us. He's tall, well built... I don't recognize him. "You lost?"

I shake my head. "I'm looking for Oscar. I'm an old friend."

The man scoffs. "Oscar doesn't have friends."

I smile. "No, he has customers. And I'm one of those too."

The man shakes his head. "Dunno what you're talking about. Fuck off."

I sigh. "Look, we all know what's in this warehouse. I came here a few years back, and I'm looking to do some... shopping. Now let us in. We're getting wet, and I have money to burn."

"I told you to—"

"I know what you told him to do," interrupts Ruby. She walks up the steps and stands in front of the man. He's easily a foot taller, but she's unfazed. She just looks up at him. "But like he told *you*, we're returning customers. Now go and get Oscar, so we don't have to add the recruitment of new security to his to-do list."

I smile. I like her.

The guy glances at me and raises an eyebrow in silent query.

I shrug. "Don't look at me. I was just going to break your arm."

He shuffles uneasily on the spot. His eyes dart back and forth, the doubt evident on his face.

"I thought that was you."

I look in the direction of the new voice and see Oscar standing in the doorway, leaning against the frame. He's smiling.

I walk up the steps, brushing past the security guard without giving him the courtesy of making eye contact.

I extend my hand, which Oscar shakes. "Good to see you again, my friend. You lost weight?"

He hasn't.

He laughs. "I appreciate the compliment, but you can shove it up your ass! You don't need to butter me up, and your money's no good here."

I nod. "I appreciate that, Oscar. Thank you."

He gestures to Ruby with a nod. "And who have we here?"

"This is a friend of mine. She's a... colleague."

"Ah, I see."

She steps forward and nods a professional greeting. "The name's Ruby."

"And where's your other friend?" he asks me.

"Josh? Oh, he's, ah... we don't work together anymore."

He frowns. "Everything all right?"

"Oh, yeah, everything's fine. We're still in touch. He's actually upper management over at GlobaTech Industries now. Would you believe that?"

He raises an eyebrow. "Really? Shit, I bet he's a busy boy."

"Yeah... that's kinda why I'm here. Can we talk inside?"

His face changes to a look of familiar concern. "Why do I get the feeling you're about to do something suicidal?"

I shrug. "Fairly safe odds under any circumstances."

He smiles and turns, disappearing inside his office.

I turn to Ruby, who's looking a little confused, and smile. "Come on. You're gonna love this part."

She follows me inside and shuts the door behind us. His office is still the same as I remember—minimalistic and untidy. Oscar is standing behind his desk. I move over, allowing Ruby to look around. She appears confused, frowning as she surveys the room. I catch Oscar's eye and smile, remembering fondly how I reacted when I first came here.

She looks at me first, then at Oscar. "I thought you sold, y'know, guns and shit?"

He smiles, then breaks into a loud laugh. She turns to me for an explanation, but I just shake my head and grin. I'm not ruining it for her.

Oscar takes a remote from his pocket and makes a point of showing it to her before pressing a button. The whirring of gears and machinery sounds out, and the wall behind him splits vertically down the middle, sliding away to each side.

Ruby steps forward, her jaw loose and eyes wide, watching as the hidden warehouse slowly reveals itself.

"Holy fucking shitballs..." she whispers.

I laugh. "Yup. That was pretty much my reaction the first time too."

Oscar smiles proudly as the doors stop. He steps aside and gestures for her to go in. "Go ahead, Ruby. Knock yourself out."

She practically runs into the warehouse like a kid in a toy store. We both watch her go, then he turns to me. "So, what brings you back here, Adrian? Didn't think you'd wanna risk showing your face around these parts after your last visit."

I scratch the back of my head and smile sympathetically. "Needs must, I'm afraid. How's it been around here?"

"It was a goddamn free-for-all in the first few weeks." He moves to sit on the edge of his desk, then crosses his arms across his chest and rests them on the top of his stomach. "Trent's assets were fought over and claimed by all the little guys who never got a chance when he was running things. The headless corpse you dropped on the cops caused a real shit-storm... You should be careful moving around the city —just a friendly piece of advice."

I wave my hand dismissively. "I got bigger problems than local PD."

He raises an eyebrow. "Who've you pissed off now?"

"The CIA."

"Jesus! Do I want to know?"

"You probably already do. You must've seen the news about 4/17?"

"Yeah, that's a fucking tragedy. I can't—wait. Please tell me you weren't involved with *that*?"

I take a deep breath. "I'll give you the abridged version. The less you know, the better—trust me. The whole thing was a front. A conspiracy. It wasn't terrorists who hijacked that satellite. The CIA was behind the attacks. In fact, the CIA *director* was the piece of shit who pressed the button that launched the missiles."

"Get the fuck outta town! How do *you* know *that*?"

"I was in the room when he did it. Held at gunpoint by a squad of agents and a bunch of terrorists who were hired to take the fall for it."

He stands, visibly disturbed. "Holy shit, Adrian!"

"Oh, it gets better. The president masterminded it all. He's been using the CIA and all the other acronyms as his own personal army-slash-hit squad... tying up loose ends, orchestrating it from the shadows as part of some master plan. I'm the only one with proof, which is why the half of the world *not* nuked back to the Stone Age is now trying to kill me."

He shakes his head and laughs with disbelief. "Sucks to be you, huh? So, what brings you here? From what you've said, even if I gave you everything I have behind me, it wouldn't be enough to protect you."

I nod. "Josh can't help me this time. He's too visible at GlobaTech. I'm putting together a team of assassins to help me kill the president. I've got one guy on board who's meeting up with me in a few days. I've just brought Ruby into the fold. We need weapons. Money's no object."

"Adrian, I..." He stands and begins pacing back and forth in front of his desk, staring at the floor. "I can't be linked to something like this."

I shake my head. "You wouldn't be. No one will ever know where the weapons came from. But there's nowhere else I can go with this. I really need your help."

Oscar sighs heavily. "Shit, Adrian. Shit!"

Ruby appears and stands in front of one of the large metal shelving units. She's holding a rocket launcher in one hand, resting it on her shoulder. Oscar turns, following my gaze.

"Adrian, I fucking *love* this place!" she exclaims.

She disappears again, heading down an aisle to her right.

Oscar and I look at each other, and he raises an eyebrow. "She's a little bit crazy, isn't she?"

"Heh... you have *no* idea."

He sighs again. "Ah, shit. Come on."

He gestures for me to follow him, then turns and walks into the warehouse.

9

MEANWHILE…

Cunningham hung up the phone and sat back in his chair, gazing around the Oval Office. He just received word from the director of the FBI that Adrian Hell had evaded capture in Baltimore a few hours ago after springing an inmate from an asylum for the criminally insane. Once again, he managed to disappear in the chaos, and the president was becoming increasingly frustrated with everyone's inability to apprehend one man.

He sat forward, leaning on his elbows and resting his head in his hands. On his desk was a stack of papers awaiting his attention and signature, but he didn't have the patience for them. He was growing tired of having to deal with all the things that went along with being president. He just wanted to get on with the mission at hand but knew he couldn't. Everything had been meticulously planned for many years, and with the time finally upon him to strike, he

86

knew he had to exercise extreme discipline to do things the right way.

His conversation with the North Korean leader had gone well, and he was expecting to implement the next stage of his plan soon. Again, timing was crucial, but everything should be in place for when he was ready.

A knock on the door distracted him from his musings.

"Yes?" he called out.

Heskith entered and walked across the plush navy carpet toward the Resolute desk. "Mr. President, I've got General Matthews on the line, asking for a moment of your time."

Cunningham raised an eyebrow. "Is Adrian Hell dead?"

Heskith shook his head regretfully. "No, he's not."

"Goddammit!" He banged his fist on the desk, the rage exploding inside him. "I *told* him—"

Heskith held up a hand. "I know, sir, and I explained that to him in no uncertain terms. But you should listen to what he has to say. He might be on to something."

Cunningham relaxed back into his chair, resting his elbows on the arms and bridging his fingers in front of his face. He sighed. "Fine."

Heskith nodded and stepped forward. He leaned over the desk and pressed a button on the phone, then placed it on speaker.

He said, "Tom, you're on with the president now."

The sound of Matthews clearing his throat rasped down the line. "Mr. President, let me first apologize for—"

"Save it, Tom," the president replied, cutting him off. "Just tell me what you have."

There was a moment's silence on the line.

"Okay, sir. Well, I sent a team to the restaurant in Maine, where we tracked Adrian Hell. We spoke to a man there named Ashton Case. He wasn't very cooperative, but we determined he's a hitman who works for a local gangster and is old friends with Adrian."

Cunningham exchanged a glance with Heskith, silently asking if what was being said was relevant. Heskith nodded.

"Go on," said the president.

"He gave Adrian a list of four names—three male, one female. Two were unknown to us, but the other two, we recognized. The first was the female, currently serving time in the Stonebanks Institute in Baltimore. At least, she was..."

Cunningham sat up in his chair. "Didn't we almost take Adrian Hell down there a couple hours ago?"

"That's right. We weren't successful, but we do know that he broke the woman out of the institute and disappeared with her."

"I hope you're coming to a point soon, Tom, because I'm losing my patience."

"Sir, our analysts believe Adrian's... recruiting. He's putting together a team for something."

"Any ideas what?"

"We can only speculate, Mr. President, but given the information he has and everything that's happened recently, the most obvious guess is that he's coming for you, sir."

Cunningham glanced at Heskith again. Although, this time, there was more concern than frustration. "How real is this threat?"

There was another pause on the line. "Sir, I strongly advise you to increase your security."

Cunningham stood and paced back and forth behind his desk. He looked at Heskith. "What do you think?"

His chief of staff shrugged. "It's sound logic, sir. Given everything we know about this guy, I'd take Matthews's advice on this one. At least until the next phase is underway. Then it won't matter what he does."

Cunningham nodded. "Make the arrangements, would you?" He looked back at the phone. "Is there anything else, Tom?"

"Sir, there is one more thing. The other name on the list that we recognize... he's an assassin we've had our eye on for a while. We liked him for a hit a couple years back in Moscow but never got enough solid intel to back up the suspicion. If Adrian's planning on recruiting him, it would definitely be cause for concern."

"So, what are you suggesting here, Tom?"

"Mr. President, I have an idea that could do away with our Adrian Hell problem once and for all. It's risky, and I wanted your blessing before going ahead with it."

Cunningham looked up at Heskith. "You know about this?"

Heskith nodded. "I do, sir, and it's a solid plan—if it works. If it doesn't, it could leave us wide open. I suggest you keep your distance and know as little about it as possible. But it's your call."

Cunningham stroked his chin, feeling a day's worth of coarse growth on his palm. He had little faith left in Matthews's ability to do anything. He believed the pressure of being so involved in 4/17 had become too much for Matthews to handle, which made him a liability. That said, he was eager to remove Adrian Hell from the picture, and if Heskith believed this plan was a viable option, that was good enough for him.

"Tom, do what you have to," he said finally. "You officially have my blessing. You're to liaise with Gerry on this one. I don't want any details beyond whether or not it's worked. Do you understand? Use back channels when communicating, and above all else, make sure the White House is kept out of it. Am I clear?"

"Absolutely, sir," he said, sounding excited. You won't regret it."

"This is your last chance, Tom. If this blows up in your face, you will not receive any support from this office."

"I understand. Thank you, Mr. President."

The line clicked off, and the room fell silent for a moment. It was Heskith who spoke first.

"What's next, sir?"

"I need to read through these papers." He tapped the pile of reports on his desk. "And then I need to speak to Secretary Fielding before the next phase goes live. In the meantime, I want you to find out everything you can about Adrian Hell. I want his entire life story. There might be something we can use against him."

"Don't you think Matthews can get the job done?"

"Let's just say his track record does little to inspire any confidence. I want this done as a precaution."

"Yes, Mr. President. I'll see to it personally."

"Thank you, Gerry."

Heskith nodded, then walked back toward his office. He closed the door gently behind him, leaving Cunningham alone.

The president walked over to a small table against the wall and took the stopper from the crystal decanter that held a sixty-year-old single malt. He lifted it to his nose and took in a deep, appreciative breath. The coarse, burning aroma of the whiskey, which had been a gift from the prime minister of the United Kingdom when he took office two and half years ago, lingered in his nostrils. His mouth watered, and he poured himself a generous measure into a matching tumbler in front of him. He cradled it in his hand for a moment, then took a large sip and walked back to his desk. He sat down in his chair and carefully placed his drink on a coaster with the presidential seal printed on it. He took the first report from the top of his pile and opened it in front of him.

"GlobaTech Industries' deployment and financial records," he muttered to himself. "Let's see the secrets behind your magic, shall we?"

10

ADRIAN HELL

Oscar agreed to help us out. We left with a large bag of weaponry and the promise that he'll deliver more to us if we need it, whenever and wherever I ask. He refused to accept any money, basing his charity on the fact that if he's sponsoring my attempt to change the world, the publicity he'll get if I succeed will earn him untold fortunes.

I appreciate his faith in my ability to do this if nothing else.

We didn't want to risk exposing ourselves any more than we already had, so we decided to lie low in Allentown overnight, then move on in the morning. We're holed up in a cheap motel on the outskirts of the city. It's a basic place. There's a parking lot facing a row of identical rooms, each with a double bed, crappy TV, and basic bathroom.

Ruby's been in the shower for almost an hour.

I'm lying on the bed, staring up at the broken ceiling fan, trying to think of a plausible and effective way to assassinate the leader of the free world. I've never struggled with how to carry out a hit before. Some jobs have been harder than others, granted, but the difficult part was always carrying it out, never deciding how to approach it in the first place. This is new, unfamiliar territory to me. I would give anything to have one conversation with Josh. He would know what to do in a heartbeat.

I rub my hands over my face, wiping away the fatigue. I haven't slept in forever. I just can't silence my mind long enough. I mean, forget trying to kill Cunningham for a moment. I still need to figure out what the guy's actually trying to accomplish. I know Josh is probably all over that too, but I need to know so I can prepare for it.

Why do all this? Why kill nearly half a billion people and make a quarter of the world's land mass uninhabitable? He already had it all. America's the richest country in the world. He single-handedly eradicated organized drug-related crime. Unemployment, the homeless, and poverty are all at an all-time low. Why destroy other countries?

Ah, fuck it. My head hurts.

I stand just as the bathroom door opens. Ruby appears with a towel wrapped around her.

"Oh my God, that felt good!" she declares loudly.

The towel isn't doing a good job of covering her body. It's high on her thigh and low on her ample chest. My gaze is drawn to her upper body. The image is burned into my mind of her back in her cell, as naked as the day she was born, covered in a frightening network of self-inflicted wounds.

Wounds which no longer seem to be there...

"Hey, I'm up here," she says, smiling.

Flustered, I look at her emerald eyes, which are playfully taunting me. "Sorry, I was—"

"You were staring at me again. This is becoming a bit of a habit, isn't it? Here..." She grabs hold of her towel in both hands and opens it like a curtain in a theater, revealing her naked body. "You want a better look?"

I put my hand up to block my view and turn my head away. "Jesus, will you *stop* flashing me? Do you even know what dignity is?"

Ruby closes the towel again, laughing. "Dignity's for pussies." She gestures to her body. "*This* is as much a weapon for me as a gun is."

"And a mighty fine weapon it is, but that's not why I'm looking. What happened to your scars? The ones that *keep your demons in*, or whatever it was you said..."

"Oh, those?" She smiles. "Just before I got myself committed, I had a makeup artist friend of mine put them on for me. I figured they'd help with the charade." She moves over to the chair by the window and sits down, crossing her legs with unnecessary exaggeration. "It's just a body wrap, essentially. Like those fake tattoo sleeves you can get."

I sit back down on the bed, facing her. I'm impressed with her commitment to the role. She still has a glimmer of insanity behind her eyes, but as I look at her now, she's a far cry from the woman I rescued this morning. She looks normal... feminine. Not a hint of the feral, twisted killer I first saw.

"So, talk me through the whole *criminally insane* thing. What was your reasoning behind it?"

Ruby shrugs. "I slipped up on a job and got caught." She leans back in her chair. "If I had been tried, I'd have been given the death penalty without question. I knew I needed to get out of it and lie low for a *long* time. I didn't have a lawyer, but I'd watched enough TV to know that pleading insanity was probably my only option. I ran through the routine in my head over and over again. Then, on my last court appearance before sentencing, I got in character. They sent me to Stonebanks in Baltimore."

I smile. "Well, I've seen you play the part, so I can understand their reaction."

"Once I was inside, I thought it could work quite well. I figured I could sneak out whenever I had a contract and hide out there between jobs. No one would ever think to look for me in an asylum, right?"

I nod. "Kinda like a Winter Soldier thing? Nice idea."

She frowns. "Who?"

I really need to lay off the comic-slash-movie references when Josh isn't here. It just confuses people.

I shake my head. "Never mind. So, what went wrong?"

"It turns out I played my part a little too well. They put me in solitary on a priority watch, which made it impossible for me to get out. Luckily, the last visit before my ass was hauled off to the funny farm was from my friend, who managed to put the body wrap on me for the scars, so at least I could keep up the act once I was inside and be left alone. Not sure what I would've done long-term if you hadn't come for me, though."

I shrug. "It was a stroke of luck for both of us there, I think. But, ah... I gotta ask, seeing as we'll be working together. The hit you got caught on... a guard in the asylum said you torched a retirement home full of old people. That's a bit much, isn't it? Even for someone in our line of work."

Ruby smiles, like she's forgiving my ignorance. "Yeah, I *did* torch a building full of old people. And that's all anyone knows, officially."

I raise an eyebrow. "And unofficially?"

"The care home I destroyed was a front for a pedophile ring, and it was full of child molesters. Every single one of those twisted fucks had spent their lives ruining other people's lives and had gotten away with it. The father of a kid who killed himself after years of abuse spent thousands of dollars investigating it, and it led him to that retirement home. The job came to me and I did it for free. And I hope each and every one of the sick bastards is still burning."

I clench my jaw muscles, empathetically angry at the thought of people being allowed to live after committing such atrocities. I also feel a swell of pride for Ruby, in a purely professional capacity. I'm pleased for her that she was able to use her abilities to take on what I would consider a noble cause and provide that grieving father with the closure he needed. It's good for us to sometimes use our skills and our job to do something honorable and just. It's a shame there aren't more of us around who think the same way.

I feel myself glaze over, lost in a moment of rage and understanding.

"Are you... okay?"

"Huh?" I snap back into the moment. "Yeah, I'm good. Sorry. And I'm glad you've got my back on this. Don't get me wrong—as I'm sure you can appreciate, I tend not to trust people much. But professionally speaking, I'm glad you're on the team."

She smiles. "No one could pass up this payday, whoever the target. Speaking of which, have you got any ideas on how we're going to do this?"

I shake my head. "Nothing concrete, no. We've got another couple of stops to make yet. There are two more people on the list I want to try to recruit."

"Yeah, I was gonna ask... where did you get my name from, anyway?"

"I went to see Ashton Case. Figured he'd know some people crazy enough to wanna help me out. You'll be pleased to know your reputation for being certifiable is strong in the community. He said to use you as a last resort... said you were off the reservation."

I smile and Ruby laughs. "Yeah, I'm *almost* as bad as you!"

"Hey, my reputation was given to me. I just work to maintain it. It's good for business."

"Smart strategy. Guess that's why you're a legend..." She smiles at me, her eyes twinkling.

"Well, I can't take all the credit, but I won't argue."

"So, who else has signed up so far?"

"Just the guy I went to see before you. Jonas Briggs..."

She claps her hands like an excited teenager. "Ooh, I've heard of him! He likes his poisons if I remember right?"

I think back to the needle he held to my neck when he first confronted me. "Yeah, that's the guy."

"Bit of a loner, but he's got a solid reputation."

"Well, I thought he was a prick, to be honest, but he seems useful and he's on board. We're meeting him in Atlantic City a couple of days from now."

She nods. "So, where's our next stop?"

"North Carolina... Greensboro."

I see the change in her expression. Her smile drops instantly and her body tenses. She uncrosses her legs and shifts in her seat.

"North Carolina? Please don't tell me you mean—"

"The European. Yeah, is that a problem?"

Ruby sighs heavily. "I'm not sure. Fernando and I go way back."

JAMES P. SUMNER

Fernando?

She smiles regretfully. "He's, ah... he's my ex."

I close my eyes as a wave of disbelief and a sense of impending dread wash over me. I let out a sigh of my own. "Great."

"We haven't seen each other for a long time. Eighteen months, easily. He took a contract in Greensboro, doing some exclusive work for a gangster who opened up a chain of companion clubs. He was new to the game but had a lot of cash—and a lot of enemies. Fernando took the guaranteed payday and started working for him, taking out the competition. But he got a little too friendly with some of the girls working there, and we broke up."

I massage the bridge of my nose between my thumb and index finger, quickly running through all the possible ways this could be a pain in my ass.

"There's no ill feelings between us that I know of," Ruby continues, seeing my distress. "I wasn't exactly the doting girlfriend. It's the nature of our business, I guess. But I actually liked him, and it hurt for a while when we separated."

"Okay, just promise me this won't be a *thing*, all right? On top of everything else, I can really do without the *Jerry Springer* crap."

She stands quickly and salutes, which causes her towel to drop to the floor. "Promise, Chief!"

I fall backward on the bed, staring at the ceiling again. "God help me."

11

ADRIAN HELL

We left our motel at dawn, hitting the road for the seven-hour drive to Greensboro. As daylight chased us, another cloudy day revealed itself. Thankfully, the rain's held off so far, but it's thinking about it.

I didn't sleep much for a variety of reasons. First, I was on the floor. Ruby *graciously* offered to share the bed with me but, given the outstanding lack of discretion she's shown so far, I didn't hold out much hope of surviving the night.

As I lay awake, I started wondering what Tori would make of all this. She's amazing, and surprisingly understanding of everything, but my current situation would test even the most patient of girlfriends.

Then I was focused on missing her. Since leaving her behind in Texas, I've purposely tried to forget about her. It just makes things easier, I guess. I'm on a dangerous journey that I'm not convinced I'll live to see through to the end. The last thing I need is the distraction of worrying about my loved ones. It's the same reason I'm keeping my distance from Josh. I know he has his professional reputation to think about, but I'm just worried I'll put him in danger.

Another reason I didn't sleep well was I still didn't feel completely safe from any potential *attempts* by Ruby to... entertain herself, shall we say. Maybe I'm flattering myself, but I think I at least have grounds enough for concern, given how she's behaved so far.

Consequently, it's taken a couple of hours on the road to really get my head in the game. I've been driving mostly on autopilot since we left Allentown. Ruby stayed awake all of ten minutes after setting off, and she's been sleeping ever since. The traffic's been light, although we've just hit I-81 going through Harrisburg, and it's starting to get busier.

I glance across at Ruby. She stirs, opens her eyes slowly, and stretches in her seat, speaking through a yawn. "Are we there yet?"

I smile. "No, there's a long way to go, I'm afraid."

She doesn't respond.

After a few minutes of shuffling in her seat, I feel her staring at me.

"What?" I ask.

"Tell me something," she says, sounding curious. "You've seen me naked more than once. And I'm pretty sure you had an eyeful in the sewers. Why haven't you tried to get it on with me yet? Most men would've by now."

I shake my head. I hate this type of conversation.

I don't take my eyes off the road. "I'm not *most men*. I've got someone waiting for me, whom I love very much. I'm not interested." I turn to look at her, smiling weakly. "No offense."

She regards me for a moment and then smiles, finally looking away. "That's nice. I'm happy for you."

"Thanks. Although, I'll admit it's not the best thing right now."

"Why?"

"Because I can't see her. I'm toxic at the moment, and anyone near me is putting their life in danger. To protect her, I have to distance myself from her. And... and it's hard, y'know."

She's silent for a minute. "Jesus... you *are* a pussy, aren't you?"

I look over and see she's smiling playfully. I frown. "Be aware that I have yet to develop any reservations about shooting you."

She pouts. "What about the whole *no women, no kids* rule?"

I laugh. "That's not a rule! This isn't a movie. If you've done something awful enough to warrant someone sending me after you, then you're going to die. Simple as that. Yeah, I won't shoot a kid, but that's my own choice. I know plenty of people who probably would. Besides, you're not a woman. You're a killer."

She shakes her head. "*I'm* not a woman? Do you want me to prove you wrong? Because you know I will..."

"No, I'm good. Thanks. You're lovely, but I'm driving and, y'know, too much of a good thing, et cetera..."

We share a laugh, and the lighter mood helps me relax more. Makes me think back to the good ol' days when I was talking to Josh on the phone, traveling solo around the country. Despite working hard over the last few years to ensure my days of doing that were over, right now, I'd give anything to trade this in and go back to those simpler times. Just for a little while.

We shoot past a sign for Chambersburg.

Hang on a minute.

We're heading straight for...

"Shit."

Ruby looks over. "What is it?"

I'm the first to admit geography has never really been my strong point. Further proof of how reliant I was on Josh—he would always tell me where to be and how to get there, so I never paid much attention. But I've just realized something...

"We're gonna drive straight through Virginia..."

Ruby shrugs. "That a problem?"

I nod. "The CIA wants me dead. Langley's its home. Plus, we'll be within spitting distance of the White House before that."

"So, we'll just keep a low profile. It'll be fine. You worry too much. You'll get an ulcer or something." She settles back in her seat, closing her eyes.

I sigh. "I think you're missing the point. The CIA—and presumably, the president—knows I have evidence to bury them. That's *why* they want me dead. They also know I'm a good assassin. It doesn't take a genius to figure that at some point I might try killing someone. It's kind of my go-to solution to most problems. So, the closer we are to them—"

"...the more security there'll be." She nods as she finishes my sentence. "So, what do you want to do?"

"Not much we can do, I guess. Whether you like it or not, we need someone of The European's caliber on our side. And we don't really have the time to detour a couple hundred miles west just to avoid the more direct route on the slight chance we might—"

Lights flash in my rearview, and sirens follow a moment later, distracting me. It's a squad car with two officers in it.

"—be seen. Fuck!"

Ruby sits up straight in her seat and looks over her shoulder. "Are they signaling to *us*?"

"Yup."

"What are you going to do?"

I shrug. "Try my best not to shoot them and hope they don't look in the back."

The big bag of goodies we got from Oscar is in the back, under some tarpaulin.

I pull over to the side of the road and roll my window down. The cops fall in behind us. They both step out of their car, look around, and adjust their belts to look casual but threatening. They exchange a glance and then approach the truck.

I look at Ruby. "Let me do the talking, okay?"

Let me do the talking... Jesus, we're screwed!

They draw level with us, and the guy on my side leans down. He looks older than me, with gray hair and a weathered face. He's maybe in his mid-fifties. "License and registration please."

"Is there a problem, officer?" I try to sound as normal and innocent as possible while pretending to search for things I obviously don't have with me.

"I hope not, son."

I look over at Ruby. She's doing her best to flirt silently with the younger officer at her side, but so far, he seems to be resisting her charms.

"I don't have them with me. Sorry—must be in my other jacket. What's this about?"

The cop stands up straight and takes a step away from the truck. He reaches forward and opens my door. "Can you step out of the vehicle, please, sir?"

I sigh. "You're not gonna tell me what this is about? This could be viewed as harassment. You know that, right?"

He doesn't bite, remaining calm and stubborn. "Sir, would you please step out of the vehicle?"

I do, albeit reluctantly.

"Is this your truck?"

Oh.

I shrug. "I'm driving it."

"Answer the goddamn question, and don't get cute with me."

"Yes, it's my truck."

"This vehicle was reported stolen from a parking lot in Baltimore yesterday afternoon."

I glance back at the old, brown rust bucket that has served me well these past thirty hours or so. I catch the eye of the other officer standing by Ruby's door. His face is expressionless. I can't tell if that's disinterest or genuine ignorance. Either way, whether this is me springing a trap or just running out of luck, I can't afford to get delayed by the police. And I definitely can't let these assholes put me in the system. All hell would break loose.

I need to do something, and I only really have one approach...

I turn back to the cop in front of me. "Doesn't look stolen to me. It's right here."

He looks away for a second with frustration, letting out a heavy sigh. "All right, smartass. Move to the front of the vehicle, turn around, and put your hands on the hood."

I shrug again. "Make me."

He moves his hand to his holster, unclipping the piece of material securing his firearm in place. "Don't test me. Move around the vehicle... and put your hands on the *goddamn* hood!"

I pace slowly to the front of the truck, lean forward on the hood, and spread my legs. I look up and glance through the windshield at Ruby, who's staring at me, silently asking what I intend to do.

Good question.

If I let these pricks arrest me, it's game over. If I knock him out and run, it's game over. Either way, I'm screwed.

But knocking him out is more fun.

I flick my gaze to her door and wink at her.

The cop moves behind me. I look over my shoulder at him. "Put your hands on me, and I'll break them."

The younger one by Ruby's door looks over. His hand disappears to his side, hovering over his firearm.

"Threatening a police officer with violence?" says the one behind me. "That's it. I'm placing you under arrest. You have the right to remain silent—"

"You first!" I spin around clockwise and bring my elbow up, slamming it into his face. He staggers back, losing his footing and falling to the ground.

Behind me, I hear Ruby's door open. I look back in time to see her ram it into the other cop's body. He stumbles backward. She steps out, moves toward him, and kneels down out of sight behind the truck.

I turn back to my cop, who's reeling on the ground. I crouch beside him and pick up his weapon. "Look, I'm sorry about this. I really am. This isn't personal. But there's some shit going on right now that's so far above your pay grade that you can't see it for the sun. You understand? You're just in the wrong place at the wrong time."

I hit him again in the face, which knocks him out cold. I stand, tuck the gun in the waistband of my jeans, and turn around. Ruby's walking toward me, holding the other cop's gun.

"You good?"

She nods. "He's out. Figured you wouldn't want him too injured…"

"Thanks. After all, it's not their fault. Come on."

She sighs. "Pussy."

I walk over to the squad car, aware that the road isn't exactly quiet. People are going to remember seeing this —and us.

"What are you doing?" she calls after me.

I duck inside, reach under the dash, and fumble around until I find the wires for the computer built into the center console. I yank them out and grab the radio. I stand up and turn to face Ruby.

"Just making sure they can't tell anyone they've seen us." I drop the radio to the ground and stamp on it.

She smiles. "Good thinking!" She points her gun at the front tire and fires once.

"Jesus! What are you *doing*?"

She shrugs. "Now they can't follow us, either."

"Yeah, but you could've just let the air out or something! Firing your gun isn't exactly—"

She raises an eyebrow and smiles.

"—discreet… never mind." I sigh. "Christ, you're worse than *me*."

"Is that a compliment?"

I shrug. "Depends on your point of view, I guess."

I walk past her and get back in the truck. She climbs in beside me.

"We need to ditch this car. Chambersburg's only a few miles away, so we'll detour there."

"Can we get something to eat? Maybe change our clothes again?" she asks.

I ease away from the roadside to rejoin the line of traffic. I check my mirror, but there's no immediate movement that worries me. "Yeah, why not?"

Ruby insisted we stop at a Dunkin' Donuts for breakfast. I'm not happy. Apart from being sick to death of seeing them everywhere I go, it's just not natural! I mean, I'm sitting here with a donut in front of me, which has been sliced horizontally and had bacon and egg shoved inside it! This isn't food! It's just a confused dessert *pretending* to be breakfast! When I die from the inevitable heart attack this is likely to bring about, I'm really going to hate myself. If I weren't so hungry, there's no way I would ever come here and order this shit.

"Just eat it," says Ruby, who is sitting across from me.

I look up at her, unable to hide my disgust as she takes a bite of her meal.

She shrugs, swallowing her mouthful of food. "What?"

"What do you mean, *what*? You're eating a goddamn cheeseburger inside a donut. How am I the only one who finds that criminal?"

She takes another bite, not bothering to finish chewing before replying. "It's not a donut, it's a bagel, you fucking moron. Besides, I've been incarcerated in an insane asylum for almost a year. This shit is heaven!"

She swallows again and takes a sip of her drink—some weird slushie with fruit in it, apparently.

I push my meal away from me. "Whatever. I can't believe I let you talk me into coming here."

"You're such a snob!"

"No, I'm not. I just feel that filling my arteries with this shit is depriving the CIA of their chance to kill me. I mean, they've been working so hard…"

She shakes her head. "Whatever. What's our next move?"

I take a sip of coffee, which is tolerable at best, and think about it. "Well, we're still a few hours away from Greensboro. We'll change clothes quickly, switch cars, then get the hell outta Dodge. The longer we stay in one place, the greater the chance of us getting caught."

A member of staff walks past our table. She's a young woman, early twenties. She catches my eye as she begins cleaning the table beside us.

"Is everything all right with your meals today, folks?" she asks, smiling.

I can't do it. I can't lie to her. No, my meal's not okay. It's a travesty—an insult to all food. It's unnatural, and despite years of perfecting the art of self-loathing, even *I* don't hate myself enough to put my body through the torturous experience of eating whatever the fuck I just paid eleven bucks for.

I sigh and grit my teeth. "It's… ah… it's fine. Thanks."

She frowns at me. I'm guessing I wasn't able to keep the disdain out of my voice. The waitress turns to Ruby, who smiles at her. "Ignore him." She gestures to me casually. "He's just grumpy because he hasn't been laid in a while."

I fix her with a stare I usually reserve for people I'm about to shoot. The young employee goes bright red and walks away, avoiding my gaze.

"Thanks for *that*."

She shrugs. "Well, it serves you right."

"For what?"

"Being miserable."

"Being mis—it's a donut with fucking *bacon* in it!"

She looks at me like I'm an alien. "It's a goddamn bagel, and it's delicious."

"Oh, whatever." I stand and stretch my back a little. "I need to make a call. Wait here."

I head over to the back near the restrooms, where it's quiet. I take out my burner phone and dial a number from memory. As it rings out, I turn to quickly survey the restaurant.

I can't believe how busy this place is. We were lucky to get a table when we arrived. Our booth's over by the window, which means we can see who's approaching. I'm surprised more cops haven't shown up, given this place is donut-themed. Unbelievab—

"Hello?"

I smile at the dulcet British tone. "Josh, it's me."

"Adrian? Where are you?"

"I'm standing by the restrooms in a Dunkin' Donuts in the middle of Chambersburg, Pennsylvania."

"What the hell are you doing in one of *those*?"

"I have no earthly idea. I was dragged here by Ruby."

"Ruby?"

"DeSouza. She's a…" I lower my voice and casually look around. "She's one of us. She's agreed to help me on my next job."

"Ah, right. So, you settled on the recruitment plan, then?"

"Yeah. Didn't have much choice. How are things with you?"

"Busy. My new team's on a mission, and I'm running intel for them."

"Can't you just hire someone to do that for you nowadays?"

"I could, but it's hard finding people I can trust, y'know?"

"Yeah, I know that feeling."

"So, what can I do for you, Boss?"

I smile again. "Nothing, really. Just... y'know, checking in."

"Adrian, do you... do you *miss me*?"

I scoff. "No, 'course not."

I do a little, but I'm not telling *him* that.

"Ah, you miss me! Boss, I'm touched. Really, I am."

"Kiss my ass."

He laughs. "Listen, have you seen the news today?"

"No, why? Am I on it?"

"Not this time, no. Not *yet*, anyway. I suppose it's still early..."

"Hey, screw you, all right?"

He laughs, but it soon fades. "There's a lot of tension overseas. Lots of rebel activity in certain regions, and refugees from all over are killing themselves trying to find a new life in other countries."

"Shit. I suppose you had to expect this after everything that's happened. Still doesn't make it any easier, though. How are your employees finding it?"

"We're coping, for now. Our peacekeeping forces have come under fire in certain parts of Eastern Europe and Africa—local rebels, mostly. It's nothing we can't handle. It's just becoming a more regular problem."

"Has anyone made any more significant advances anywhere?"

"No, thankfully. But there've been rumblings. All you have to do is look at a map to see where the danger could lie. Russia and China are out of the game. Pakistan fared slightly better, but it'll still be years before it's back on its feet. It's the people who haven't been affected that are more dangerous. Guys in places like Japan, India, North Korea, parts of South America... they were all relatively unscathed. They'll feel threatened, I'm sure. I think it's just bubbling away beneath the surface, waiting to erupt."

"Christ. Well, if and when it does, I'm sure GlobaTech will be there to help deal with it. And even Cunningham wouldn't be able to sit back and let that happen, surely? He must've known this was an inevitable side effect of his plan."

"Yeah, maybe."

"So, how are you holding up, dealing with all this?"

"Well, Schultz is handling most of the bureaucracy, which is good of him. He's working around the clock to get anyone and everyone on our side. He's the face of Globa-Tech now. I'm organizing the logistics in the background, as well as helping you out where I can."

"Yeah, I appreciate everything you're doing for me, Josh. That intel you secured in Prague will hopefully be the final nail in Cunningham's coffin."

"I've got a good team. You'd like them. You know Ray Collins?"

"Ray? Yeah, nice guy. I was grateful for his help back in Pripyat."

"Yeah, he's something, all right. And you remember Jericho?"

"Stone? Jesus, how's he doing after Colombia? I can't believe he's not dead."

"He's still pissed about his unit turning on him, and he's not *your* biggest fan. Although, I think he's secretly thankful you kept him alive."

"Don't mention it. Look, I might not get a chance to call again for a while. I'm heading to North Carolina. Gonna see if I can convince The European to help me."

"The European? Isn't he supposed to be a bit of a dick?"

I chuckle. "Yeah, that's what I thought. But he's a damn good killer all the same."

"Fair point."

"I've already got a guy called Jonas Briggs on board. We've arranged to meet in Atlantic City in a couple days. I told him I'd keep in touch with him between now and then."

"Be careful with that, Adrian. Remember, calls and texts from a cell phone can be tracked."

"Yeah, I know. I use this cell phone sparingly. We've both got the log-in details to an e-mail account. We're leaving messages to each other in the drafts folder."

"Holy shit, Boss! Did you... were you actually paying attention to me all those times I told you technical things?"

I laugh. "You sound surprised. You know I'm actually pretty talented, right?"

"Yeah, but... y'know... I just didn't think you fully understood that stuff."

I shrug. "I don't. But I know enough to get by. You'll always be here for the rest."

"I'm so proud! Well, just remember to keep your head down, okay? Being all covert and whatnot is one thing, but the CIA has boots on the ground actively looking for you. Just be careful out there, man."

"Yeah, I am. Don't worry. Though, I must admit, it's getting harder to keep a low profile with Ruby in tow."

"What's she like?"

I think for a moment. "She's flashed me twice since I busted her out of an insane asylum."

There's silence for a moment. "She *flashed* you?"

I shake my head at the fact he completely ignored the part about her being incarcerated. "Twice."

"You get all the luck..."

I laugh. "That's one way of looking at it. Listen, do me a favor, would you?"

"Keep an eye on Tori for you?"

"I figured you were doing that anyway, to be honest."

"I am."

I smile. "Thanks. No, I was gonna say, do you have an e-mail account I can contact you with?"

"I do, yeah—of course. Why? What can't you say over the phone?"

"It's nothing I *can't* say. I just don't have the time to say it all. I've... I've got a plan, Josh. Based on the team I've got, I have a plan to end all this. But I need your help."

"Jesus, this must be big if you're planning in advance. You never do that."

"I know, but even *I* know this isn't something I can make up as I go along. Can I send you the details and what I need?"

"Yeah, sure. Leave me a draft, and I'll get right on it."

"Thanks, man. I'm hoping you'll agree it *could* work. It's easily the most dangerous job I've done. If anything happens to me... if I don't make it out the other side of this thing—"

"Quit with the emotional shit, Boss. You'll be fine. You've got this. You're, y'know... you."

"Thanks. But I'm being serious, Josh. If this goes south, I want you to go to The Ferryman. Tori's got the code to the safe there. My last will and testament is inside."

"Adrian, I..."

"All the money's yours, Josh. Every cent."

"Jesus! Adrian, I dunno what to say... I mean, what about Tori? I thought you'd be—"

"She's getting the deed to the bar."

"Shit. Listen, I'm touched, man. Seriously. But you can't

think like that, okay? Get your head in the game. Forget about that crap for now. You start thinking about failing, you *will* fail. Understand?"

"I hear you."

"Having said that, if you fail, I'll be loaded! I think I might start helping Cunningham..."

I laugh. "Fuck you!"

He laughs too, and I take a moment to remember this conversation. It feels natural talking with him. If this is the last time we speak, I want to remember the way we were. Everything we've been through together, summed up in a few sentences.

"Hey, have you ever eaten in one of these donut places?" I ask him.

He scoffs. "Are you fucking kidding me? Those places are unnatural. They're like a travesty to all food!"

"That's what I said!"

There are a few seconds of silence.

"Good luck, Adrian. Whatever happens, I've got your back until that piece of shit is in the ground. Remember that."

"Thanks, Josh. For everything. See you around."

"Damn right."

I hang up and let out a heavy sigh. I compose myself before I head back over to the table.

It's time Ruby and I hit the road.

12

ADRIAN HELL

The rest of the journey was uneventful, which I'm grateful for. We borrowed a handy little 4×4 on the way out of town, and we only stopped once for gas on our five-hour trek down Route 29.

I contacted Jonas via the e-mail account to let him know we were still on track to meet him tomorrow in Atlantic City. He replied saying he was finishing up a contract and expected to be on the road by tomorrow evening at the latest. I also left a message for Josh with my plan, but he hasn't answered me yet.

The rain chased us nearly all the way to Greensboro but gave up about a half-hour ago. We're parked across the street from a nice-looking bar on the corner of West Market and North Cedar, facing the college. The clouds overhead occasionally make room for some sunlight, but mostly, it's just dull.

In the interest of saving time, instead of following Ash's

vague information on the last known whereabouts of The European, I persuaded Ruby to simply call him and find out where he is. She said she wanted to meet up, and when she was met with skepticism, I gave her the nod to say she was with me and we were here on business.

That twisted his arm, and he gave us this address and a time—which is five minutes from now. His only stipulation was that we would both be unarmed, which I expected. It's common when two people in our world meet on business for them to show a certain level of professional courtesy and respect toward each other, to compensate for the understandable lack of trust.

So, we laid low, grabbed another bite to eat, and eventually made our way here.

By all accounts, The European has a reputation for being a world-class piece of shit, but there's no denying the man's skills as a professional. He's adept in most methods of killing. He's still young—compared to me, at least—but he's experienced and effective. Potential allies are few and far between at the moment, and if I can get him on board, we'll be in a good position to move forward with my plan.

And I'm sure twenty million dollars will help convince him if he's reluctant.

That said, despite everything, I haven't forgotten the fundamentals that gave me *my* reputation, either. Namely, my almost-perpetual cynicism and overwhelming distrust of anyone and everyone.

I'm looking over at the club, which is a nice building. It's a corner plot, with one main entrance guarded by a huge doorman. Presumably, there's a back entrance too, but that's it. No other way in or out. I have to assume The European is familiar with the place. Ruby said he's been working exclusively for some gangster in the city, so he's definitely going to know the area better than me. I'll be meeting him on his turf, in his own backyard...

I don't like it.

I was prepared for Jonas, using myself as bait to get to him. Ruby was pretty straightforward because if I had any doubts about her, I could simply leave her in her cell. But this guy... I don't know... he's got my spider sense jumping all over the place.

"You want me to go in and meet with him?" Ruby asks, presumably noting my visible hesitation.

I shake my head. "No, this is my responsibility. I just like to know everything about a new situation before I put myself in the middle of it."

"What's to know? He said he was interested in the work and to meet him here to discuss it."

"Yeah, I know."

"But..."

I smile and turn to look at her. "*But...* I don't like it. Just my gut feeling."

"Are you sure that's not you ovulating?"

I roll my eyes. "Because I'm a pussy... yeah, yeah—I get it. No, it's because I'm incredibly good at what I do. I haven't survived at the top of this business for as long as I have by being reckless. That's all I'm saying."

That's a complete lie. I've survived at the top of this business for as long as I have because of Josh, *despite* my borderline suicidal levels of recklessness.

But I'm not going to tell her that and ruin a perfectly good point.

She holds her hands up. "All right. Take it easy. So, what do you want to do?"

I shrug. "I have no option but to go inside to meet him. I want you to stay here, out of sight. Give it fifteen minutes, and if there's no sign, come in armed." I fix her a look, staring right in her eyes. "I hope there won't be any confusion or misplaced loyalties, should it come down to it."

She shakes her head and shrugs casually. "Please... I have no loyalty to *either* of you. But you're paying me a lot of zeroes to have your back, and he's not. There's my loyalty, okay?"

"Fair enough." I reach behind me, take out the gun I stole from the cop, and hand it to Ruby. She takes it without question. "Right, I'm going in."

18:21 EDT

I nod courteously to the doorman as I pass him and walk into the bar. The interior is artificially lit, but it's bright and looks pleasant enough. It has a blue and green theme throughout, with neon highlights decorating the bar area. Tall bar stools are positioned around columns to the right as I enter.

There's a small step down and then the place opens up, expanding back with chairs surrounding tables down the middle and left side. The right is taken up by the bar, and the restrooms are just beyond that.

The bar is half-full. It's probably a bit early for the evening crowds to descend. I scan the room and see a mixture of people enjoying their drinks—a group of young women off to the left, some couples on the right, a large party in the middle, laughing together... and one man sitting alone with his back to me, wearing a suit I can tell from here is worth a small fortune. It's tailored and shiny, light gray in color.

There he is.

I take a breath and walk over, fighting to retain what little diplomacy I have left. I don't like it, but I need him on my side in this, so I have to play this delicately.

I draw level with him, stop, and point to the seat opposite. "Join you?"

He looks up and smiles. "But of course." His voice sounds slimy and fake, and his accent has a hint of French mixed in with it. "It is good to see you, Adrian."

I smile humorlessly as I sit down. "I bet."

"Please, there is no need for any hostilities between colleagues. Can I get you a drink?"

I hold my hand up. "I'm good. Thanks."

He nods. "Of course. Straight to business, then?"

I regard him for a moment. He's a good-looking guy. There's no denying that. He's clean shaven, with chiseled, boyish features. He has thick, dark, styled hair and... has he had a manicure? Christ!

In addition to his fancy suit, he's wearing a black silk shirt with the top two buttons open. Resting on the table in front of him is a set of keys. There's a keychain on it with the Ferrari logo.

He sees me looking and smiles. "It's in the parking lot out back. The 488 Spider in British racing green. A beautiful machine. Zero to sixty in a fraction under three seconds. Six-sixty under the hood. It sounds like... like a tiger riding a bat out of hell." He laughs to himself.

Prick.

I don't care about your car, you fucking arrogant douche! I clench my jaw muscles.

Relax, Adrian. You need to stay calm.

I sigh and offer a weak smile. "You should be a car salesman."

He laughs again, clapping his hands together. "There's that famous sarcasm of yours. Tell me, how is your British friend doing these days? John, isn't it?"

"Josh. And he's fine. Bit busy at the moment, though."

He nods. "So, what brings you to my city?"

"*Your* city? Okay... I'm here to offer you some work."

"I already have plenty of work, thank you."

"Mine will pay better. Trust me."

He shrugs. "I don't know... I am paid *very* well."

"Not *this* well."

He strokes his chin for a moment. "How much are we talking?"

I frown. "Aren't you interested in what the job *is* first?"

He shakes his head. "I am interested in what the job is worth to me. For the right price, I will kill anyone. I do not care who."

"Okay. Twenty million."

A slight look of surprise reaches his eyes, betraying his otherwise calm and collected demeanor. "Dollars?"

"Yup."

"That *is* an impressive payout. And this is just my share?"

I nod. "Everyone on the team gets the same twenty million, yeah."

"And who do you have on this... team? Besides my darling Ruby, obviously."

I roll my eyes. "So far, just her and a guy from New Hampshire called Jonas Briggs. Got one more stop to make after we've finished here and then I can start planning the details. Are you interested enough to sign up?"

He absently strokes his eyebrow with his middle finger, staring blankly at the table in front of us.

"For you to be prepared to part with eighty million

dollars in total, this hit must be big. High profile... near impossible. Am I right?"

I shrug, giving nothing away.

"I am surprised there is a job in existence that would be deemed too much for the legendary Adrian Hell to handle on his own. I admit, I'm intrigued..."

Oh my God, what an asshat!

I lean forward, rest my forearms on the table, and lower my voice. There's no music playing in here, and I don't want anyone to overhear our conversation.

"I'm going to kill the person responsible for the 4/17 attacks."

He matches my body language and strokes his eyebrow again. "Now this, I do not understand. Did the president himself not announce almost two weeks ago that the person behind the attacks was in custody?"

I nod. "He did. But he's lying."

"And why would the president lie?"

I hold his gaze so that he can see the truth in my eyes. "Because the president is the one responsible."

He stares at me for a moment, then sits back quickly in his chair. He claps his hands slowly and laughs. "You are good, Adrian. *Very* good! You almost had me convinced. But there is no way anyone would make a serious attempt on *his* life. And there is no way anyone would believe your frankly outlandish claims."

I shrug and lean back myself, adjust my position in the chair, and get comfortable. I can see this conversation going on awhile.

"I have proof."

He stops laughing and raises a curious eyebrow. "Proof?"

I nod. "Aside from the fact that I was in the room when the big red button was pressed, I have documents that prove the president was behind it all. I *could* go into the finer points of it all with you, but if I'm honest, there's no need. It won't change the fact that he needs to be taken out. That's the job, *Fernando*. Are you in or out?"

He's quiet for a few moments. "And you're offering me twenty million to help you?"

I nod. "If we succeed, the money's yours."

"And if we don't?"

I shrug again. "Then we'll probably be dead, so the money's irrelevant."

He smiles humorlessly. "While you say I should be a salesman, Adrian, I fear that is not a skill set we share."

"To be honest, I'm growing tired of making my sales pitch. Call me old-fashioned, but this situation, to me, is the ultimate example of simply doing what's right. And with everything that's at stake, I like to think of it as a no-brainer."

"If that's true, why such a lucrative payday?"

"Because the right thing to do is rarely the easiest... or the smartest, in my experience. People like us... sometimes we need a bit more convincing."

"True. And what's in it for you? You're not getting paid for it."

"No, I'm not. I tried to leave this life behind, and that bit me on the ass. But I'm not here for the money. I'm here because it's right. Because it's necessary. And I'm the only one who knows the truth. So, I view it as my responsibility to do what other people can't." I check my watch. Ten minutes. Ruby should be here in another five. I need to wrap this up. I don't want her to come in here or these two to have a *thing*. "So, what'll it be?"

More silence and chin stroking, which I'm sensing is

more for show than anything. He knows what he's going to do.

"I'm afraid I must decline your... generous offer."

I frown, genuinely surprised. "Really? Even after everything I've told you... even knowing what's at stake?"

He nods and smiles. "Yes. I will be honest with you. I'm already working a contract in addition to my exclusive work in the city. I appreciate you taking time out of your busy life to explain your job offer to me, but I'm afraid it was wasted breath."

To quote any *Star Wars* movie, *I've got a bad feeling about this...*

My gut is knotting up with frustration and adrenaline as my spider sense goes off the scale. I tense every muscle in my body, counting down in my head how long I have until Ruby comes in here with a gun.

I grit my teeth. "Well... if you're not interested, I'll just be on my way."

The European leans forward again, holding a hand up. "I'm... heh... I'm afraid you can't do that, Adrian. Sorry."

I raise an eyebrow. "Excuse me?"

"You know, it's ironic, really. All the people in this world who want you dead, yet you're still your own worst enemy."

I sigh. "I'm really starting to dislike you."

I'm starting to worry too, but I keep that hidden. I don't have time for concern right now. I suspect I'm about to have a bad day.

"Yesterday, I was approached by someone with a job offer even more lucrative than yours. They wanted me to take out five targets. Discretion wasn't necessary but success was. And get this... they offered me seven-point-five million per target. *Per target*, Adrian! That's thirty-seven and a half million dollars total!"

I fight to keep any trace of concern from my face. "That's good work if you can get it. Congratulations on the contract."

"Thank you."

"And how's it going for you?"

He shrugs. "Honestly? Easier than I thought. I've taken two of them out so far."

"Well, don't let me keep you..."

He smiles. "You're not." He reaches inside his suit jacket and takes out a cell phone. He taps the screen, swipes to the right a couple of times, then places the device on the table and spins it around to show me. "Here's my first target."

I look at the screen.

Fuck.

Fuck, fuck, fuck!

It's Ashton Case. He's lying on the floor with a hole in his head and a pool of blood surrounding him.

I consciously think about how I should react. I'm surprised but... not that surprised. Yes, it's a shock to see Ash dead. And I feel responsible because I dragged him into this. But at the same time, I knew from the moment we pulled up outside that something wasn't right here. I *knew* it. And I hate when I'm right about shit like this and don't listen to myself.

Fuck.

I stare into The European's stone-gray eyes. I make a mental note of the time, the date, the weather outside, the color of the barman's tie—every single detail about this exact moment. I decided this sonofabitch is going to die, and I want to remember everything about this moment for when the time comes.

He smiles at me and swipes the screen. "And here's my second."

He's not trying to hide how much he's enjoying this. Piece of shit.

I stare at the screen again, but this time, I frown. "Who's that?"

He pauses for a moment, confused, but then acts like he's just realized something. "Ah, you must not know this person. He was the last name on the list Mr. Case gave you."

Oh.

I shrug, trying to remain calm while I think of all the ways I'm going to hurt him before I let him die. "Well, I appreciate you showing me. Saves me a trip."

"Ha! So arrogant…"

"Thanks."

"You won't talk your way out of this, Adrian. Once I've disposed of you and my dear, sweet Ruby—whom I assume is waiting outside?—I'll be heading to finish off Mr. Briggs before collecting my paycheck. Would you care to tell me where he is? It'll make things much simpler."

I need to stall him, either until Ruby gets here or until I've thought of a way to deal with this without endangering the people in here. I'm not armed, but I don't want to get into it with him right now because I have no doubt that he is.

I hold his gaze and try to sound as casual as I can. "Sure. He'll be in the bar of Caesar's in Atlantic City two days from now."

He's momentarily taken aback but quickly recovers. "Thank you. That's most… considerate of you."

I shrug. "Hey, I'm a nice guy. What can I say? So, tell me… who offered you the contract?"

He smiles. "You have a lot of enemies, Adrian."

"Yeah, I know. But I doubt many of them would condone hiring a contract killer to come after me."

He smirks, and it makes me want to hit him. You know how there are certain people who have a face you just *have* to punch as soon as you see it? Well, this guy's one of them.

"Do you honestly believe that?" he asks. "After everything you've just told me?"

I raise an eyebrow again to stop my eyes from going wide and giving away the fact that I'm on the back foot here. I quickly work it out in my head. The CIA caught up with me in Maine as I was leaving Ash's restaurant. They must've contacted the mothership before I took them out, and word would've gotten to someone in a position of power about what I was doing. They somehow got a copy of Ash's list, contacted the one name on it with any serious reputation, and offered him an obscene amount of money to take me and everyone else out.

I look into his eyes again. He's nodding at me. "That's it, Adrian. Put the pieces together…"

I sigh. "The president?"

He shakes his head.

I frown. "General Matthews?"

He smiles. "You're smarter than you look, Adrian."

"Yeah, I hear that a lot."

"Now, as pleasant as this has been, I should go. I imagine Ruby will be coming in any moment, correct?"

I say nothing.

"Of course, she is. You'll have a backup plan in place. I should go and say hi." He stands. I immediately move to follow, but he quickly steps around the table and places one hand on my shoulder, while the other opens his jacket, revealing a silenced handgun.

I *knew* he would have a gun. Does honor mean nothing anymore?

"I wouldn't do that if I were you."

"Why? You gonna shoot me?"

He smiles again. "Not at all. You don't simply *shoot* a living legend such as yourself. That is not a fitting end for someone of your professional standing. No, for you, I have something far more... grandiose planned."

"Gee, you shouldn't have..."

He pats my shoulder. "It was no trouble. Underneath your seat is a bomb. It's a device of my own design, containing a brick of C4 and a pressure-activated dead man's switch, which you engaged when you sat down. It's quite simple, really. You stand up, the bomb goes off. You'll take this entire building out along with you." He condescendingly pats my cheek with his palm a couple of times. "I believe some CIA people are on their way to disarm the bomb and collect you. Sit tight until then, okay?"

He backs away, fastens his jacket again, and waves.

Oh my God...

There's so much anger coursing through me right now, it actually hurts. Every fiber of my being is screaming at me to run over to him, shove my hand down his throat, and pull his lungs out through his mouth.

But I can't.

I tentatively feel beneath my chair with my hands.

I pat it gently, feeling for a—

Yup. That's a big fucking bomb!

Shit.

I fix him with the coldest stare I've ever given anyone. "I'm going to kill you. Understand? I'm going to kill you, and it'll really hurt."

He nods. "Okay, Adrian. Good luck with that."

He turns and waves behind him, strolling out of the bar without another word.

"Fuck," I mutter.

I look around at all the people in here, blissfully unaware that my ass is the only thing stopping them from becoming a hole in the ground.

I look outside through the small window in the door. I can just about see the hood of our 4×4. No sign of Ruby. I hope she's—

Holy shit!

A deafening explosion fills the air, shattering the glass in the door and rocking the foundations of the building. Everyone screams, jumps to their feet, and runs around in circles in sheer panic.

I stay planted to my chair, fighting the urge to run outside in search of Ruby.

Smoke billows across the street from what I assume are the remains of my ride. Sirens fade into earshot over the crackling of the flames.

Now what do I do?

13

ADRIAN HELL

Man, I wish Josh were here... stuck in a chair with a bomb strapped to his ass instead of me. I mean, seriously—what the hell am I supposed to do now? I can't stand up, and I can't exactly sit here doing nothing.

I'm pissed at how easily The European screwed me too. I should have listened to my gut. This would never have happened a couple of years ago. Maybe I'm getting sloppy. Or worse still, old.

I let out a low growl of frustration.

I need to get my head in the fucking game. If I carry on the way I have been, I'm going to end up dead.

Shit!

Right... focus, Adrian.

I take a deep breath. And another.

Okay. I have no reason to doubt that slimy little bastard when he said the CIA are coming for me, so I need to figure

129

a way out of here before they arrive. Otherwise, it's game over.

I look around the bar. It's emptying quickly, but there are still some people seemingly too scared to move. Makes sense, I guess. The explosion was outside, so I'm guessing their instinct is to stay indoors.

A young couple are at the next table over from me. They're maybe in their mid-thirties. I look across at them. "Guys, you need to get out of here. Get as far away from this building as you can. Do you understand?"

The woman's crying, gripping the hand of her man tightly. He's trying his best to comfort her, but I can see that he's just as scared as she is. His arms are trembling, and his breathing is fast and shallow.

He stares at me. "W-why aren't *you* running?"

"Don't worry about me, all right? Just take care of your girl. Get out of here, and make sure you take everyone else still in here with you."

The woman looks up and stares at me through her teary, red eyes. "Th-then come with us."

"I... I can't, all right? Like I said, just get out of here as fast as you can. It isn't safe."

They both stand and move slowly away from the table. The guy frowns, his fear giving way to concern. "Wait... what's wrong? Who are you? And why aren't you trying to run like everyone else?"

I sigh. I was only trying to help, not make a big deal of things. Jesus...

"Look—that was *my* car that exploded outside, all right? I think my friend might've been in it at the time. I'm not sure. The guy I was just sitting with blew it up, and he put a bomb under my chair. If I move, this whole building goes up in smoke too. I can't let that happen, which is why I need you guys to run like hell. Get as many people as you can who are still in here to go with you. Please!"

Their eyes go wide, and any fleeting concern soon reverts back to panic. They turn on the spot and bolt for the door, shouting to the few remaining people they pass to follow them.

It worked. Everyone's leaving. But as the door opens, the approaching sirens get much louder. They must be right outside...

"Adrian?"

I frown. Is that..."Ruby?"

She appears from behind me, stands at my side, and looks down, confused. "What the fuck are you doing?"

I scoff. "What am *I* doing? What are *you* doing? How are you not dead?"

She shrugs. "I saw him coming and dove out of the car just before he shot the gas tank. I waited till he'd gone, and when I didn't see you come out, I circled around back to see where you were. Why are you just sitting here like an idiot?"

I sigh and let my shoulders slump with shame. "There's a bomb under my chair. If I stand up, it goes off."

"Piss off! There's no way..." She crouches down and looks under my chair. "Holy shit!" She stands up and punches my arm. "There's a bomb under your chair!"

"I know! And hey!" I nod at my arm. "Do you mind?"

"Oh, sorry. So, what's your plan?"

"My plan? Ruby, if I had a plan, do you really think I'd still be sitting here?"

"Huh, fair point. Well, listen, there are cop cars and fire trucks everywhere out front."

"I figured. Your ex-boyfriend also mentioned the CIA are coming, so we really have to find a way out of here and fast."

I shift uncomfortably on my seat while trying to keep all my weight on it. "Any bright ideas?"

She frowns. "Wait, how does Fernando know the CIA is heading here?"

I let out a tired sigh. "Because the director of the CIA hired him to kill me, you, and everyone else on my list. Ashton Case is already dead, as is the remaining person we didn't get a chance to approach. He knows where Jonas is going to be, but I bought him a day, so hopefully he'll move on before *Fernando* gets there. We need to find your ex and kill him."

"That bastard! I'm gonna—"

"Ruby? Can we please focus on *my* problem? We'll get angry at him later, okay?"

She sighs, tucks her gun at her back, and crouches beside me again. "Okay, *fine*. Gimme a minute."

"Whoa, what are you doing?" I grip the edge of the seat in both hands, my body tensing.

"Relax. I'm just going to defuse this thing…"

"You're gonna *what*? What do you know about bombs? And why are you being so casual?" I look down, trying to see what she's doing. "Ruby? Ruby! I don't like you messing with this thing! Just—"

She stands. "Okay, you can get up now."

I raise an eyebrow. "Huh?"

She smiles. "You can stand up. I've disabled the dead man's switch. The bomb won't detonate if you get off the chair."

"But how did you—"

"Hey, I'm not just a pretty face, you sexist asshole. I dated this guy for a few months. He might've shown me a thing or two. I mean, don't get me wrong. I showed *him* a thing or two as well, if you know what I…"

I glare at her.

"You know what I mean. Never mind. Look, just trust me. Get up, so we can get out of here."

I take a deep breath. And another. I try to stand, but my legs don't agree with what my brain's telling them to do. Despite my initial reservations, I'm starting to like Ruby. I think trusting her might be a way off, but I'm open to the idea. One day. But...

Ah, fuck it.

I jump out of the chair and into a crouch, shielding my head with both arms. I hold my breath.

One second. Two seconds. Three... four...

Nothing.

I look around and see Ruby standing with her arms folded across her chest. She doesn't look happy.

"Thanks for the vote of confidence, dickwad."

I scratch the back of my head nervously. "Heh... sorry. It's not that I don't... I just wasn't sure if... I'm..." I give up. "Thanks for saving my ass, Ruby. Heh... *literally*!"

She continues frowning and pouting at me for a few moments, then her face relaxes. "You're welcome. Now can we get out of here?"

I nod. "Yeah."

She turns and heads for the back. I follow but stop after a few steps as an idea hits me. "Ruby, hang on a sec."

She stops and looks back at me. "What?"

I glance back at the chair. "How good *are* you with bombs, exactly?"

She paces slowly toward me, frowning. "Why?"

"I'm just spit-balling here. We've got CIA agents heading here to kill us, right? There's no way they're going to keep us alive a second longer than they need to if we're caught. Their orders would've been clear, probably given by either the CIA director or the president himself." I shrug. "Would be nice to get one over on them."

She smiles, with a hint of disbelief in her eyes. "Are you suggesting we take them out?"

"I'm suggesting you set that bomb to count down and go off in, say, three minutes? If it goes off before they get here, there's a chance they'll think we were taken out by the blast, which buys us time. If it goes off once they arrive, there's a good chance we'll take them out, which would be both useful and entertaining."

Ruby raises an eyebrow and starts pacing back and forth, staring at the floor. I'm not sure, but I think she's experiencing doubt...

"What is it?" I ask.

"Killing people I'm paid to kill is one thing, but killing G-men is something else. We're not stupid, Adrian. That's a whole other level of heat we'd be bringing—"

I hold my hand up to stop her. "Ruby... it's a little late for that, don't you think? In case you haven't noticed, those G-men are already coming to kill us. And they're doing so because President Cunningham wants them to. It doesn't get any worse than that. This is what you signed on for. It's literally us against the world right now."

She takes a deep breath and nods slowly.

"Besides, it was only a week or so ago that I took out over twenty NSA agents with a proximity mine..."

"You *what*?"

"Hey, it was me or them." I shrug. "Fuck 'em."

She chuckles desperately. "Christ... okay, gimme a sec here."

She carefully picks the chair up, flips it over, and rests it on its side, revealing the bomb. It looks... impressive. Explosives aren't my strong suit. I never really used them or found a good enough reason to learn how.

Ruby's hands move delicately and expertly over the device, figuring out the wiring and reconfiguring it to suit our own violent needs. She carefully starts moving things around. I hold my breath instinctively.

"Three minutes on the clock?" she asks.

I nod. "Yeah, that should do it."

She reconnects a couple of wires in different places and presses a few buttons.

"Okay, and... done." She stands and looks at me. "We should probably leave."

I glance down at the device, which is now showing two minutes and fifty-four seconds.

"Yeah, good idea."

We both run over to the back of the bar, through the storage area, and toward the rear entrance. I ease the door open slowly, peeking out as I do. There's a track that runs along the back of the building like an alley. There's a squad car parked at one end with its nose facing the parking lot opposite, but I can't see any cops. Cautiously, I look the other way, which leads away from the main street, toward some railroad tracks. It looks clear.

"Come on," I call over my shoulder.

We step outside, careful not to make too much noise. We check all the angles, quickly and professionally. Then I reach behind me, grab Ruby's wrist, and break into a jog. She keeps pace without a word, and we make it to the tracks without being seen.

We both glance left when we reach a clearing and see West Market Street beyond, overrun with cops, firemen, and terrified passersby. The railroad crossing is blocked off, which should mean the tracks have been cleared.

"C'mon. This way."

We set off along the tracks as quickly as we can. We run under West Friendly Avenue, where it opens into a wooded clearing. We keep going full speed for another thirty seconds, then stop, turn around, and catch our breath. Ruby's leaning forward, her hands resting on her knees. I'm standing upright, hands on hips.

I'm reminded for a second of the morning jogs I used to go on with Styx, chasing the sunrise around Devil's Spring with my dog keeping pace next to me.

I take in a deep, heavy breath and sigh away the painful, raw memory.

A thunderous explosion rings out, illuminating the dull, early evening sky with a bright orange flash before clouding it with billowing smoke. The ground shakes beneath our feet. Even though we're probably a good half-mile away, I can hear the sound of glass and brick showering down on the immediate area.

I hope the innocent people were smart enough to get clear of the building before that thing went off. Even the cops—I mean, they're just doing their jobs. It's nothing personal with them.

Now the CIA guys... I hope *they* got blown to shit. Fuckers.

"Okay..." says Ruby between breaths. "What... now?"

I shake my head, unsure. "I guess we keep running."

19:27 EDT

As I suspected, any trains due through here were diverted because of the chaos behind us, so we've had a clear run. We walk along the tracks at a steady pace. We're both tired and hungry. Plus, as time has passed, I think we've both become notably disillusioned. We might have escaped relatively unscathed from The European's unexpected attempts to take us out, but that doesn't make me feel as happy as it should.

The CIA, not content with sending teams of agents across the country to kill me, has now hired a professional assassin to try as well. I wouldn't normally be too concerned, but when that shit-stain blew up our ride, he took our weapons along with it. That means we're defenseless, except for the gun Ruby has at her back.

We're also hours and miles behind him, and he's on his way to kill the one remaining ally I've got: Jonas Briggs. I just hope Briggs's natural paranoia buys us enough time to reach him before The European does. I can't afford to lose anyone else.

I look over at Ruby, who's walking silently beside me. We haven't said much since we started walking. Not much we *can* say, really. She's staring at the floor with her arms crossed.

"You all right?" I ask her.

She nods. "Yeah..."

"Really?"

She smiles. "No." She sighs. "What the fuck is going on, Adrian? What have you gotten me into?"

I tense my jaw muscles. I'm not angry at the accusation, but I feel guilty that it *is* my fault she's caught up in this. I thought hiring help was the smart thing to do, but so far, all I've succeeded in doing is getting two people killed—one of whom I considered a friend.

Goddammit.

"Look, I know this is far from an ideal situation, but it's

the way it is. When you pick a fight with the U.S. government, things tend to be a little one-sided."

She looks at me challengingly. "You speaking from experience?"

"Heh... kinda." I shake my head. "My life sucks."

I start laughing. It's the only option I have to stop me from shooting myself. After a moment, she joins me. We're walking side by side, laughing with increasing gusto until our sides start to hurt. We calm down and take a few deep breaths, pausing in the middle of the tracks, surrounded by shallow woodland.

"So, come on, tough guy—spill. What's your story? I mean, most people in our world know who Adrian Hell is. But how have you managed to go from *that* guy to *this* guy." She gestures to me with her hands. "Public enemy number one."

I smile. "That's a long story."

She shrugs. "It's a long fucking walk."

I stare ahead of us, seeing the edges of the tracks join together in the distance.

"Yeah, I guess it is."

20:13 EDT

"...and then you *climbed* up the side of *Alcatraz*?" asks Ruby, sounding shocked.

I smile. "Yup. That was... quite an experience."

"*The* Alcatraz?"

I nod.

"Jesus..."

In the last forty minutes or so, I've told her about my first interaction with GlobaTech Industries in Nevada and about my unexpected, short-lived partnership with the FBI in San Francisco.

I shrug. "Life's been a little... unorthodox these last few years, to say the least."

"No shit! I thought I had it bad being locked up in Stonebanks."

"Are you still regretting your decision to leave with me?"

"I don't know. I mean, this sucks, but... hearing about the things you've done, the things you've been through, and why you're here now... I guess it's the right thing to do, isn't it?"

I try to hide a small smile of pride as I see the difference in her compared to twenty-four hours ago. "I think so, yeah."

She chuckles. "You sure know how to pick a fight. I'll give you that."

"Thanks."

"You're not good at identifying compliments, are you?"

"I just tend to assume most things are meant as one. It's easier."

She shakes her head. "You're an idiot."

"Thanks!"

"Oh my God..."

We come up on a building that looks like a warehouse from behind, but as the trees clear, a sign becomes visible. I point to it. "It's an auto shop."

Ruby looks across at me and smiles. "Perfect place to borrow a car."

I smile back. "My thoughts exactly. Come on."

We move carefully through the undergrowth until we reach the chain-link fence at the back of the property. We scale it quickly and quietly and drop down behind the building. I scan the area for any security cameras, but I can't see any.

We move so that our backs are against the wall, tentatively edging around the southeast corner. I feel Ruby's arm move behind her, presumably going for her gun.

I put my hand on her elbow. "No need for that. Even if there's anyone here, they won't be a threat."

She shrugs me away. "Instinct. Sorry."

"Yeah, I get that. Don't worry. Come on."

We move around, staying close to the wall as we make our way down the side of the building. As we reach the northeast corner, we stop again, drop into a crouch, and peer around. There's no sign of life. The place must be closed for the evening.

At the front of the shop is a parking lot, a gas pump, and an air machine for tires, which is at the opposite end from us.

Ruby nudges my arm and gestures to the handful of vehicles standing in the lot. "Jackpot," she whispers.

I take one last look behind us before scanning ahead. There's a security camera above the door to the office, which is maybe six yards along the front of the building from where we are. I can just about see another one at the far end, above the metal shutters.

I lean in close and whisper, "We need to be careful here. If we get caught on camera, there'll be a trail of breadcrumbs leading everyone right to us."

Keeping low, I move forward, away from the building and the camera's line of sight. A few moments later, I hear Ruby behind me. We make it almost to the street and then head parallel to the shutters until we reach the cars.

I stop by the hood of a generic tan sedan and look back at Ruby. "This one's fine."

She shakes her head. "Uh-uh." She points past me, and I follow her gaze. "*That* one."

She's pointing to a 1978 Silver Corvette C3 Coupe.

I shake my head. "No."

She barges past me to the car and runs her fingertips along the side. "Yes! God, yes!" She turns and looks back at me. "We *have* to drive this car!"

I walk over to her. It's a nice set of wheels, I admit. A real classic, and it looks sexy as hell. But...

"Ruby, we need to stay discreet. *This*... this will be like a beacon attracting every G-man and LEO to us like moths to a flame."

She shrugs. "Let's be honest, Adrian. They're gonna find us sooner or later anyway. At least in this, we get to have some fun! Plus, we'll get to Atlantic City a helluva lot faster. Come on... live a little!"

"If we live a little, we might end up dying a lot!" I sigh. I can't physically summon the strength required to argue my point any further. "Ah, fuck it. Knock yourself out."

She squeals like a teenage girl at a pop concert and jumps at me, throwing her arms around my neck. She pulls me down to her height, hugging me tightly.

"Thank you!"

She lets me go and moves around to the driver's door. It takes her a few moments to get inside and a few more to disable the alarm and hotwire it. She starts it up and guns the engine. The loud roar reminds me of The European's sales pitch about his new Ferrari.

I climb into the passenger seat beside her, slightly cramped in the small space.

"New Jersey, here we come!" she says, smiling with genuine excitement.

I shift in my seat as I struggle to find any level of comfort. "Just get us there in one piece, please."

She scoffs and smiles. "Pussy."

She pulls onto the street and heads right, putting her foot to the floor and weaving through the light traffic until we hit the freeway.

I stare out the window, watching the low skyline of Greensboro fade into the distance as dusk falls.

I'm glad to see the back of this place.

14

MEANWHILE...

President Cunningham strode urgently into the Situation Room through doors held open by one of the Marines stationed outside. On his heels was Gerald Heskith. As they entered, the people sitting around the table got to their feet. Cunningham was in no mood for pleasantries. It was yet another irritating occasion when he needed to act like any other president would, despite knowing the horrific truth that others didn't.

"Take your seats," he said to the room before sitting at the head of the table. Heskith sat to his immediate right. "Somebody talk me through exactly what happened."

An analyst sitting to Heskith's right cleared his throat. "Mr. President, there were two explosions on a street in Greensboro, North Carolina a little over two hours ago."

He paused to nod at the man sitting across from him, who stood and walked over to a workstation at the back of the room. Within seconds, the large screen on the wall facing the table flickered to life, showing a topographical map of the area, as well as satellite feeds and local news reports.

The analyst continued. "The first was a vehicle, and we believe a single gunshot to the gas tank triggered the explosion. The second was the building across the street, roughly seven minutes later. The entire structure was destroyed, and the buildings on either side suffered extensive collateral damage."

Cunningham stroked his chin absently. "Casualties?"

The analyst let out a taut breath. "Twenty confirmed dead, with the same number missing or injured. Emergency services secured the scene within minutes..."

Heskith looked down the table at the man sitting at the opposite end. Dennis Atkins, the National Intelligence Director, was a short man who had retired from the Navy to take up the position offered to him on Cunningham's council.

"Director Atkins, has anyone come forward to claim responsibility for this?" he asked.

Atkins shook his head. When he spoke, his voice was deep and deliberate. "No, Gerry, they haven't. There's been no indication thus far that this was an act of terrorism."

"So, what are we looking at here?" asked Cunningham.

"At the moment, we don't know. The evidence from the scene is being worked over by the FBI, and I've asked to be personally kept in the loop on this. As soon as we have anything, I'll let you know, Mr. President."

Heskith had a notepad in front of him. He quickly scribbled a single word on it, then turned it to show the president.

Cunningham looked first at Heskith, then at the pad, and frowned.

Matthews?

The president sighed heavily. This attack certainly wasn't something he had anticipated as part of his ongoing agenda. So, he had to proceed like anyone else in his position would.

He addressed the room. "Okay, in light of everything recently, I want this treated as an act of terrorism until proven otherwise. I want to know who was behind it, and I want the chairman of the Joint Chiefs of Staff to personally put together a retaliatory response strategy within the hour. We're trying to help, but we cannot allow anyone to attack us, whether it's because of misplaced blame for what happened or something else. It is our responsibility to lead the world toward a new future. And we must show that we are strong, which means we will take swift and decisive action against anyone who threatens that future."

The analysts around the table exchanged nervous glances.

"That'll be all," he said. "I'd like the room for a moment, please."

Everyone stood and walked toward the door except Heskith and Atkins, who knew to remain seated. Once the last of them had left the room and the door was closed, Cunningham addressed his intelligence director.

"Dennis, what really happened?" he asked.

Atkins fixed his commander-in-chief with a focused stare. When he spoke, each word was measured. "Mr. President, may I speak freely?"

"Please do."

"Thank you, sir." He cleared his throat. "Mr. President, you need to strongly consider removing General Matthews from his post as CIA director." He pointed to the screen. "This was *his* mess."

Cunningham let out an impatient sigh and clenched his jaw to subdue his anger. He glanced at Heskith briefly before replying. "You know that for sure?"

Atkins nodded. "Over half the casualties caught in the second blast were CIA agents sent to apprehend Adrian Hell, whom we believed would be there."

Heskith held up a hand. "Sir, you may want to consider leaving the room before this de-brief continues."

Cunningham shook his head. "No, I want to know. In a little over twenty-four hours, the second phase of our plan begins. If there's anything that could jeopardize that happening, I want to be aware of it."

Atkins nodded. "Very well, sir. General Matthews approached one of the assassins from the list we recovered back in Maine and recruited him before Adrian Hell got the chance. His mission was to kill everyone else on that list, including our primary target. What you're seeing here is this assassin's failed attempt to do just that. He checked in with his assigned handler at the agency to advise that he's heading to Atlantic City to eliminate his final target."

"So, he doesn't realize he failed in Greensboro?" asked Heskith.

Atkins shook his head. "It appears that way, yes."

Cunningham scratched the back of his neck and shook his head. He regretted not asking more about this endeavor before consenting to it. "And why did the CIA have a team there?"

"The assassin explained that he'd trapped Adrian Hell in the building by securing a bomb to his chair. The CIA unit was to disarm it upon arrival and take Adrian into custody. Unfortunately, Adrian managed to escape and rig the device so that it exploded as the agents were entering the building."

Heskith shook his head. "Sonofabitch..."

"Okay." Cunningham leaned forward in his seat. "Dennis, from now on, you will personally take control of both Cerberus *and* the operation to take out this bastard. I want him dead, and I want whatever information he has on his person destroyed."

"Yes, Mr. President."

He turned to Heskith. "Gerry, I want you to reach out to this assassin. Warn him about Adrian and tell him to finish his job in New Jersey as planned. Then give him his new target. Do I make myself clear?"

Heskith glanced down at the name he wrote on his pad. "Yes, Mr. President."

"Good." He turned back to Atkins. "Director, thank you for your time."

"Of course, Mr. President. I'll be in touch."

He stood and took his leave. The room fell silent. Cunningham leaned back heavily in his chair and stared at the polished surface of the mahogany desk. Next to him, Heskith allowed the president a moment of reflection, then produced a file, which he slid across the surface of the table.

"Sir, this is everything I managed to find on Adrian Hell."

Cunningham opened the file and skimmed through it. The more he read, the wider his eyes became.

"I spoke with Julius Jones about this over at Langley," continued Heskith. "He knew Adrian way back when. They founded the D.E.A.D. unit together. When he left to pursue a career as a gun for hire, most of what little paperwork existed about him was destroyed."

"This man's a living, breathing weapon..." observed Cunningham.

"He's a dangerous adversary, yes."

"Matthews should've done his homework."

"Maybe. But his plan to send a snake to kill a snake was still a sound strategy under the circumstances. I'm sure it's only a matter of time before we take him out, sir."

"I'm leaving it in your capable hands, old friend. See that Director Atkins gets this information."

"I will, Mr. President. So, how are our friends overseas?"

"They're waiting for our word." He let out a long, calming sigh. "I tell you, Gerry, this has been a long time coming. And despite GlobaTech's involvement, it's still played out pretty much as I expected."

"It was a smart move, awarding them the job of providing foreign aid. Though, they probably thought we did it in exchange for them keeping their mouths shut about what they knew."

"Well, I never wanted to include them in anything, but because of Adrian Hell's interference, I had no choice but to let them conduct their investigations and provide assistance. The public was crying out for it. I knew we could control the flow of information, so they would never find anything incriminating. But then they figured out how Cerberus fitted into it all. I was forced to play my hand early and make my statement about El-Zurak being apprehended."

"I wouldn't worry, Mr. President. It doesn't matter what intel Adrian has. We'll stop him before he can use it."

"How do you know he hasn't already?"

Heskith shrugged. "Honestly, sir? If he made his intel public, I'm sure we'd have found out by now. I know how his mind works. He believes he's only alive because of it, so he'll keep it close to his chest, thinking he's safe."

"See to it you're right, Gerry. It's all falling into place, and I want to make sure nothing else gets in the way. We're ready to take the next big step forward, and we can do so without any of the sacrifices we were expecting to make to our own military forces. It's beautiful! Is Fielding ready?"

"He is, sir. He's ready to give the order on your command."

"Good. I trust Atkins will deliver Adrian Hell to us soon. And I'm leaving Matthews's retirement to you." He took a breath and allowed himself a small smile. For the first time in a long while, he could see a clear picture in his mind of the endgame.

He flipped idly to the back page of Adrian's file, frowning as he glanced over it.

"Adrian owns a bar in Texas?"

Heskith nodded. "He does, sir. He retired there a couple of years ago."

"Hmm. I wonder if he has anything else waiting for him back in Texas…"

15

ADRIAN HELL

Ruby and I are sitting at a table by a window overlooking the small parking lot and the busy intersection in front of the Applebee's on the corner of North Michigan and Baltic. Sunshine is periodically glimpsing through the gray clouds above, looking to put an end to the dismal weather of the last few days.

We left our ride at the convention center and continued on foot through the city. The car served us well and made the thirteen-hour journey a little less of a chore.

It's busy inside, with a mixture of late breakfasts and early lunches. We're sharing a pot of coffee between us, and I've got a plate of actual food in front of me—bacon, eggs... the works. I look at Ruby, who's regarding her stack of pancakes with reluctance.

"What's the matter? Do you want me to shove them inside a donut for you?"

I smile as she gives me the finger.

"I'll shove them somewhere in a minute..." she mutters.

I chuckle and take a sip of my drink. "Right, we need a plan. I've contacted Jonas and brought him up to speed on everything since Greensboro. I've told him not to get here until midday tomorrow, which gives us a full day to find The European and take him out. I think it's safe to assume he's already in the city. He's not expecting Jonas until tomorrow, so he'll be lying low somewhere. I'm not sure he knows we're still alive, so we might be able to get the jump on him if we can find him. Any ideas?"

She shrugs as she finishes a mouthful of food. "I don't know. Can't we just wait for Jonas to get here and use him as bait?"

I shake my head. "Nice idea—and a little ruthless—but no, we can't afford to just sit and wait. We need to start taking the fight to these bastards. The European is their weapon now, which means we need to find him and take him out of the game."

"Yeah, fair point. Hey, speaking of ruthless—why did you tell Fernando where Jonas would be, anyway? You practically handed him over on a silver platter..."

I shake my head. "No, I told him because this way, we know roughly where that prick will be. It saves us wondering and looking over our shoulders. We know where he is and what he intends to do, so that's an advantage for us."

"Okay, so what's *your* bright idea for taking him out before Jonas arrives tomorrow?"

I sigh, take another sip of coffee, and stare absently out the window. "I'm working on it."

Outside, the traffic is heavy, and the sidewalks are cramped. I hear the roar of a loud engine and glance across in time to see a sports car drive into view. The driver's revving the shit out of it, presumably trying to show off, despite doing the same ten miles an hour that everyone else is in their cheaper, more modest vehicles...

My first thought is that the person driving is a guy, early thirties, probably wearing a suit. He likely works in an office, where he's paid an obscene amount of money for talking shit to strangers. A little presumptuous, maybe, but I'm sticking with my first impression that the guy's an asshole.

But my second thought is a stroke of genius. The sound of the engine made me think about The European's fancy Ferrari...

"Ruby, do you know much about cars?"

She shrugs. "I can drive one..."

"Your ex drives a top of the line Ferrari. Wouldn't something so exclusive have a built-in GPS tracking device? Like, as an anti-theft measure or for Triple A?"

"Possibly. Sounds like something they would do nowadays. Why does it matter?"

"Because... if someone were able to hack the signal, they could pinpoint the location of the vehicle. I think."

"You *think*?"

I shrug. "Not my area of expertise, but it sounds clever, doesn't it?" I smile as I stand. "Besides, I know a man who can..."

"Where are you going?"

I gesture outside with a nod to the window. "I won't be a minute."

I head out the door and take out my burner phone. I dial Josh's number as I pace away from the junction, so it's a little quieter.

He answers on the second ring. "Yeah?"

I frown. His British accent sounds tense. Josh never gets tense...

"It's me," I say. "You all right?"

He lets out a tired sigh. "Yeah, I'm fine. What's up?"

"I'll tell you in a minute. Seriously, man, what's wrong? I know when something's bothering you."

"Mate, you don't wanna know about my problems. Trust me. You've got enough of your own."

"Yeah, I know, but—"

"Adrian, seriously. I'm running one of the largest corporations in the world single-handed, despite having practically no experience in such things. At the same time, I'm deploying soldiers from a private military—which, at last count, isn't too far behind this country's own armed forces in terms of the number of boots on the ground—to all corners of the globe to keep the peace in nations that have very recently been blown in half. I'm just... I'm just *stressed*, okay?"

I don't say anything. I can just about imagine the pressure he's under. Everyone has a bad day, and everyone sometimes needs to vent in order to stop things from getting on top of them.

I'll just give him a moment.

He sighs heavily. "Look, I'm sorry. It's just been one of those days, y'know? And at this level, *one of those days* is pretty fucking bad. What can I do for you?"

"Y'know what? It doesn't matter. I'll sort it."

"Adrian, don't be a dick. What do you need?"

I roll my eyes. "Well, I was wondering if you'd be able to track down the location of a specific car if I told you the owner's name. Maybe hack into its GPS signal or something."

I'm met with silence.

"Josh?"

"Huh? Sorry, I just fainted for a second because you

asked me something incredibly smart and technical. Who are you? And what have you done with the assassin?"

I smile. There he is.

"Just when I thought I was starting to miss you, you remind me how much of a douchebag you are." We pause for a second to laugh. "I did tell you that I listen when you talk. So, can you help me or not?"

"Man, you've changed. Pretty soon you won't need me at all!"

"Now we both know *that's* never going to happen, Josh!"

He laughs. "Yeah, I guess you're right. Okay, gimme a sec. Seriously, you have no idea how good it is to be given something easy to do for a change! What's the guy's name?"

"Fernando Garcia."

"Fernando... Isn't that—"

"The European? Yeah, it is."

"What, have you *lost* him? What's going on?"

I sigh. "Okay, long story short, he's already been hired by General Matthews to kill me and everyone else on the list I got from Ashton Case. Ash is dead, as is the last name, whom I didn't even get chance to approach. I'm in New Jersey now. He knows Jonas Briggs will be here tomorrow, so we've got twenty-four hours to find that talking colostomy bag and take him out."

Josh lets out a low whistle. "Christ, and I thought *my* life sucked..."

"It does, Josh. Massively so."

"Gee, thanks."

I shrug. "Just calling it like I see it."

"So, wait, is Ruby still with you? Is she okay?"

"Yeah, she's fine."

"Well, that's something. Okay, what car does he have?"

I think back. "It's a... Ferrari... something."

"Aww, and you were doing *so* well..."

"Hey, I'm thinking! It was something to do with a spider..."

"The 488 Spider?"

"Yeah, that's it! In British racing green—I remember now."

"Nice car. Hey, what's the difference between The European's Ferrari and a hedgehog?"

"I have no idea..."

"On a hedgehog, the pricks are on the *outside!*"

I laugh out loud. I really didn't want to because it just encourages him, but that was pretty funny.

"All right, let me see here..." he says casually. I hear the rapid tapping of keys in the background. "And... got him. The GPS last transmitted from the hotel parking lot of the Trump Taj Mahal in Atlantic City. Where are you?"

I subconsciously glance over my shoulder to get my bearings. "I'm about seven or eight blocks west of there, outside an Applebee's."

"Okay, well... now you know where he is."

"Thanks, man. I'm gonna go and, y'know... kill him and stuff. Listen, I appreciate the assist, Josh."

"Always happy to help, you know that."

"I know. Speaking of which, have you had a chance to look over my plan yet?"

"Yeah, I've had a look. Where the hell did you come up with that?"

"It just kinda came to me, I guess. I thought about the skill sets of everyone involved and went from there. What do you think?"

"I think it sounds like a perverted squirrel's favorite pastime."

I frown. "Huh?"

"Fucking nuts!"

I close my eyes and shake my head. "That's terrible."

"Hey, I gotta laugh, man. Otherwise, I'd cry."

"Yeah, I know what you mean."

"All right, joking aside, your plan is actually insane. You know that, right?"

I think about it for a moment. "Yeah..."

"That being said... I reckon it could work. There are a lot of moving parts, though. It won't be easy."

"Nothing worth doing ever is. Can I leave it with you?"

"You got a time in mind for this thing?"

"Any time after tomorrow. I need Jonas for part of it, so as soon as possible after we link up with him."

"Okay, I'll get back to you."

"Thanks, Josh. Listen, you take it easy, all right? I know it probably doesn't feel like it right now, but the whole world isn't on *your* shoulders. Remember that."

"I appreciate you saying that, but it kinda is. I mean—"

"Josh, you have an entire company at your disposal. You don't have to do everything yourself. Well, unless you're doing something for me..."

He's silent for a moment, then laughs. "The more things change..."

"...the more I get shot at!"

He laughs again. "Take it easy, brother."

"You too."

I hang up and turn to face the restaurant. I see Ruby in the window, watching me as she sips her coffee.

What was that?

It was faint, high-pitched... like a ping. It's a familiar sound...

I frown as a small hole appears in front of Ruby. The edges of it spider-web across the glass. My primal instincts tell me straight away what's happening, but I can't do anything. Time slows to a crawl as I stand on the crowded sidewalk. My feet feel like they're sinking in quicksand. I look on helplessly as the coffee cup explodes in her hand. A split-second later, she's punched off her seat from the impact of what I can only surmise is a high-caliber sniper round.

Shit!

11:14 EDT

My first reaction is to look in the direction opposite the restaurant to see if I can pinpoint where the shot came from.

I can't.

I just see traffic and people running and screaming. That's been happening a little too often lately when I'm around.

The next reaction is to get to Ruby. I don't want anyone else going to her aid in case she's still alive and there's a follow-up round being loaded into the chamber of a sniper rifle at this moment. If anyone's catching a random bullet, it's me.

I sprint across the parking lot and burst through the door. I'm met with chaos and shouting, but I take a deep breath and ignore it. I mentally drown out all extraneous noise until the only thing I can hear is the sound of the blood pumping from Ruby's body.

I push through the crowd of people huddled around our table. Ruby's lying on the floor. There's a small pool of spilt coffee at her side. Several fragments of the cup she was holding are scattered all around.

There's a thick puddle of blood behind her head and torso. Her eyes are wide and unblinking. I look at her chest. It's rising and falling with rapid, shallow breaths.

Well, that's something...

I crouch beside her. "Ruby? Ruby, talk to me—are you okay?"

Nothing moves except her eyes, which flick to me. She furrows her brow.

I shake my head, silently cursing myself at the woefully inept attempt at helping. "Yeah, of course, you're not... never mind. Sorry."

I can see the entry wound on her right shoulder, just below her collarbone. I carefully put my hand behind her and reach down her back, feeling for an exit wound. My finger touches the wet, sticky flesh an inch or two below her neck.

"Okay, the bullet went through and through. That's a good thing. Can you move?"

She takes a few extra breaths, mustering up the energy to speak.

"Do I... have... to?" she manages, wincing with each syllable.

I shrug. "No, you can stay here and get shot some more if you want? Or you can wait for the EMTs and the police. See how that goes. Or you can get your ass up, so we can find the sonofabitch who just shot you. Your call."

"I... hate—"

"Me? Yeah, I know you do." I smile, and she just about succeeds in returning it. I move my arm behind her head and grab her hand in mine, preparing to lift her. "Okay, this is gonna sting like a bitch..."

I lift her up, and she unleashes a scream of agony that might actually raise the dead. I shift around to her left side and put her arm around my neck. I move my right arm around her waist to support her.

"Come on," I say. "You can do this."

In front of me, the crowd of onlookers slowly moves out the way. A guy steps forward and looks at me. "Hey, buddy, shouldn't you call the police or an ambulance? She's just been shot!"

I stop and stare at him, unable to hide my frustration as I struggle to hold Ruby upright. "Look, you and everyone else here might not be able to comprehend the full extent of what's just happened, so let me clarify." I cast a glance over the crowd around me and raise my voice, so everyone can hear. "My friend's just been shot by someone with a sniper rifle. You all know what one of those is, right? And I genuinely believe the intention is to kill her. Now I happen to have a good idea who pulled the trigger. I also happen to know he's a good shot. That means this non-lethal wound wasn't an accident. It was intentional, so she'd feel pain. That leads me to believe that he's still looking down his scope at us all, lining up his next shot, which he may or may not have decided is the one that will finish her off. And you bunch of assholes are standing here watching..."

I pause, looking around once more to see if any of what I just said is sinking in. The silence and blank stares tell me it probably isn't...

Okay, I'll try the shock tactics instead.

"Guys, you have a sniper aiming at you... *run!*"

The silence holds another second or two. Then the screaming restarts with renewed volume and vigor. People start running in every direction out of panic before focusing long enough to aim for the door.

There we go. Idiots!

I hear another ping as a second bullet penetrates the

window. I drop to the floor on instinct, dragging Ruby down with me. I land on my back, and she falls on top of me, momentarily winding me. Off to my left, a man hits the floor with a smoking hole in the center of his forehead. His eyes are wide and blank. The screams grow louder again. I lose valuable seconds staring at the innocent blood running from his skull like a faucet.

Goddammit!

I look at Ruby. Her face is inches from mine. She's in visible pain, wincing from her gunshot wound. I hold her in place on top of me, trying to press her as low as possible for cover.

"You okay?" I ask.

She nods but can't manage to form words.

"We need to move. Suck it up, all right? You can bleed later."

As gently as I can, I slide out from under her, move to a crouch, and scoop her up again, placing her arm around my neck as before. Practically dragging her, I push us through the stampede and out the doors, stepping onto the sidewalk. I head toward the back of the building, out of sight, down North Ohio Avenue.

Judging by the position of the bullet holes in the glass, the sniper—whom I'm going to assume is The European— is somewhere east of the convention center and north of Applebee's. There was practically no angle of elevation on the holes, which suggests he's at street level, so presumably shooting out the back of a stationary vehicle. I didn't hear a shot, which means he's not using anything as big as a .50 cal'. Maybe a Savage, or a Remington.

Now that we're out of sight, it'll take him a few moments to get back behind the wheel and follow us. By that time, hopefully, I'll be ready for him.

We turn onto Arctic and head toward the strip mall at the opposite end of the plaza from Applebee's. I don't want to try losing him in a crowd because he's already proved he won't let something trivial like an innocent life get in the way of taking us out. I just need to get someplace where he can't follow me in his vehicle, yet stay close enough to him that his rifle becomes ineffective.

Ruby's dragging her feet next to me and breathing heavily. I glance sideways at her and see her fighting to stop her eyes from rolling up in her head. The wound is far from fatal, but exertion and blood loss can take their toll on a person. She needs to rest.

We make it to the plaza. I head for a nearby bench and gently lower her onto it.

"Rest here, okay? I'll be back."

She flops back heavily as she sits. She looks around for a moment, dazed, before focusing her gaze on me. "Where... what are you—"

I place a hand on her left shoulder. "Relax. I'm going to—"

Tires screech behind me. I spin around to see an old station wagon sliding to a stop in front of the plaza. It came from the left, did a one-eighty, and stopped with the driver's door against the curb. It opens, and a man wearing a tailored shiny suit and sunglasses which probably cost more than most people make in six months steps out. He doesn't shut the door; he just walks toward me, unbuttoning his suit jacket.

The European. Fernando Garcia.

Ruby's ex-boyfriend.

Assassin... Asshole... Dead man.

I move to meet him, anxious to close the gap before he

has time to produce the gun I can only assume he's reaching for.

Yup... he's pulling out a handgun as I get within arm's length of him.

Without a word, I grab his right wrist with my left hand, controlling his weapon. Holding on, I step into him and shove him backward with my shoulder, which sends him arcing counterclockwise, swinging away from me.

I follow up with a strong right hook, aiming for his throat. He sees it coming and uses his own momentum to move back and avoid it, dropping his gun in the process. I overbalance and stumble forward, momentarily losing my footing and, consequently, my grip on his wrist.

Uh!

I didn't see that kick coming. It just caught me in the gut... knocked the wind out of me for a second...

I'm keeling over but look up as I go down, expecting a follow-up shot.

I see his right hand swinging down. I try to lift my arm to block it, but it has little effect. The blow goes through my guard and hits me on the side of the head. I land hard on the ground, lying on my side, feeling groggy.

I close my eyes for a split-second, allowing my instincts to take over. I'm on the back foot and can't consciously think fast enough to regain the upper hand. I need help...

I need my Inner Satan.

I open my eyes again. On cue, all traces of humanity are gone, replaced by the urges of a primal, long-buried killer who's eager for a taste of the old days.

I spring to my feet, immediately stepping in close. He seems unfazed, moving like the calculated professional I know him to be, planning his next moves. In the back of his mind, he'll be thinking of a way to get his gun back.

Fighting is like chess, remember?

Without breaking stride, he steps through and throws another kick with his right leg. I catch it, hooking his ankle in my left arm. Not wanting to let up for even a second, I launch a straight kick with my right leg, catching him squarely in the gut. I let go of his ankle and let his momentum take over, carrying him back a few feet.

He lands awkwardly but recovers straight away. He uses the momentum to roll backward, feet over head, finishing in a crouch with a hand on the ground for balance. His sunglasses have fallen off. His gray eyes stare at me, full of hatred.

His gaze flicks to his left, seeing his gun. I know it's there, but I don't want it. And I don't want him to get it, either. Too many things can go wrong when you're armed in public.

I sense he's going to lunge for the weapon. I see his muscles tense beneath his tight-fitting suit. My resurgence will have taken him by surprise, prompting panic. That will lead to desperation and, ultimately, a mistake. That is exactly what I'm hoping for.

I dash forward, heading to my two o'clock to cut him off. We collide, and he throws a right hand. I block and counter with a right elbow of my own. He deflects it, bending his left arm up beside his head. He unleashes a body shot with his right hand and connects with my side.

Thankfully, it just misses my kidney. I stagger back, unable to absorb the power behind the blow completely. I clutch at my waist, wincing as I gasp for breath. The European smiles at me with evil intent in his eyes.

He's a lot closer to his gun than I am. If he gets to it, I'm dead.

Sirens sound out loudly, interrupting our standoff. We

both straighten up and turn to see three patrol cars slide into view.

We lock eyes.

"We will finish this dance another time, Adrian," says The European, smiling.

"Bet your ass we will," I reply, forcing myself not to blink as I stare him down.

He scoops up his gun and sets off running away to my left. I watch him go, knowing I'm too late to make my own escape now that the cops are here.

I sigh. "Sonofabitch…"

I look over at Ruby, who seems to be struggling with her wound. She catches my eye and holds my gaze, a look of regret and apology on her face.

I simply smile and shrug. I always knew my luck would run out eventually. I glance over my shoulder as the cops exit their vehicles, draw their weapons, and move in a practiced formation, approaching me from all sides.

I turn clockwise to face them, slowly raising my arms out to the sides.

"The guy you want went that way," I say loudly, gesturing quickly with my head in the direction The European ran.

They don't care. They ignore what I say and form a semicircle in front of me.

"On your knees!" shouts one.

"Hands where we can see 'em!" says another.

I have no choice but to comply.

Shit.

It was all going so well…

16

ADRIAN HELL

They didn't mess around with the arrest. There were six officers in total. Five of them cuffed me and loaded me into the back of a squad car, while the other read me my rights. They rushed me back to the PD in a neat formation—one car in front, one behind, me in the middle, sirens blaring.

The Atlantic City Police Department is on the aptly named Atlantic Avenue, only a few blocks from where I was picked up. Within minutes, I was escorted through the doors and straight into an interrogation room. They never took their eyes or their guns off me.

The real kick in the balls came when they took the flash drive from around my neck. It was a strange sensation because I felt genuinely lighter—as if it had been this enormous weight *literally* around my neck. But I also felt deflated and beaten. That evidence is the key to ending this, and it was entrusted to me. Without it in my possession, I'm letting everyone down. Tori, Josh—everyone.

They secured me to the table in a sparsely furnished room and left me alone. I've been here maybe ten minutes, staring around the room, bored. It's a standard layout—square, gray walls, security camera, no clock. It could be any interrogation room in any precinct. There's an empty chair opposite me. The table's fixed to the floor. I'm sitting with my back to the door, and the two-way mirrored wall is on my right.

I feel calm. I know how this works. Having taken time to consider my options here, I've come to the unfortunate conclusion that I don't actually have any. There's nothing to think about, nothing to plan, no next steps...

I am completely, unequivocally fucked.

The police have me in custody, and I have no doubt that every government agency in the country will be aware of it. Usually, they would be fighting one another to see who can get here first and claim the prize. But not this time. This time, everyone's drinking the same Kool-Aid. Everyone's united under one badge, and President Cunningham's made sure I'm going down as the most wanted man in history.

Fucking prick.

I feel my heart rate increase as I think about him. My jaw muscles clench as the frustration and anger build inside me.

I can't wait to shoot him.

The door bursts open, distracting me. I casually look to my left and wait for whoever's just walked in to stride into view. Probably some fat desk sergeant here to tell me the CIA are on their way to question me.

Question me, my ass.

I'm seething with rage, struggling to control it as it erupts inside.

I swear I'll burn this entire *fucking* building to the ground before I let them take me anywhere! Goddamn—

"Adrian Hell."

Huh?

Two men appear next to me. Both are in suits and wearing their jackets open with their badges clipped to their belts. FBI badges. One man's Caucasian, and he takes a seat opposite me. The other's a black man, maybe mid-thirties, and he stands just to the right of the table.

I know them both—one better than the other. I didn't expect to see either of them again. In fact, I know people went to great lengths to make damn sure I didn't. For their sake.

"Adrian, would you care to tell me what the hell you think you've been doing?" asks Special Agent in Charge David Freeman. His voice is as gravelly as I remember. Maybe even a little more so. I might have driven him to smoke more. He needs a shave too, and his naturally tanned skin looks weathered. He seems tired; I can see the fatigue in his eyes.

I raise an eyebrow and glance at Special Agent Tom Wallis, standing next to him. He nods once, discreetly, but says nothing. He looks tired as well.

Welcome to my life...

I take a deep breath. I know what's going on here, even if I don't understand how they managed to get involved. They can't be seen to be familiar with me because Ryan Schultz saw to it that any involvement either of them had was explained away. The only thing that can't be denied is that Wallis was in the room when Matthews pushed the button, and the official explanation is that he was there trying to catch me. Consequently, he's been dancing to Cunningham's tune ever since.

It's a big risk, them coming here.

But I'm glad they did.

I casually glance over my other shoulder, up at the camera, and then directly at the mirror before answering.

I shrug. "Honestly? An assassin was hired to kill me. I was defending myself."

Freeman frowns. "And who would hire one assassin to kill another?"

"Another?" I smile. "Who said *I* was an assassin? I was just looking after my friend. Is she okay?"

Wallis clears his throat. "Your friend has been taken to a hospital. She's stable, but we'll need to question her as soon as possible."

I breathe a silent sigh of relief. At least Ruby's all right —for now.

"Adrian, you're wanted in connection with the murder of over twenty NSA agents and seven CIA agents, *and* for suspected links to the terrorist organization responsible for the 4/17 attacks. We're here to detain you, pending a full investigation. You will be appointed legal counsel once you arrive at the FBI field office. Any questions?"

I shake my head. "No. Just make sure *all* my possessions are brought with us."

Wallis steps forward and unlocks my handcuffs, allowing me to stand. I do, and he turns me around, cuffing my hands again behind my back.

"Let's go, asshole," he says, guiding me toward the door with his hand on my elbow.

With Freeman just behind us, we walk through the precinct and out the back to the parking lot, where a choco-late-colored Crown Vic is waiting. Wallis guides me into the back seat, walks around the trunk, and climbs in beside me. Freeman slides in behind the wheel, starts up the car, and pulls out of the lot, heading west.

. . .

12:09 EDT

I hold off a couple of minutes before saying anything, as if waiting until we're a safe distance from the precinct would make any difference whatsoever.

"Guys, what the hell are you doing here?"

Freeman glances in the rearview, catching my eye. "Saving your ass. You're welcome, by the way…"

"Yeah, thanks. But you coming in here to help me is a helluva gamble."

"We know," says Wallis, next to me. "We didn't have a choice. We've both been under scrutiny from the top since 4/17, and we've had no other option than to actively do what we can to help track you down. The plan was that once we did, we could get you before anyone else."

"Well, at least your plan worked."

He shakes his head. "No, Adrian, it didn't. *We* didn't find you."

I frown. "Then who did? And how come you're here?"

In the front, Freeman lets out a defeated breath. "The CIA is using Cerberus to track you. That's how they keep catching up with you. As part of the counterterrorism unit I run, we have access to that information as well. We've been keeping one step behind the CIA, letting them do the legwork, so they can lead us right to you. When the bulletin hit about you being apprehended, we knew we had to step in. How the hell did you get caught?"

I shrug. "My own fault, I guess. I've been putting together a team to help me take down Cunningham. The CIA got to one of the people on my list before I could and hired him to take the rest of us out. You said they had

Cerberus trained on me this whole time. Now I see how they managed it."

"So, this assassin was the guy you were fighting when you were picked up earlier?" asks Wallis.

I nod. "Yeah, a very competent all-rounder called Fernando Garcia. Also known as The European. Just so you know, he isn't going to stop until I'm dead. It doesn't matter who's with me."

Silence falls as Freeman navigates the dense midday traffic. He takes the turn for the expressway that will take us all the way to the New Jersey Turnpike.

"So, what's your plan, exactly?" I ask.

"Get you out of Atlantic City, for starters," says Wallis.

I shake my head. "No way. I'm not leaving without Ruby. And the only other member of my team is meeting me here tomorrow. I can't afford to lose him too. Not now."

"We need to get you somewhere safe, Adrian. Somewhere we can regroup and—"

"This isn't a debate, Wallis. You just said the most powerful satellite in the world is being used to track me. There *isn't* a safe place. Not anymore. And neither of you are really in a position to help me finish this. I need my team... what's left of it, anyway."

"Okay, so what's *your* plan?" asks Freeman, sounding like he's losing patience with me. "Seriously, what do you intend to do to fix this?"

I laugh. "Do you really wanna know?"

He pauses for a moment. "Yes. Tell me."

I shrug. "Okay. I have a plan to get me and my team inside the White House. Then I'm going to do what I've been saying I'll do all along—kill the president."

Wallis lets out a heavy sigh and shakes his head. "Jesus..."

Freeman shakes his head. "I had to ask. Okay, what do you need?"

I look at Wallis. "First, get these cuffs off me." I shift in my seat and turn away from him slightly. He takes them off, and I bring my hands around, sit back, and massage my wrists to get the blood flowing again. "Thanks. Okay, we've established I can't hide, so I'll stop trying to. I need to get Ruby, meet with Jonas, and make my way to Washington."

Freeman looks at us both in the rearview again. "That... ah... that might be a little difficult."

I frown. "Why?"

"Because your friend was taken to a secure wing of the AtlantiCare Medical Center, which is a few miles in the opposite direction. She's under twenty-four-hour guard until she's well enough to be moved. There's no way you'll get to her. I'm sorry."

"Don't be sorry, Freeman. Just turn the damn car around."

"Adrian, you can't be serious?" asks Wallis. "It's suicide going back there. The CIA will have a kill order, and we can't protect you."

"I'm not asking you to. And everything I've done in the last three weeks has been borderline suicidal, so that's nothing new. This is the only way. I'll worry about getting Ruby. Just get me there and then get out of here before what little cover you've got is blown."

Wallis sighs and stares at the floor. I feel sorry for him. He didn't ask to get caught up in any of this, and he's been doing his best to stay alive while watching my back. At the moment, that isn't easy for anyone.

"Ah, shit..." says Freeman.

"What?"

"We've got company. Lots of it."

I frown and look over my shoulder out the rear window. There are three black SUVs spread across the three lanes of the expressway, following us.

The CIA couldn't be more conspicuous if they painted their standard-issue vehicles bright yellow and put a Playboy bunny on the roof, holding a sign that says, *Agents on Board.*

I remember the good ol' days when you never knew they were there. Old school spies and black ops units appeared like ghosts a second before they took you. Nowadays, they shout it from the rooftops and take out ads in the fucking newspaper. And don't get me wrong... it's not because of a decline in quality. It's simply that they don't give a shit. Cunningham rules the world. Why should anyone who works for him care about the consequences of their actions anymore? It's not like anyone's going to reprimand them, is it?

This is bad. Really bad. I glance quickly at Wallis and Freeman in turn. Both look worried and justifiably so.

I need a plan...

I could—no... that wouldn't work.

There's always—no. Damn it. That wouldn't work, either.

Ah, I've got one!

Well, that was quick, even by my standards.

But... wait—no, I can't. Can I? There must be another way...

Shit.

There isn't another way.

Oh, man, this is going to suck.

Not for me, obviously.

For these two.

I look at Wallis. "Do you trust me?"

He frowns. "I don't like it when you ask me things like that..."

I smile. "I've got a plan that means we all get out of this. But you're not going to like it."

"What is it?" asks Freeman.

"Oh, you're *definitely* not gonna like it! But there's no other way. And no time to argue. Do you both trust me?"

Freeman looks at Wallis in the rearview, and they both nod to each other.

"Do what you need to," says Wallis. "If the CIA stops us now, we're all dead."

I nod. "My thoughts exactly. Okay... give me your gun, Tom."

He hesitates.

"Come on," I urge. "Time's a-wastin' here."

He sighs and pulls his FBI-issue Glock 22 handgun from his shoulder holster. He holds it out to me. I glance quickly over my shoulder again to size up the SUVs. They're closing in fast. I can just make out the facial features of the driver on our tail, which means he should be able to see me as well.

I need to make sure he sees everything...

I look at Wallis and smile apologetically. "You're a good man, Tom. Thanks for everything you've done for me."

He frowns. "I don't underst—"

I grab the gun with my left hand, raise my right elbow, and lunge sideways into him, connecting with his jaw. I hit him where his mandible meets his ear, and he slams against the side of the car, slumping unconscious in his seat.

I face the front, carefully positioning the gun against the back of the driver's seat.

"What the fuck are you doing?" yells Freeman.

I lean forward. "Sorry, David. I think you're a dick, but you don't deserve this. It's... it's the only way."

I fire once. The gunshot is muffled by the back of the seat. The bullet hits him exactly where I intended—the right side of his waist, through and through. It's a fairly shallow flesh wound that avoids anything major. It'll bleed like Niagara Falls and hurt like hell, but he'll be fine.

He falls forward, hitting the wheel with his forehead, which causes the car to swerve to the right. I put my hand against the headrest and push myself back in my seat, bracing for the inevitable impact.

This was a stupid idea...

17

ADRIAN HELL

12:22 EDT

The car slides across the outside lane, narrowly missing the oncoming SUV. We do a complete three-sixty and slam side-on into the grass verge that runs alongside the expressway. My attempt at bracing counts for nothing. I'm thrown sideways and land on Wallis, who is crushed against the door on the right side.

Ah!

My head bounces off the window, jolting my neck. I feel a trickle of blood making its way down the side of my face. I sit back for a moment and try to relax my body. I glance forward, feeling a little dazed. Freeman is slumped over the wheel. He's breathing. Through the windshield, I see the three black SUVs slam on their brakes up ahead, ignoring the traffic and desperately trying to come back and claim their prize.

Exactly like I want them to.

I look down and check the mag of Wallis's Glock. Minus

175

the round I put in Freeman, there are thirteen loaded and one in the chamber. I slide across the seat, put a hand on the door, and check through the rearview to make sure I'm clear. The road behind me is practically empty. I guess my friends from the CIA have already blocked the road.

I open the door, climb out, and stretch quickly. I shake my head to clear it. I glance back over my shoulder at Wallis, sprawled on the back seat, unconscious. I feel bad for him. Freeman I can take or leave, but Wallis has always been good to me. I wish I had another option right now.

I walk slowly into the middle of the road and face the three oncoming vehicles. The sun is tucked away behind some light clouds, and there's a strong breeze blowing across from the east. I relax, standing casually with my arms by my sides. I grip the Glock tightly in my hand.

I'm not entirely sure how to go about this. I guess I'll just have to play it by ear. But whatever happens, there's no way I'm leaving here with *them*.

The vehicle on my right slows as it gets within a few hundred yards of me. The one in the middle follows suit, but the one on the left maintains its speed. It must intend to go past and stop behind me...

No chance.

I whip my arm up, turn my body slightly, and fire once at the front tire of the vehicle. The sound of the bullet is partially drowned out by both the noise of the traffic on the other side of the expressway and the wind. But it's still loud.

It finds its mark, as I knew it would. The SUV's probably doing forty-five, maybe fifty. The front left side drops sharply as the tire disintegrates, and the back swings out. The driver struggles to retain control. I stand my ground, holding my breath as the vehicle goes flying past, inches away from me. It turns side-on, and the remaining tires screech loudly and throw up smoke. I turn slightly and watch as it—

Holy shit! It's just flipped into the air!

It crashes down heavily on its roof and slides farther away from me.

I can't pass up this chance...

I widen my stance, tense my body, and steady myself. I take aim, both hands on the gun. I take a deep breath and quickly drown out my surroundings until all I'm aware of is my target. I'm aiming for the gas tank...

I line up my shot and fire three rounds in quick succession.

There's a deafening blast and a rush of air as the vehicle goes up in flames. The force of the explosion lifts it off the ground once more. It lands, and I hear the exposed framework creak over the crackling of the deadly flames engulfing the metal carcass, like a starving man attacking a buffet line.

I allow myself a split-second of celebration for having just improved my odds of getting out of this in one piece. Then I spin around to face the remaining SUVs, which are stopped at an angle probably twenty feet in front of me, nose to nose.

I close my eyes for a moment, then adjust my grip on the Glock as I think about the next step. It's eight on one—and not just any eight. These are CIA agents who will likely be under orders from up high to kill me. I think the time for interrogation has passed.

I take a couple of deep breaths.

In...

Out...

In...

Out...

I open my eyes and feel my Inner Satan slide behind the wheel.

Adrian's sitting this one out. These assholes are mine!

I know I'll only have a few valuable seconds before they retaliate, so I need to make sure every shot counts.

I walk forward, raise my arm, and open fire before they have a chance to get out of the vehicles. The windshield shatters, exposing the targets trapped within. The driver catches a bullet in the forehead. He slumps against his door as a thick splattering of blood covers the glass next to him. The passenger scrambles for his weapon, but he has no chance. I aim and fire, putting a bullet through the center of his heart. He's pushed back against his seat, and a crimson pool expands across his shirt.

I turn my attention to the other SUV. The agents have had time to organize themselves a little, so the four of them are climbing out of the vehicle as I put them in my crosshairs.

My first three shots take two of them out. The driver and one of the men from the back seat remain. By my count, I have five bullets left, and there are four assholes still standing.

Cutting it close...

I dive off to my right as they return fire; my instincts kick in even though I've barely had time to register the sound of the gunshots. I hit the ground and roll away to the embankment, quickly get to my feet, and take cover behind Freeman's Crown Vic.

Bullets squeal and ping off the bodywork around me. I chance a quick look over the hood and see them both pause to reload. Behind them, the two remaining passengers from the first SUV move wide to my left. I'm guessing they'll try to outflank me while I'm pinned down.

I duck back behind the car and quickly check the mag. I was right. There are five rounds left. Okay, I've got four targets—two on either side. I can't try to pick them off at the same time because it'll take too long to aim. There's little sense in clearing out the guys on the left, as they're in the open. The guys on the right have the cover of their vehicles, plus their fallen colleagues are over there with weapons and ammunition they're not using anymore.

Right, it is...

I raise my arm over the hood and fire a blind round to the left, just to give them something to think about. I leap to my feet and fire off two more rounds at the guys on the right. The first finds its mark, hitting the driver center mass, just below the throat. He drops quickly, bouncing off the hood and onto the ground. The second shot misses. The remaining guy must have good reflexes because he's already down behind an open door.

Shit.

Two left...

Fuck it.

I get up and run toward the guy on my right. As I do, I switch hands, extend my left arm, and fire my two remaining bullets at the guys over by the flaming wreck. Again, the first hits the target. I see one of them hit the ground and clutch his thigh. The blood loss from a wound like that will likely finish him off.

The second one is wide but prompts the last man standing to duck away momentarily, buying me a much-needed reprieve.

I reach the guy on my right just as he's breaking cover to shoot at me again. I throw the empty Glock at him as I approach at full speed. He flinches long enough for me to get within arm's length. I slam into the open door, shoulder first, knocking him off his feet and sending his gun flying from his hand. I move around the door and pounce on him, not wanting to give him any time to recover. I stomp down hard on his stomach, causing him to jolt upright from the ground. As he does, I crouch and throw a punch, hitting him squarely on his jaw. His head snaps back, bounces off the blacktop, and knocks him out.

I'm covered by the door now, so I reach over and pick up his weapon, quickly checking the mag. It's a Sig Sauer P220. It has a small barrel and is a common handgun for law enforcement agencies. There's almost a full load too, which is good news.

I glance around the door to see where the last remaining asshole is, but there's no sign of him.

I look back at the guy and check his pockets. There's no ID, just a billfold containing a couple hundred dollars. I suppose if these guys are part of a special operations group, any mission to take me out would be off the books. I see the brazen, couldn't-give-a-fuck-anymore attitude stemming from the White House and filtering down to all the acronyms, and it pisses me off. The public remain oblivious because Cunningham still needs to be seen doing everything by the book, so there'll be no record to link this back to him. It's not so much the fact they're playing by their own rules that gets to me. It's the arrogance they show while they're doing it—like they're untouchable.

I'll show them *untouchable*... bastards!

I stand and make my way into the middle of the expressway. I'm not bothered about cover now. There's only one guy left. What's he going to do?

I hold the gun loose by my side. I feel a wave of calm wash over me. The hard part's done, and my Inner Satan can rest again.

"Hey!" I shout. "Get your ass out here, front and center."

I stop and wait for any movement. After a moment, the remaining guy appears from behind the trunk of the Crown Vic. Sneaky bastard was going to try to get the jump on me...

He's aiming steadily and professionally at me, using both hands to line up his shot.

"Drop your weapon!" he shouts back.

I laugh. "Fuck me—you're optimistic, aren't you?"

"Drop it now!"

I raise the Sig Sauer, one-handed, and aim at him. "No."

He hesitates, just for a second. Pussy.

I fire once, shooting his right hand. His gun flies from his grip, and he yells in pain as the bullet penetrates his palm. He clutches at the fresh hole in his hand and staggers backward.

I take a couple of steps toward him, keeping my gun raised. "Who sent you? Was it Matthews? Or did Cunningham finally decide to get his hands dirty?"

He's standing still, grimacing from the pain and staring at me with a mixture of anger and fear. He doesn't look like he's going to answer me, though.

Stubbornness can be really painful sometimes...

I line up another shot and fire once, hitting him in his foot. He screams and falls to the ground, unsure of which bullet wound to tend to.

"You're not going to make me ask again, are you?" I say to him. "Don't make the mistake of thinking you've been lucky so far with those non-lethal wounds. They were deliberate, and the next one will be decidedly more painful and life-threatening."

He growls through gritted teeth and stares at me. He's maybe ten feet away, close to the Crown Vic. His breathing is deep but rapid. "Fuck... you! We'll... we'll get you. Sooner or... later."

"Yeah, so you people keep saying. Tell me, how's that working out for you so far?"

He says nothing.

I shrug. "Yeah, that's what I figured. I'm gonna bring it all down. Do you understand me? Cunningham, Matthews, the entire presidency... I'm gonna reduce it all to dust. I'm past caring whether everyone was involved, or if it was just the brass in the offices on the top floor pulling the strings. I have the evidence to bring the entire administration to its knees, and I'm gonna show it to the world."

The guy frowns. "What... what are you... talking about?"

I scoff. "Don't act like you don't know!"

He simply shakes his head. His face softens as his anger gives way to something else. Confusion?

"Okay, wait. Why do you think you're after me?"

He grimaces again before answering. "Because... because you're a terrorist..."

"Uh-huh... and who told you that?"

Again, he says nothing.

"Well, maybe you're proof that not everyone involved is necessarily guilty of conspiracy. You think I'm responsible in some way for 4/17, right?"

He nods slowly.

"Well, I'm not. In fact, I started out trying to stop the people who were. Then I found out President Cunningham is actually behind it all. And I have proof. Categorical, undeniable proof. That's the real reason you've been sent to kill me. To silence me. And every attempt to do so has failed. General Matthews is getting so desperate that he's actually hired a professional assassin called The European to try it."

He doesn't believe me. That's fine. It doesn't matter, really.

"So, here's how it's gonna work. You're going to go back to your bosses at Langley and tell them you failed. Tell them I'm still alive, and I'm coming for all of them. Say that I have proof the CIA manufactured intelligence to frame me and did so on the president's authority. And I'm going to tell everyone."

I step toward him and lean down, then hit him around the face with my gun, knocking him out.

I walk over to the Crown Vic, duck inside the back, and take my flash drive from Wallis's pocket. I put it back around my neck and feel reassured once more that I'm in control. I move to the front and open the driver's door. I bend over, lift Freeman's arm, and place it over my shoulder. He's conscious but barely.

"Come on, Freeman. I've got you," I say as I haul him out of the car.

"You're... an... asshole..."

I smile. "Yeah, I know. But this way, the sole surviving agent will head back to the CIA and say I escaped by force, which stops either you or Wallis from being associated with me. It had to be believable."

I heave him upright, and he leans against me, staggering as we walk toward the only SUV that's still roadworthy.

Freeman tries to speak again. "Wh... where... are—"

"I'm getting you to a hospital," I say, saving him the breath. "Just relax, all right? I'll leave Wallis here. He's fine."

I load him into the back seat of the SUV, quickly gather up all the weapons and ammunition I can see, then climb in behind the wheel. I gun the engine, spin the SUV around, and speed off, away from the carnage I just caused.

18

ADRIAN HELL

I slide to a halt outside the emergency entrance of the AtlantiCare facility on Pacific Avenue. It's a brilliant white brick and glass building that looks newer than it probably is. I step out of the SUV and rush to open the rear door.

Showtime.

I look over at the open doors leading into the emergency room. "Hey! I need some help over here!"

I move to the rear door and open it. I reach inside and grab hold of Freeman's arm.

"Sir, step out the way," says a female voice behind me.

I turn and move to the side. Two EMTs in green coveralls are rushing toward me, one on either side of a gurney. Both are women. The one nearest to me steps toward the vehicle, helps Freeman out, and then looks at me. "What happened?"

"I saw him on the expressway. There was a pileup, but he

looks like he's been shot. He's an FBI agent. I got him in my car and came straight here."

The EMT nods. "Okay, let us work." She turns to her colleague. "Gunshot wound to the right abdomen. It's through and through. Let's get him inside right away."

They expertly lay him down and wheel him quickly toward the entrance.

I walk alongside them. "Is there anything I can do?"

"We've got it from here," says the other EMT, "but you'll need to hang around. The police will have to be informed, and they'll want a statement from you."

"Yeah, of course. Thanks."

I slow down and watch them disappear inside. I quickly look around to check for any suspicious, not-so-well-disguised G-men, but I can't see any. I walk casually inside, making sure my jacket covers the gun I've got tucked at my back. I head over to the front desk and catch the eye of a nurse who's talking on the phone. She holds up her finger and smiles, signaling she won't be a minute. I smile back and lean on the counter, glancing idly around at the waiting area.

As places like this go, it's really nice—nothing like how I envision a normal hospital to look. The furniture doesn't have that basic, bulk-bought style. The seats are chocolate brown and made of a soft material that appears more comfortable than a standard waiting room chair. The floor is carpeted, and there's no smell of disinfectant anywhere. TV screens are positioned strategically around the area, with local news channels on some and internal information on others.

"Help you?"

I turn back and see a nurse standing in front of me behind the counter. She's short and a little overweight, with nice eyes and a friendly tone. I get a faint waft of her perfume, which smells like coconut. I get the impression she enjoys her job.

"Hi—yeah, I hope so. A friend of mine was brought in here earlier with a gunshot wound to her shoulder. I'm just checking up on her. Can you tell me where she is please?"

"Sure, I'll check. What's their name?"

"Ruby."

She moves over to the computer and taps away at the keyboard. "Second floor, room twelve," she says after a moment. "She'll be resting after the surgery, but you should be able to see her."

"That's great. Thanks."

I think about taking the elevator but decide against it. I don't want to voluntarily trap myself in a metal box, just in case. Instead, I head away from the front desk toward some double doors at the end of the corridor, where a sign directs me to the stairs.

I take them two at a time and push open the doors at the top. I come out into a smaller, open plan waiting area. Freeman said she was being held in a secure wing, so I'm guessing there will be at least one cop outside her room. I need to be discreet; my face will be well known now.

I approach the desk. The young man sitting behind it looks up. He's clean shaven, with boyish good looks and a professional smile.

"Can I help you?"

I smile a greeting. "I'm looking for room twelve. A friend of mine's in there."

He nods. "Sure, it's that way." He points to his left. "Last door on the right."

"Thanks."

I walk cautiously toward the corridor and peer around the corner as casually as I can.

Shit.

There are two cops outside the door.

I won't be able to get in there without causing a ruckus, and I really need to lie low—especially if I want to get Ruby out of here in one piece.

I look around in search of inspiration. I see two doctors come out of a room set back on the left, away from the waiting area. I wait for them to disappear out of sight, then, curious, I walk over. It's a break area for staff.

Hmm.

I glance over my shoulder at the front desk. The guy's distracted by some files in front of him. I grab the handle and quickly push the door open, then step inside and close it again.

It's a square room with vertical blinds at the window directly opposite the door. There's a couch against one wall and a circular table with some chairs around it a little farther along. There's a small kitchen area by the window in the far corner. It smells of fresh coffee, and my mouth waters at the prospect of sitting down with a cup of Joe and forgetting about my troubles.

Huh... I wish!

The room looks great, but it doesn't help me. I sigh and turn to leave. Hanging on the back of the door are two white lab coats, complete with name tags of doctors.

I scratch at the ever-thickening coarse hair on my chin and smile to myself.

Light bulb!

13:19 EDT

. . .

I approach the door to Ruby's room, smiling at the cops standing on either side. They look bored out of their minds. They're wearing knife vests over light blue, short-sleeved shirts. Their guns are strapped to their waists.

I stare at both of them in turn, nodding a curt greeting as I move to open the door. The one on the right shuffles sideways slightly, allowing more space for me to pass.

"Afternoon, Doc," he says to me.

"Afternoon, Officer," I reply courteously.

I open the door and step inside, closing it gently behind me. It's a generic room—clean and smart with little decoration. The bed is facing me, and machines are on either side, idly beeping at regular intervals, which is comforting. Two windows allow in plenty of natural light.

I move over to the side of the bed and glance down at her. Ruby's lying still with her eyes closed. Her chest is rising and falling slowly. There's a thin plastic tube running under her nose, and her right shoulder is bandaged. Her arms are resting on top of the covers. I place my hand on hers.

"Hey, you awake?" I ask.

"Huh?" she responds groggily.

She slowly opens her eyes, blinks, and stares around the room, disoriented. Finally, her gaze rests on me. She looks at me blankly for a moment, and then frowns. "Why are you dressed like a doctor?"

I smile, happy to hear her voice. "I'm in disguise." I place a finger to my lips and whisper. "Shh, don't tell anyone."

She shakes her head and chuckles. "Did simply putting on a white coat *actually* work?"

"Strangely, yes, it did. You've got two of New Jersey's

finest right outside. I just walked straight in, and they practically saluted me."

She smiles at me for a moment, but it slowly fades. "I thought you'd be long gone. What happened after they arrested you?"

"Long story, but I have a couple of FBI agents helping me. Well, as much as they can, anyway. They came to collect me, but the CIA weren't far behind."

"Did you... did you kill any of them?"

"Any CIA guys?" I shrug. "Yeah... all of 'em. Well, all except one. I left him alive, so he could deliver a message for me to his boss."

She sighs heavily. "Jesus..."

"How're you feeling?"

"I'm all right. No lasting damage. It was the blood loss that worried them the most, I think."

I nod. "Good because we need to get out of here."

She smiles weakly. "Do I have to?"

I take a breath and shake my head sincerely. "No, you don't have to. Look, joking aside, if you want out, I fully understand. I'll make sure you're well compensated for your efforts, and I'll do what I can to get you a clean break. But I know things are—"

I stop because I notice the look on her face. She's staring at me, her green eyes wide and playful. Her mouth is fighting to hide a smile. "Can you not tell when a woman is just after a little sympathy?"

I absently scratch the back of my head and look away. "Ah... no?"

"You're an idiot."

I smile at her. "Thanks."

She tuts and sighs. "Come on, get me out of here already. I've got an ex-boyfriend to kill."

I laugh, switch off the equipment surrounding her bed, and help her unplug herself. She pulls the bed covers back, slowly swings her legs over the side, and rests her feet on the floor.

I place a hand on her shoulder. "Take it easy, all right? Don't want you injuring yourself."

"I'll be fine. Stop being a pussy. I just need a minute."

I hold my hands up defensively and step away, giving her space. I watch as she slowly pushes herself to her feet. She stands still for a moment, composing herself after what looks like a rush of blood to the head. Then she turns around and leans over the bed to reach for a glass of water.

I roll my eyes and look away for a moment. "Ah, Ruby?"

Still leaning over, she looks back at me. "What?"

"You, ah... you have one of those gowns on that doesn't have a back. And..." I sigh, struggling with the subtlety. "You don't have any underwear on."

She frowns, glances back at herself momentarily, and then at me. She shrugs. "What's your point?" She smiles and turns away, retrieves the water, stands up straight, and takes a sip.

I massage my forehead with my hand.

I don't think I've ever seen the same woman naked *this* many times and had it be a problem for me.

Ruby walks tentatively over to me. "So, what's the plan?"

I frown. "Plan? What plan?"

"To get me out of here?"

"Oh. No, I didn't make a plan."

"What do you mean? How can you come in here without an escape plan?"

I shrug. "Look what happened last time I tried to get you out of somewhere. Figured there wasn't much point in planning anything."

"What the... I can't believe you'd be so—" My smile stops her, and she shakes her head. "Asshole! Don't mess with me like that!"

I scoff. "Oh, because you've never done that to me, have you?"

"That's different. I'm a woman."

"Whatever."

"So, what *is* your plan?"

"We're just gonna walk out the front door and drive off."

Ruby looks at me blankly for a moment. "*That's* your plan? Just... walk out of here?"

I nod. "Yup."

"Jesus! I think I preferred it when I thought you didn't have one."

I laugh. "Just follow my lead." I tug on my lapels. "And respect the white coat, bitch."

She smiles.

I walk over to the far side of the room, where a wheelchair's parked against the wall. I push it over to her and gesture with my head. "Get in."

She sits down, somewhat begrudgingly, and leans back, looking up at me. "Are you sure this will work? Your track record with ideas isn't great."

"Are you kidding me? My shit always works... sometimes."

She looks forward. "We're *so* dead," she mutters.

I push her to the door, step around, and open it. I stick my head out and look at the cop on the left. "Hey, would you mind getting the door, please? I'm taking Miss DeSouza for a couple of follow-up tests."

The cop turns around and, without a word, holds the door open for me.

"Thanks."

I move back and push Ruby into the corridor. I set off toward the elevators, walking purposefully, like I figure a doctor would.

I frown as I hear footsteps behind me. I glance over my shoulder and see both cops following us.

Shit.

"Do you need anything?" I ask them.

The one who held the door shakes his head. "No, sir. But your patient is wanted for questioning, and until the Feds arrive, wherever she goes, we go."

Wonderful.

I smile at them. "Of course. Sorry."

We move into the waiting area, and I make a point of casually looking to my left as we pass the front desk in case the guy sitting there decides to point out the fact that I'm not *actually* a doctor.

We make it to the elevator, and I lean over and press the call button. It arrives after a moment, stopping with a ding. The doors slide open, and I push Ruby inside, positioning her wheelchair so that she's next to me, facing the doors. The two cops step in and stand in front of us.

"Which floor?" one of them calls behind.

I glance forward. There are only six buttons. "Top floor, please."

I can see Ruby staring quizzically at me in my peripheral vision. I turn and wink at her.

The doors slide shut and we begin our ascent. We pass the third floor. I start planning my next few moves. I'll need three, I think. Two targets, close quarters... yeah, three should do it.

We pass the fourth. Then the fifth.

And...

I kick the cop in front of me in the back of his knee, hard.

First move.

As he buckles, I slam into him with my shoulder, sending him head-first into the doors. He drops to the floor, out for the count.

Second move.

I hit the emergency stop button as I launch my elbow at the cop in front of Ruby, who hasn't yet managed to react to what's happening. It connects with the side of his throat, and he falls backward. He slides to the floor, making a horrible wheezing sound, like a gurgle.

Third move. Job done.

"You good?" I ask Ruby, who's staring at me with the same bemused smile she gave me when I took out the guards at Stonebanks, back in Baltimore.

"Yeah, I'm good. I'm just—"

She stops and frowns at the cop at her feet, still making the noise and clutching his throat. She slams her foot into his face, and he falls silent.

"*That* was annoying."

I smile. "Right, we need to change."

She looks at me, frowning again. "Change? Into what?"

I nod at the cops on the floor.

She shakes her head. "Oh, no. No way. I'm not putting a uniform on. Not a fucking chance."

"You got any better ideas?"

"But..." She sighs. "Well, no, but they'll be too big for me. It'll look ridiculous... and obvious."

Oh, yeah.

"Okay, well..." I reach down and take both of the cops' guns from their holsters. "Put these under your gown, at least."

I hand them to her, and she smiles, glaring at me with an insane mischief in her eyes. "Ooh, kinky!"

I raise an eyebrow. "Now? Really?"

She shrugs. "What? A girl's gotta have *some* fun…"

I restart the elevator and hit the button for the ground floor. We reach the top, and thankfully, the doors open and close without anyone trying to get in. As we begin our descent, I drag the cops to the back and push Ruby to the front.

"We need to be quick, okay?" I say to her. "I've got an SUV parked out front."

She nods. "Got it."

The doors open and we walk out. I push her toward the entrance, walking fast and looking away again as we pass the front desk.

We're almost at the doors now. Just a few more steps and we're in the—

"Hey! Wait a minute!"

—clear. Fuck!

I look over my shoulder. The nice lady behind the desk is standing and pointing at me. "Get back here! You can't just walk a patient out of here! Security!"

And we're out of here…

I run toward the SUV, pushing Ruby in front of me. "Back seat!"

She steps out of the chair as I bring it to a stop. The guns fall onto the ground.

She crouches for them. "Ah, shit, sorry!"

"Forget them. Just get in the goddamn car!"

She stands and climbs onto the back seat. I slam the door shut behind her and scoop up both guns. I push the wheelchair away with my foot and climb in behind the wheel. I drop the guns on the seat next to me, fire up the engine, and drive off. The tires screech loudly and throw up smoke behind us.

"You okay?" I shout back as I check the mirrors to make sure we're not being followed.

"Yeah, I'm fine." She sounds short of breath.

I catch her eye in the rearview and raise an eyebrow, asking a silent question.

She sighs and rolls her eyes. "My shoulder hurts like hell, all right?"

"We'll pick you up some painkillers on the way."

"Where are we going?"

I open the glove box and fumble around until I find a cell phone. I toss it onto the back seat.

"Get the number for Caesar's, then call them and book us a suite."

"Erm... Adrian? Don't you think we should *maybe* consider leaving town?"

I navigate the traffic as best I can, forcing myself to slow down so that we don't look like we're fleeing a crime scene. "No, we need Jonas if we're going to stand any chance here. Running away is no longer an option."

I hear her sigh behind me. "Okay, I'll make the call."

"We'll take a detour on the way to get you some clothes and aspirin. And when you're done, I'll call Oscar and see if he can deliver another bag of supplies to the suite for us."

I take a right and stop at a set of lights. I can hear Ruby on the phone behind me. I check the time on the SUV's dashboard.

Once we meet up with Jonas, we'll start planning how to take the fight to these bastards, instead of simply waiting for them to come to us and defending ourselves. But right now, tomorrow seems a long way off.

19

MEANWHILE...

President Cunningham was alone in the Oval Office. After his daily briefing with the senior staff earlier that morning, he pushed his other appointments back a day. He knew many of them would be largely irrelevant, given everything that would happen in just a few hours.

He sat behind the Resolute desk, his navy blue suit jacket hanging on the back of his chair. He stared blankly at the documents in front of him, seeing the words on the page but not registering their meaning.

He was angry at himself for allowing traces of doubt into his mind. It wasn't doubt about what he was doing and why but more about whether it would work. Everything had played out as expected so far, with the obvious exception of Adrian Hell. He was confident that particular situation would be handled soon now that he had passed that responsibility on to Director Atkins.

But while things had turned out as planned, the *way*

they had was, at times, anything but smooth, and that worried him. Director Matthews, for example. Everything he had tasked that incompetent idiot with had been done, but it seemed to be more through luck than strategy. Adrian Hell... the mission in Prague with his D.E.A.D. unit... even the management of El-Zurak and his men. It could've been done far more efficiently, and now he was concerned he was losing control. He hated second-guessing himself.

But he also knew that once the next phase was under-way, the rest of it would play out by itself. There was only one way it could possibly end. Knowing he was close to the stage where he no longer had to do anything provided him with some comfort. It made him think of a father teaching his son to ride his first bicycle. The training wheels were off, and he was holding the back of the seat with his hand while his son pedaled. Then, when the time was right, he would subtly let go and watch his child ride off into the world.

He knew he would soon be able to relax and watch as everything slowly crumbled around him, ready to be rebuilt stronger than ever before, with him heading up the transition into a new era of peace for mankind.

A knock at the door interrupted his musings. He looked up as Gerald Heskith entered the room and walked hurriedly toward him.

Cunningham frowned. He detected the stress from Heskith's body language—the fast walk, the furrowed brow, the tensed jaw. "Gerry, what's wrong?"

"Mr. President, I'm sorry to disturb you," he said, sounding uncharacteristically flustered. "But we have a... situation that requires your immediate attention."

"What is it?"

"It's Matthews, sir. He's gone."

"Already? That's great news, surely?"

"No, Mr. President—you don't understand. He's alive. He's just... disappeared. I spoke to Julius Jones over at Langley. He said Matthews left carrying a briefcase a few hours ago, saying he'd be back later today. Jones said the whole thing didn't sit right with him, so he went to Matthews's office to look around. The entire room had been cleared out. Every piece of paper in there—gone."

Cunningham stood quickly, sending his chair rolling away behind him. He pointed a finger at Heskith, his anger overshadowing any sense or reason. "You find him, Gerry. Do you hear me? Find him!"

Heskith nodded, holding his hands up defensively and taking a subconscious step away from the desk. "We're doing everything we can, sir. I've spoken to our new... contractor. He's tracking him down as we speak."

Cunningham sighed and paced back and forth behind his desk. "He had everything, Gerry. Do you understand? *Everything*. This Adrian Hell business is one thing. The information *he* has is cause for concern, I know, but we'd be able to explain it all away in time. But Matthews has everything. In lots of detail. If he gets a sudden bout of conscience, we're finished."

"I understand, sir. Leave it with me. It's best that you don't know any more about this."

Cunningham let out another long sigh, then sat back down. He could feel the tension building between his eyebrows just above the bridge of his nose. He used a finger to quickly massage away the beginnings of a headache.

He looked up at Heskith. "Fix this."

The chief of staff nodded and left without a word. President Cunningham leaned back in his chair and stared blankly at his desk once more.

· · ·

17:45 EDT

After a tense couple of hours, Cunningham retired to the residence early. His anger and concerns had eventually given way to butterflies ahead of the history-making events that were only a few hours away.

He sat facing the fireplace, cradling a glass of brandy in his hand and staring thoughtfully at the flames. The smell from his glass was strong but pleasant. Brandy was one of the few luxuries he allowed himself. He gave up his life to politics, knowing his destiny was always to be exactly where he was, doing exactly what he was doing. He had seen it so clearly from a young age. He had foregone a typical child-hood, having few friends and even fewer relationships. He had no interest in getting married or having children. He just had his mission. But brandy was the exception. He had started drinking it in his mid-twenties and fell in love with it from the first sip. He kept his glass on the mantel above the fireplace, so it remained subtly warm for when he poured himself a measure—a trick one of his old college professors taught him.

He cradled his tumbler, occasionally sipping at the expensive amber fluid. Next to him, the day's newspaper lay on the mahogany table in the glow of the lamp, waiting to be perused.

But he couldn't focus on reading. All he could think about was what the world would look like tomorrow and whether there would be any more surprises that would threaten everything he had worked for before then.

The business with Matthews really angered and worried him. He knew Heskith would handle it, but that wasn't the point. The risk of exposure was massive, and he couldn't shake the feeling that his luck might run out before tomorrow.

He took some deep breaths and another sip of his drink, trying to relax. He wasn't there yet, but he was in the home stretch. He checked his watch and smiled.

Just under four hours to go.

20

ADRIAN HELL

Caesar's is incredible! I've never stayed anywhere as nice as this. The suite Ruby booked is a premium deluxe something-or-other in the Centurion Tower, with a view of the ocean from the room. There are two queen-sized beds facing a large TV screen and a section of the suite that consists of armchairs and a low table, like a living room. The bathroom, on the left as you enter the suite, is wall-to-wall marble. Cold yet opulent.

Ruby lay on one of the beds, resting. That bullet must have really shaken her. She's not taken her clothes off once since we got here...

I've been pacing up and down the room since we arrived earlier this afternoon. We've kept a low profile. We haven't ventured out of the suite once, and we've ordered room service when we've needed food or drink.

Tomorrow, with some luck, Jonas Briggs will arrive, and we can finally start planning. I feel like I've been trapped in purgatory. Every time I look forward, something crops up behind me and keeps me rooted to the spot. I've been running for weeks now, and I'm fast approaching the point where I'm ready to just stop, turn around, and shoot whoever's chasing me.

"Will you sit down? You're giving me a headache."

I'm standing at the window, looking out at the balcony and the city beyond, all lit up and bustling with activity below. I glance over my shoulder at Ruby and smile apologetically. "Sorry. I'm just anxious."

"Well, learn to relax a little, would you?" She reaches over for the remote and clicks the TV into life. She settles for the first thing she finds, which looks like a sitcom. She pats the bed next to her. "Come on. Sit down. Enjoy."

I look at the space beside her and raise an eyebrow.

She sighs. "I'm not going to eat you. Man up, will you?"

I roll my eyes, move around the bed, sit down, and rest against the plush headboard. I let out a deep breath and close my eyes for a moment.

"Attaboy," Ruby says. I can hear the smile in her voice. "Now..."

Her hand rests on my leg, high up on my thigh. My eyes snap open. I spring to my feet and stare at her.

She starts laughing. "I'm kidding!"

I shake my head and run a hand through my hair. "Look, it's been hard enough with you flashing me every two seconds..."

She raises an eyebrow. "Has it now? There's hope for you yet, Adrian!"

Her playful smile does little to help matters. "What? No, not like that! Just... okay, look—I'm on the edge, all right? I'm *this* close to losing my fucking mind! I have to kill the president, and the entire country is gunning for me. I haven't taken one step toward getting this fixed, and people are depending on me. I'm sick and fucking tired of running. I just want everything simplified and broken down. I want to be pointed in the right direction and told where to shoot. That's it! I don't need any more drama or temptation or fucking *anything* getting in my way. Just…"

I run out of words. My breathing's fast, yet heavy. I feel a surge of adrenaline in my veins. I feel my breaking point. Everything just spilled out of me, triggered by the slightest push.

What the hell?

Compared to some of the shit I've been through in my time, and despite what's at stake, this situation doesn't really feel any worse than any other. What the hell's wrong with me?

I focus my gaze on Ruby, who's staring at me with wide eyes, filled with… not anger… not even shock. Is it sympathy?

She stands, walks around the bed, stops in front of me, and looks up at me. She puts her arms around my waist and rests her head on my chest, squeezing me gently.

I don't know how to react. My adrenaline hasn't subsided yet, and I'm holding my arms out to the sides, not sure if I should embrace her or push her away.

"I'm sorry," she says quietly. "Okay? I'm sorry."

I slowly move my arms around her as my heart rate slows. I hold her close to me as I fight another foreign concept: emotion. I feel overwhelmed, like what I'm doing is *too* big. I don't honestly know if I can do this, regardless of how much help I might have.

I push her away slightly and hold her by her shoulders at arm's length, staring into her eyes. "Ruby, if we fail…"

She tilts her head, smiling wryly. "If? If? Adrian, if your auntie had balls, she'd be your uncle!"

I frown. "Huh?"

She shrugs. "I dunno—something my old man used to say. The point is, since when do we deal with *ifs*? We deal in blood and bullets, Adrian. That's it. I don't blame you for losing sight of that. Shit, I can't imagine what's going on in your head right now. But I'm telling you—blood and bullets. Understand? Nothing else."

I walk away and gaze blankly through the window. The lights across the skyline blur together as my mind wanders.

A knock on the door disturbs me. I spin around, catching Ruby's eye. "You order room service?"

She shakes her head. "Nope. Could it be Oscar?"

I relax a little. I forgot about him. I called him earlier, and he said he would be here at around 10:00 p.m. I check the clock in the room and walk toward the door. As I reach for the handle, it opens from the outside.

Well, it's not Oscar...

22:11 EDT

General Matthews walks into the room and brushes past me with indifference. I watch him, completely dumbfounded. He's not in his full military garb but just a regular suit, and he's carrying a briefcase. He looks thinner than I remember. I've not seen him since... since he killed half a billion people.

I need a minute...

What the fuck?

What the *fuck*?

I blink hard and shake my head.

...

...

...

And we're back.

I push the door shut and walk hurriedly over to him. I throw a punch, which catches him on the side of his face as he turns around to look at me. He goes down and drops his case. I kick it away from him, reach down, grab him by his lapels, and haul him back to his feet. I punch him again—this time in the stomach—then push him onto the bed.

I lock eyes with him, fixing him with a cold stare filled with hot fury. I don't blink. "Ruby, get the gun. Keep it on him."

I look at her when she doesn't move and see the confused expression on her face.

"This is General Matthews."

Her eyes go wide. She moves for the gun and aims it at him.

I turn back to him. The rush of anger I feel is quick and frightening. "You piece of shit! How dare you come to me, you *fuck*! I should kill you right now."

Matthews holds his hands up. "I... I expect you to." His voice cracks with fear. "But you need to hear me out first."

Ruby steps forward, the gun unwavering in her hand. "Why the hell should we?"

"Because we're running out of time, and you can still stop this... this madness!"

Ruby and I take an involuntary step back, shocked.

I hold my hand out to Ruby, signaling for her to lower the gun. Shit just got interesting.

"Say what now?"

He shuffles himself up to a sitting position on the bed.

"I'm a dead man. I know that. I just hope I'm not too late to make amends." He points to his briefcase. "In there."

I turn to Ruby. "Watch him."

I move over to the case, which is now near the foot of the second bed, nearest the door. I pick it up, rest it on top of the covers, and click it open. It's full of files and paperwork.

I look over at Matthews. "What's this?"

"Everything," he replies. "That evidence you've got... it's okay. It'll get people asking questions. But it won't stop anyone. It won't make a real difference. And that's the sad truth. But everything in that case... it will change the course of history."

I quickly sift through the papers. None of my earlier concerns and doubts matter anymore. People say it can take just a second to change your life. They weren't kidding.

I'll admit, the majority of the documentation means little to me.

"Why are you here, Matthews? Why the sudden change of heart?"

"Because Cunningham wants me dead!" he screams. "I messed up, and now he's trying to get rid of me. At first, I was angry at you. It's your fault I'm in this position..."

"My fault? How am I to blame for anything that's going on?"

"Because you won't *die*!"

I scoff and hold my hands up. "Oh, *I'm sorry*..."

"Ever since Atlanta, I've been trying to kill you—to tie up the one loose end I had left. But you're a resilient sono-fabitch."

I shrug. "Thanks." I glance at Ruby. "That was a compliment, right?"

She shakes her head and rolls her eyes.

I look back at Matthews. "I know you've been using

Cerberus to track me. And I've lost count of how many body bags I've filled. I'm going to stop Cunningham. You know that, right? I'm gonna kill that bastard and—"

"And that won't do a goddamn thing…" He shakes his head regretfully. "That's why I'm here. He's set his sights on me now. I know he has. And nothing can stop him. It's all in the case. Everything. Every last goddamn detail of what he's planning. This is bigger than you can imagine, Adrian."

I can't hide the concern from my face. He's telling the truth. I'm sure of it. I don't like it, but he is. I lock eyes with Ruby, who looks much the same as I probably do—wide-eyed, slack-jawed, and completely speechless.

All this time, I presumed that the buck stops with Cunningham. I've been working on the basis that if I can kill him, things will go back to the way they were. But now Matthews is saying that's not going to happen…

"Then enlighten me. What's after Cunningham?"

He nods at the briefcase. "It's all in there…"

I sigh, losing patience. "Give me the abridged version. That's a lot of shit to look through."

Matthews hesitates slightly.

"Don't clam up on me now, you sack of shit!"

"He's… ah… it's Cunningham. His vision for the world… it's… I understand it. He just wants peace."

"He's got a funny fucking way of showing it…"

"He's an intelligent man, Adrian. Probably more so than you give him credit for. The Armageddon Initiative was his own creation. He knew that in order for his plan to work… for it to be accepted by the American people, he needed an enemy. In every story, there has to be a villain. Cunningham believes *he's* the hero. The first stage—hijacking Cerberus and using it on all those different countries—was planned meticulously for years. And Hamaad El-Zurak served his purpose well as the public's hate figure. Installing him as the leader of a fictitious terrorist organization was a stroke of genius. But the next stage of the plan is happening now. And yet again, Cunningham has someone else to play the part of the villain."

"What's the next stage? What could possibly be worse than 4/17?"

"Cunningham knows everything GlobaTech is doing. He knows where every man is, where every truck carrying medical supplies is, every engineer, every consultant... he knows it *all*. He's going to destroy GlobaTech's forces. He never wanted them to be a part of this. Then you started helping them, and they found out enough about what's happened to think they could buy our silence.

"But Cunningham already had it figured out. He knew he could use GlobaTech to do the heavy lifting in the first few weeks. It would look great to the people of the world that the United States was helping, and he wouldn't have to risk one member of our armed forces to do it. Now GlobaTech's forces are spread so thin, they'll be easy to wipe out. It'll leave the world vulnerable, and people will beg Cunningham to help them. Using the full strength of this country's military, we can destroy the enemy Cunningham himself put in place just so they could fail after they've served their purpose, and he will control the world as it's rebuilt from the ground up."

I can't believe what I'm hearing. I had no idea the extent of his endgame was this... this fucking crazy! Like Matthews said, you can *kind of* understand the basis for his plan. Nobody wants any more war or famine. Why can't we all just get along, right? But this? You can't just kill the world and start from scratch!

"Adrian..." says Ruby.

I ignore her, staring at Matthews. "Who's the enemy this time? Who's Cunningham using to destroy GlobaTech and start a third world war?"

"Adrian..." she says again.

"Matthews, tell me! Who's coming for us all?"

He stands and walks into the middle of the suite. The backdrop of the city is lit up behind him through the window. He stands tall and takes a deep breath. "North Korea."

Holy fucking shit...

I turn to Ruby. "I have to warn Josh..."

"Adrian!" she shouts. "We're too late! Look!"

She points to the TV, and I stare at the screen. The sitcom has disappeared, interrupted by a breaking news bulletin. The volume is too low, so I can't hear the voice of the anchorman on the screen, but behind him is a live video feed from Shanghai, according to the caption below it. It shows explosions and fire and death.

Across the bottom of the screen reads the horrifying headline: NORTH KOREA INVADES!

Ruby's right. We're too late.

21

ADRIAN HELL

I watch in horror as more and more reports come up on the screen, showing attacks all over the world. China... Russia... India... Pakistan... even mainland Eastern Europe. North Korea has popped up out of nowhere and is shooting at peacekeeping forces—namely GlobaTech—and civilians everywhere.

I look over at Matthews, whose eyes are watering as he stares at the TV screen. He's shaking his head as if what he's seeing is just a bad action movie and can't possibly be real.

"No... no..." he mutters. "I can't believe he actually went through with it..."

"Hey!" I yell. I march over to him and grab him by the throat. I walk him backward and pin him to the glass. "You don't get to be upset. Do you hear me? This is your fault. *Yours*! You're the greatest mass murderer this world has ever seen, and *this*..." I point to the screen behind me. "...is all happening because of *you*!"

He finally breaks. His whole body shakes as he weeps in front of me. For a split-second, I actually feel bad for him. But I quickly remember he's a piece of shit. I spin him around by his throat and push him into the center of the room.

I look over at Ruby and hold my hand out. "Give me the gun."

Without hesitation, she hands it to me. Instinctively, I check the mag, work the slide, and aim at Matthews's forehead. "Any last words?"

Ruby takes a step back between the beds. In my peripheral vision, I see her looking at me, but she's also got a trained eye on the TV screen. It's hard to watch but also hard not to.

Matthews stares at me with tear-filled eyes. A grim determination creeps across his gaunt face. A few tense seconds of silence pass.

I see his gaze flick past me momentarily.

I see Ruby follow his gaze, a look of shock on her face.

Shit. Something's happening behind me, isn't it?

Everything slows down. All sound fades away. I push Matthews to the floor and spin around in time to see The European unhooking himself from a rappel line. He reaches behind him and brings a gun around into view. He aims at the window.

How the hell did he—

Time resumes its normal speed.

"Get down!" I yell as I drop to the floor.

I'm not bothered about Matthews, but I hope to God Ruby's reacted as fast as I have.

The glass splinters and cracks, then eventually smashes completely. The second I hear it, I jump to my feet. I know

The European will stop firing at least for a few valuable seconds while he steps into our suite.

I meet him as he does and grab his gun hand, controlling his weapon. I raise his hand skyward and jab him in the ribs. He grunts through it and delivers a short headbutt to my face. I see it coming but not quickly enough. I turn my head a fraction, so he connects with my cheekbone instead of my nose. It was a snapped blow with little wind-up and, consequently, little momentum.

But it still hurt like a sonofabitch!

I drop to one knee, my head spinning. I glance up and see he looks just as dazed as me, despite remaining upright. I fall flat on my back and look forward as I lash my foot out with as much power as I can. I catch him off guard and connect with his knee, taking his leg out from under him. I scramble to my feet as he hits the floor, and I see his gun skid away from us, across the carpet.

I position myself to deliver a kick to the side of his head, but he grabs my front foot and launches a desperate left arm into the side of my leg. The crook of his arm hits my knee. I buckle and drop again, landing heavily on my side.

Ah, shit!

We're lying on the floor next to each other—me on my side, him on his back. He lurches up and drops his elbow on my face, hitting my cheekbone again. I feel the skin swell and burst instantly from the impact, followed by the warm rush of blood as it starts down my face.

I'm struggling to get my bearings. My leg's killing me, and the cut on my face feels pretty bad, judging by how much blood I feel coming from it. I roll over onto my front as The European gets to his feet. He scoops up his gun and looks at Ruby, then aims at...

...at Matthews? What the hell?

I frown, concentrating on trying to ignore the pain I'm feeling. I slowly drag myself up and rest on my right knee. My left isn't cooperating, and I'm not sure how much pressure it could take. Losing the ability to stand is never good in a fight...

I look up at Ruby apologetically. She catches my eye and nods once. Then I see her descend into the madness I haven't seen since Baltimore. It's in her eyes. The *crazy* floods into them like a river of madness washing over her, taking over completely and allowing her to unleash her demons.

She pounces on The European, which I don't think he was expecting. He fires a round, which thankfully misses anything of any consequence. And Matthews. He tries to aim at Ruby, but she's already got her claws into him. Literally! She's on his back, her legs around his waist, and her nails are sinking into the flesh at the base of his neck, drawing blood.

He lets out a growl and lashes out behind him, narrowly missing her head with his gun. She uses her weight and momentum to start spinning him, eventually dragging him to the floor. They land on their sides, and her grip loosens momentarily. He seizes the opportunity and flips over, pinning her down on her back. He's inside her guard—her legs are still around his waist—and he's doing his best to land punches to her face and body.

She's a talented fighter. No doubt about it. She's strong and composed... though, admittedly, at the moment she's getting her ass kicked.

Oh, spoke too soon!

She grabbed his arm by the wrist and pulled him down on top of her. Now she's shuffling her hips and repositioning her legs, placing one on his left shoulder and one under his right arm, crossing her ankles behind him. She's trapped his head and right arm, and she's pushing with her legs while pulling on his wrist. I hear her snarl and grunt through gritted teeth, fighting to ignore the obvious pain it's causing her to do it.

The pressure her thighs are putting on his neck and throat is making it difficult for him to breathe and cutting off the circulation to his brain. He's frantically throwing short jabs to her right side, but he can't put anything behind them that would do any damage.

The bastard's done.

After another few moments, the jabs slow down. Then they stop. His body starts to go limp, giving up the fight with gravity, but she keeps her grip on him. Her legs must be aching, holding him upright now that he's barely conscious.

She glances sideways at me and raises an eyebrow.

I nod. "Finish the sonofabitch."

She takes a deep breath and then quickly lets go of his wrist. She moves her left leg from under his arm and places it on his shoulder, like the other one. She crosses her ankles again and pushes once more with both legs. She lets him fall to the side and props herself up on her elbow.

From this angle, I can see his eyes rolling up into his skull. His cheeks are turning a light purple, and spit is bubbling on his lips as he tries to talk.

"You're an asshole, Fernando," she says to him. "And this is for trying to blow up me and my friend!"

She pushes herself up with her hand and violently twists her lower body, throwing her hip over and snapping The European's neck between her legs. The crack is loud in the room, as is the dull thud as his head bangs lifelessly against the floor.

Ruby lies flat on her back, resting her body and sighing with relief.

"Nice work," I say. "I've always thought you had killer thighs, but..."

She bursts out laughing and runs her hands through her hair and over her face. "Nice!"

The mood lightens for a fleeting moment but soon drops again. I push myself up, using the bed for leverage. I rest my left foot tentatively on the floor and then ease my weight down on it, testing how strong it is. I almost overbalance.

Huh... not very, it seems.

I limp toward Matthews, who has propped himself up against the wall over by the bathroom. He's sitting on the floor, his shoulders slumped forward with defeat, staring up at the TV screen.

I glance at it. The headline along the bottom has changed. Now it says: THE WORLD AT WAR!

Dramatic yet frighteningly accurate.

I look down at Ruby and extend a hand, which she takes. I pull her up, and she stretches, cracking her shoulders.

"So, we're friends, are we?" I ask, half-smiling.

She shrugs. "Closest thing I've got to one at the moment."

"Yeah..." We bump fists and turn to look at the CIA director. I point to the TV. "So, how do we stop this?"

He shakes his head, smiling humorlessly. "You don't. You can't. It's too late."

I look at Ruby and hold out my hand again. "Gun, please."

She obliges, and I take aim at Matthews. "You should know that I don't like being told I can't do something. I have a somewhat compulsive personality, and people saying that to me kinda makes me want to do whatever it is even more

—just to prove the fuckers wrong, y'know? So, I'll ask again. How do we stop this?"

He raises his arms, shrugging with frustration. "What do you want me to say? Yes, Adrian, you and your girlfriend here can head outside and take on the entire North Korean army by yourselves if you want. That's how you stop it."

I smile. "Hey, don't tempt me. The mood I'm in, they wouldn't stand a chance."

"This was Cunningham's plan... all along. He struck a deal with North Korea, saying he would bury any evidence of their troops' movements if *they* agreed to risk the wrath of the West by invading everyone."

"I don't get it," says Ruby. "What's in it for the Koreans?"

"I don't know..." says Matthews. "Maybe they want to show the world they survived 4/17 and establish themselves as a new superpower? To them, this is their chance to conquer the planet, and Cunningham told them he'd let them if they left America out of it."

I shake my head. "No. There's no way they would believe him."

"You'd be surprised what those crazy bastards will believe."

"So, what's Cunningham really planning?"

"His idea is to let them destroy GlobaTech and then *he'll* destroy *them* using the full might of the United States military. He wants to establish a worldwide martial law, which will give him total control over every nation—damaged or otherwise. He envisions other leaders bowing before him, giving him complete power, and allowing him to unite the planet under one banner."

I turn to Ruby. "Christ. Hitler didn't have shit on this guy."

"So, what do we do?"

I don't get a chance to answer. There's another knock on the door. We exchange a look, and I turn to Matthews. "You bring a friend?"

He shakes his head and shrugs. "None to bring. And I turned my cell phone off before I left Langley, so I couldn't be tracked..."

"Watch him," I say to Ruby. "He moves, kick him in the throat."

I move slowly over to the door, practically dragging my injured leg behind me. I place the barrel of the gun against the spy hole. "Who is it?"

A deep laugh sounds in the corridor outside. "Room service," replies Oscar's familiar voice.

I breathe a sigh of relief, lower the gun, and open the door. He's standing with a smile on his face, holding a large black sport bag. "Try not to lose these this time."

I roll my eyes. "Come on in."

He walks in and looks around in awe at the suite, and I shut the door behind him. He lets out a low whistle. "This place is nice..." He nods at the broken balcony doors, then at The European's body in the middle of the room. "Am I late to the party?"

"Just getting started. He tried crashing, but Ruby put him in his place."

Oscar looks at her. "How are you doing, Ruby?"

She smiles. "I'm good. Thanks."

He drops the bag on the bed just behind her. "Present for you."

I move next to him. "Have you seen the news?"

He turns and stares at the screen. "Yeah... this is all part of the shitstorm you've found yourself in, I'm guessing? What are you gonna—" He turns and sees Matthews for the first time, still sitting on the floor. He looks at me. "Who the hell is that?"

"Oh, sorry. Where are my manners? Oscar, this is General Tom Matthews, the director of the CIA. Tom, this is my friend and arms dealer, Oscar."

Matthews says nothing. Oscar stares at me, wide-eyed, and raises an eyebrow.

"It must be fucking weird being you, man. I mean, really... who did you piss off in a previous life?"

I shrug. "Probably not as many people as I've pissed off in this one. You got a cell phone on you?" He takes one from his pocket and hands it to me. "Thanks. I gotta make a call before someone comes to see what all the noise is about. Ruby, see what ol' Oscar here has brought to the party, would you?"

I pace slowly away, toward where the window used to be. I feel the cold wind rushing in from outside. I step carefully onto the balcony, avoiding the sea of shattered glass, and dial a number from memory.

I just hope to God he picks up.

22

ADRIAN HELL

I pace back and forth as best I can, impatient, conscious of how quickly we're running out of time.

Come on… pick up, Josh, you—

"Yeah?"

Man, he sounds pissed!

"Josh? It's me. Are you all right? Have you seen—"

"The news? Yeah, I've seen it. What the fuck is happening? Where did this even *come* from?"

I sigh. "The abridged version? This is Cunningham's endgame. He struck a deal with North Korea to wipe out all of GlobaTech's forces and establish itself in all the affected regions around the world. North Korea thinks it has a partnership with the United States and that the two nations will essentially divide up the planet between themselves."

"That is fucking ridiculous! Have you even heard *yourself* when you say it out loud?"

I can't help but smile. "Yeah, it's beyond insane, I know. But that's what's happening now. Cunningham knows where every single asset of yours is—public or otherwise. Josh, can you do anything about this?"

"How does he... y'know what? Never mind. I've got everyone doing everything they can. I've got more men with more firepower getting ready to deploy wherever I can get them to the fastest as we speak. Schultz is coordinating with Homeland and the NSA—two agencies we're pretty sure aren't under Cunningham's influence. They're just acting as anyone would under the circumstances. With Schultz bringing them up to speed, we're starting to slowly take back the country."

"I think that might be too little, too late. This is just the first phase."

He sighs. "And you're gonna tell me the second phase now, aren't you?"

"Cunningham's using the Koreans like he did El-Zurak. They're the bad guys, and he's going to jump to everyone's defense and kick their ass. And when he's done that, he intends to do something that, under any other circumstances, would be impossible and clearly insane."

"Which is?"

"He's going to unite the world under the banner of the United States, using our own military as a kind of global army. It'll be a dictatorship on the largest possible scale. He'll control everything."

Josh sighs down the phone again. "Bollocks."

"Exactly. But I think he's right when he says people are going to love the idea, given everything that's happening. They'll be blinded by the sense of security and won't see if for what it is."

"Yeah, good point. Just out of interest, how do you know all this? It's not on the flash drive hanging around your neck..."

"No, it's not. General Matthews tracked us down and told us everything. He said Cunningham's trying to kill him for failing to kill me. He's here with us now."

"And you believe him?"

"I do. He's given us a caseload of evidence to back it up too. But then The European burst in here and tried to take *him* out instead of us. His friends in the White House must be done with him. It explains why he came to me, anyway."

"Fuck. So, what happened with The European?"

"Ruby killed him."

"Oh, good. So, she's okay?"

"She's doing fine, considering."

The line falls silent for a moment.

"Jesus, Adrian, how did we end up involved in this shit?"

"You got me. I was just minding my own business, running my bar."

"Yeah... I bet *that* life seems a million years away right now, huh?

"You're not wrong, man. So, what's your plan? Can you hold off the North Koreans?"

"I don't know. That's a big fucking army, Adrian. We do all right for ourselves, and in terms of technology, we'll kick anyone's ass any day of the week. But man for man, bullet for bullet, they outnumber anything we've got six to one, at least."

"Are you seriously trying to tell me that one member of your elite private military can't kill six North Korean soldiers?"

"Well, when you put it like that..."

We share a quick laugh and then I remember the reason I was calling.

"Listen, Josh, I know you've got a lot on your plate, but I don't suppose you've had a chance to—"

"Put everything in place for your bat-shit crazy plan? Yeah, you're good to go. I'll leave you a message with the details. It's still mental, but it's prepared as much as it can be. The rest is up to you, boss."

"Thanks, Josh. You're a legend. Do you know that?"

"I do."

"Heh. According to Matthews, killing Cunningham isn't going to stop what's now in motion, but I'm gonna do it anyway. I'm gonna knock on his front door, walk inside his house, and put a bullet between his eyes."

Josh laughs. "Y'know what? I believe you, you big, scary bastard! It'll be like Heaven's Valley all over again."

I smile. "Yeah, except there might be a few more men."

"And the house is a little bigger *and* better protected."

"And a little whiter..."

"So, thinking about it, it's not much like Heaven's Valley at all, is it?"

I pause. "Not really, no. But taking down Pellaggio was fun, wasn't it?"

"It sure was beautiful to watch," he says fondly. "So, am I right in assuming the words *Inner* and *Satan* will be making an appearance soon?"

I think about it for a moment. I think this situation is so big, so... unique... that I can't afford to lose control. I need to rely on my skills, and I need to stay disciplined enough to do what needs to be done.

"I don't think so, man. Not this time. The world is at war. I can't lose control if I want to do this."

"Huh. Fuck me, Adrian. I never thought I'd see the day where things got so bad that even your dark side couldn't help."

"I guess it's not dark enough anymore."

"Either that or you've finally trained him to *think* as well as *maim*. And if that's the case, can you grab a gun and go kill some North Koreans, please? Because you've just become the most frightening thing I've ever known!"

"Thanks!"

Josh chuckles, almost nervously. "I'm not *entirely* sure that was a compliment. I'll be honest..."

"Yeah, Ruby says I struggle spotting them." I glance over my shoulder at her. She's sitting beside Oscar on the edge of one of the beds, staring in disbelief at the TV. "Listen, Josh. What I said when we last spoke... I know you said not to think about what could go wrong and everything, but... well, shit doesn't really get much more *wrong* than this. You're waging a war with North Korea, and I'm about to go and kill the president. Just in case either of us doesn't make it out the other side of this thing, I just wanna say... y'know..."

"Adrian... Boss... it doesn't need to be said. But I know. And the same goes for you."

I smile. "I love you, bro."

"Beers at The Ferryman when this is over?"

"Bet your ass."

"Go do your thing, Adrian Hell."

"Good luck, Josh."

I hang up and stare out at the city for a moment. I've got my plan. And it's going to work. A couple of tweaks are needed in light of the information Matthews has kindly provided, but that's not a problem.

I let out a heavy sigh.

This is it....

I head back inside. Ruby looks over as I step through the shattered balcony door. "Everything okay?"

I nod. "As much as it can be, under the circumstances."

I move over to the bed. Oscar stands and steps to the side so that I can see all the weaponry laid out behind him. There is a *lot* of firepower! I pick up a suppressed handgun. It's a Beretta, similar to my old ones but not as cool. I regard it in my hand for a moment and then turn and aim at Matthews.

"Give me your cell."

I hold out my hand. He reaches inside his pocket, takes out his phone, and hands it to me.

I look down at it. It's turned off, like he said. "What's the security code?"

"Four, seven, eight, two."

"Thanks. Now is there anything else you think I should know? Anything else that might help us stop this?"

He shakes his head. "It's all in the case. Just please, promise me you *will* stop him."

"Oh, you've got my word on that, General."

I pull the trigger, and a split-second later, Matthews's head snaps back. A deep crimson sprays across the wall behind him. He slumps forward and falls to the side.

I look at Ruby and Oscar in turn. Neither says anything.

"Pack everything up, including his briefcase." I hand the gun to Oscar. "I'm sorry about this, but you're here, which means you're part of the fight now. I need all the help I can get. I'd give you the *if you want out, now's your chance* speech, but there's no point. There is no out, understand? You grab a gun, and you don't stop shooting until everyone's dead. Whether that's us or them, that's for fate to decide. But this is it. We're gonna lie low here until the morning. As soon as Jonas arrives, we're leaving town."

"You gonna tell us the plan?" asks Ruby.

"Once we're all together, yeah."

She smiles. "Groovy."

Oscar hangs his head. "Shit…"

23

ADRIAN HELL

April 30, 2017 — 11:46 EDT

We gathered our things and found an empty suite one floor down. We broke in and spent the night, though no one slept much. We just sat mostly in silence, watching the TV. I worked my way through the documents in Matthews's brief-case, mostly to keep my mind occupied.

I contacted Jonas and left him an update. While it was good The European was finally dead, I had to assume our hotel was compromised. If he had been working for the powers that be and he managed to find us, chances are *they* know where we are too. I told Jonas to meet us in the short-term parking lot of the Atlantic City airport.

We commandeered a Mercedes sedan from the lot at Caesar's and headed there, stopping briefly on the way for breakfast. We're currently parked nose-first in a space not far from the entrance to the airport, anonymous in a sea of vehicles patiently waiting for their owners' return.

Oscar's standing next to the car, leaning against the

driver's door with his arms folded across his chest. Ruby's still inside, stretched across the back seat with her eyes closed. I'm not sure she's actually asleep, though. She's holding her shoulder, which I know is still giving her grief. I'm sitting on the hood, with my leg resting up on it. The warmth of the engine is providing some relief from the pain and stiffness in my knee—a result of my run-in with The European last night.

I've got the flash drive in my hand, spinning it absently between my finger and thumb. All this time, I've been hoping the information on this drive would cause people enough concern that it might keep me alive long enough to stop Cunningham, but it turns out it barely scratches the surface.

North Korea is still invading most of the Eastern hemisphere. The assault has been relentless, according to the news reports we've watched and heard. Even the naivest of us can see this had to have been planned months or even years in advance. It's too slick, too coordinated. Cunningham's a real sonofabitch, and the more I think about how he's played us all, the more I blame myself for not stopping this sooner. First, it was Cerberus, and now the Koreans... I'm sick of arriving at the party too fucking late.

Well, that ends right now.

"Heads up," says Oscar.

I look back at him over my shoulder, and he gestures to my left with his head. There's a car approaching, and even from where I'm standing, I recognize Jonas's squat frame behind the wheel.

Oscar moves along the side of the car and stops next to the trunk. I follow him and knock on the window as I pass. Ruby sits up, instantly awake and aware.

"Showtime," I say.

She nods and climbs out, and we form a loose line by the Mercedes. The car slows to a stop next to us, and Jonas gets out.

He regards each of us in turn with an expressionless gaze, then stretches his arms and back. He idly glances around the parking lot and looks up as a plane takes off nearby. He watches it climb until the noise is barely audible.

He looks at me and gestures to my bruised cheek. "So... how's it going?"

I shrug. "Oh, we've been having a blast. You good?"

"I'm here, aren't I?" He looks at the others. "This the rest of the team?"

I nod. "Yeah, this is Ruby DeSouza." She nods at him, which he returns. "And this is my arms dealer, Oscar."

"Arms dealer, huh? This doesn't sound like *your* usual gig..."

Oscar smiles humorlessly and casts an unhappy glance at me. "It's not."

I pat him on the shoulder. "Forgive ol' Oscar here. He's always a little cranky before lunch. Come on. We need to make tracks. You can put your car in our space. We'll take our ride."

He nods. "Okay. You figured out a plan yet?"

"I have. I'll tell you on the way."

12:35 EDT

Oscar's driving, and we're coasting along Route 40 toward I-295, which will take us into Wilmington, Delaware. I asked Ruby where her friend lives—the one who put together the body wrap she wore in Stonebanks. That needs to be our first call.

Ruby's up front, staring straight ahead in a kind of trance. I think she's psyching herself up. There's a somber atmosphere in the car. No one has ever experienced a global war before. I fought in Desert Shield, but that wasn't on the same scale as World War II, for example. What's happening now *is*. And the real kicker is that because of 4/17, the North Koreans are just walking in and doing what they damn well please. It's a worrying time. Even though we know the fighting is on the other side of the world, we can't help looking up every now and then to see if any planes overhead are waiting to drop bombs on us. The people not directly under attack are slowly being crushed by their own paranoia. The scenes on the news say it all—it's chaos.

I do have complete faith in Josh and GlobaTech. Don't get me wrong. They have a ridiculous amount of manpower and technology, but at the end of the day, they're essentially one company—not an army, a *company*—fighting an entire nation. And Cunningham's played it so that the United States doesn't look bad for not getting involved. GlobaTech has been billed as the savior for everyone, thanks to the president's marketing machine.

I've brought Jonas up to speed on everything, in light of us getting Matthews's paperwork. I think it actually opened his eyes to the scope of this thing. When we first spoke back in New Hampshire, he seemed skeptical that anyone would do this for reasons other than money and fame, but now I think he gets that this is about more than just a big payday.

I guess now is as good a time as any to tell them my big idea. This should cheer them up...

"Okay everyone, listen up." I shift slightly in my seat behind Oscar. Ruby turns around so that she's facing the rest of us. Beside me, Jonas looks across patiently. "This is what's going to happen. First, we stop off at Wilmington and get some disguises from Ruby's friend. I've seen this person's work firsthand." I glance at Ruby, who smiles. "And it's brilliant. We're not talking any extreme *Mrs. Doubtfire* shit. We're going to get a little makeover and conceal our features enough to buy us a little more freedom once we hit the capital."

"That's all well and good," says Jonas, "but how do you intend to get inside the White House, exactly? There won't be any tours, given we're at war with North Korea. That place is gonna be locked down tighter than Snow White's chastity belt."

"You're right. It is. But I've already thought of that, and it's all taken care of."

Ruby chuckles. "Adrian, I've known you long enough now to know that it's never a good sign when you plan things in *this* much detail! Your track record—"

"—doesn't mean a damn thing, sweetheart. This is the job that changes all the rules. You understand? This is the job that people in our line of work aspire to be a part of. This plan *will* work. It has to..."

She holds her hands up in silent apology.

"I've located a company that does contract work for the government. We're going to pose as an emergency on-call team from Tyger Security and say that we're there to upgrade the systems, as per a request from the Secret Service. There's a van waiting for us in Annapolis, Maryland, with uniforms and IDs for us all. Our credentials will already be entered into the system for when we arrive—all courtesy of our friends at GlobaTech."

I pause to let the first part of the plan sink in. No one speaks, so I'm assuming they're okay with it so far.

"There'll be a dispersal device in the van as well. Once we're inside, Jonas—I need you to rig it up to the air conditioning system for the West Wing. It'll pump nitrous oxide through the vents, which will incapacitate everyone in there for about twenty minutes."

"Non-lethal?" he asks, sounding surprised.

"Absolutely. A lot of the people working in that building are innocent. We need to remember that."

He shrugs. "If you say so..."

"It should buy us enough time to breach the Oval Office, then I can take care of the rest."

"What if he's not there?" asks Oscar, calling over his shoulder as he navigates the traffic. "The world's at war. Would he not be in the... what's it called? Situation Room or something?"

"I thought about that. But he's behind this, remember. He and everyone else on his staff who's involved will know there's no immediate threat to the United States, so I'm gambling on them carrying on as normal as a show of strength. They'll be on high alert, but I think he'll hold meetings in his office."

"What if you're wrong?" asks Ruby.

I shrug. "If I'm wrong, we'll find him. But I'm starting in the place I think he's most likely to be. Nothing else we can do. Now Oscar and I will travel to get the van. Ruby, Jonas... I need the two of you to handle another vital part of the plan *before* we approach the White House."

The two of them exchange a quick intrigued glance. Ruby shrugs. "Shoot."

I pat the briefcase next to me, containing Matthews's evidence. "I need you both to get inside the State Department and deliver this to Elaine Phillips."

Her eyes go wide. "Are you fucking shitting me? She's the secretary of state!"

"No, I'm not shitting you. And yes, she *is* the secretary of state. You'll have a disguise, and you should be able to at least get inside the front door with no problem. It's up to you once you're in there to get to her, give her this case, and convince her we're not crazy."

"Adrian, you *are* crazy," says Jonas.

I smile. "Thanks."

Ruby sighs. "Let's say, just for a moment, we manage to do that. Why her, specifically? Is she not on Cunningham's payroll?"

"Not according to this information. She's pretty much the only one who isn't, though. Cunningham knew he couldn't just replace her when he took office, so he kept her close and in the dark as much as he could."

"Jesus... I mean, how... what can..." She gives up and sighs, holding her hands up in defeat. "Whatever. Fine."

"That's my girl! Listen, everyone. I know this sounds impossible but look at what's happening. Look at what's at stake here. We need to succeed, okay? And I believe we can."

"No offense, Adrian," says Jonas. "But you *do* realize what you're suggesting is suicidal?"

I sigh. I can't afford for morale to drop now. "Look, guys, if I didn't think you could do this, you wouldn't be here. And for twenty million bucks, you've gotta expect some risks. I don't like this any more than you do, but unless you can think of an alternative, this is the only option that stands any chance of working. I never said this would be easy. I just said it'd be worth doing."

No one replies. They just face forward in their seats and stare out the window. I know I'm asking a lot of them, but I think we have a genuine shot at pulling this off. Silence fills the car. I can't imagine what must be going through everyone's head at the moment, apart from *I must be crazy…*

"Oscar, pull over just here," says Ruby, gesturing to a space near the sidewalk.

He brings us to a stop outside a thin, three-story house with a wooden porch. A short pathway runs alongside a modest patch of grass.

She glances back at me. "We're here."

13:21 EDT

We stand in a line, staring at the house. I have the briefcase in my hand. I'm not letting it out of my sight.

"Okay, listen, fellas," says Ruby. "Veronica is a friend of mine, okay? I don't want her getting dragged into this. She won't ask questions, so once we're done here, just… just forget you ever met her, all right?"

I move over to her and place a hand on her shoulder. She looks me in the eye, and we hold each other's gaze for a moment.

"It'll be fine," I say to her. "Come on. After you."

Ruby smiles briefly and walks toward the door, which opens as she sets foot on the first of the three steps leading to the porch.

"Ruby!" shouts the woman who's appeared in the doorway. "Get over here, bitch!"

Ruby laughs. "Ronny, you sexy whore!"

Veronica is a full-figured woman with a round face and bright red hair. She has piercings through her nose and the corner of her bottom lip. She's wearing black leggings and a plain matching sweater. Her smile is genuine and infectious.

They embrace at the top of the steps and disappear inside. The three of us exchange curious glances. I'm not sure what just happened, or what we're supposed to do now.

Ruby reappears on the porch. "Well, come on!"

We walk inside, and I shut the door quietly behind me.

The house is beautiful and stylish, with wooden floors and baseboards lining the hallway, which has stairs to the right and runs through to the kitchen at the far end. On the opposite side are two rooms, both with their doors closed.

Ruby and her friend are heading into the kitchen, and the three of us follow them down the hall. The house has a nice blend of rustic furnishing and modern appliances. The whole place feels cozy but spacious.

Veronica is sitting at a large table in the middle of the room. Ruby is standing beside her, leaning over and resting on the surface. They're exchanging pleasantries but look up as we enter.

Ruby moves to join the rest of us. "I really appreciate you helping us out like this, Ronny. I know it's a lot to ask."

She shrugs, smiling. "Anything for you, babes. You know that." She pats her on her shoulder, and Ruby winces. "Shit, are you okay?"

Ruby looks away. "It's nothing. I... I got shot there yesterday."

"Say what? Bitch, why aren't you in the hospital?"

"I was. I stayed a few hours, had surgery, took some painkillers, and we left."

"We?"

I step forward, smiling politely. "I needed her help. She's a tough cookie. She'll be fine."

Veronica eyes me warily. "Uh-huh. So, babes," she says, turning back to Ruby, "who are your friends?"

We're quickly introduced, and I explain what we need

from her. Veronica nods along, listening with a professional ear.

"Okay," she says finally. "I can do that." She addresses the group. "The trick with a convincing disguise isn't to try altering your entire appearance completely. It's to distort certain *aspects* of your appearance so that it looks natural but different enough from your normal features."

I nod. "Makes sense..."

I've never thought about the science behind this, and it's actually quite interesting.

Ruby's friend walks over to me and stops at my side. She's at least a foot smaller than me. She stretches up, gesturing to my face with her pinky finger. "What we do first is add a prosthetic nose. This is probably the most recognizable feature, so altering that will completely change the dynamic of your face." She points to the scar I have running down under my eye. "Next, we'll cover up any obvious blemishes—anything people will see and remember." She turns to me. "That's a beauty. Mind if I ask how you got it?"

I shrug. "It was a gift from an old acquaintance."

She raises an eyebrow. "And what did you give them in return?"

I look her in the eyes but say nothing. My lips form a thin line, and my jaw muscles twitch. My silence tells a thousand tales.

She chuckles nervously. "Okay... so, finally, we accessorize. Fake glasses and facial hair for the guys and different makeup for the lady. Something subtle but a new look. You won't recognize your own reflection."

"This is great," says Ruby. "Thank you *so* much for this!"

Veronica moves over to her. "Don't mention it. So, who's first?"

We all exchange glances.

"I'll do it," says Jonas after a moment. He smiles. "Make me pretty, will you?"

Veronica rolls her eyes, then grabs him by the hand and leads him out of the kitchen. "I'm good, but I'm not a miracle worker, honey..."

They disappear into the first room along the hall, and the door closes behind them. I take a seat at the table. After a moment, Oscar and Ruby join me.

"You okay?" she asks.

I nod. "Yeah. You?"

"Yeah..."

"Your friend is quite a character."

"She's the best."

"I'll make sure she's taken care of once this is over."

"I appreciate that, Adrian. Thanks."

She stands and leaves the kitchen, heading for the room where Jonas is getting his makeover. Oscar moves into her seat and clears his throat.

"Adrian," he says in a hushed tone. "This plan of yours to get inside the White House... it sounds great an' all, but have you thought about how we're going to get out again?"

I look him in the eye, tensing my jaw muscles again. I let out a heavy sigh. "Yeah, I need to talk to you about that..."

24

MEANWHILE...

President Cunningham paced back and forth in front of his desk. He looked concerned, even a little nervous, though not for the reasons people might think.

It had been almost eighteen hours since news broke of North Korea's global invasion. He knew it was coming, but he also knew the first twenty-four hours would be critical. He didn't expect them to fall at the first hurdle because many of the countries they were attacking were crippled beyond any immediate recovery. His concerns had more to do with how significant the attacks were. He needed the world to see that not only were they being threatened but also that they had no hope. The first and only line of defense anywhere was GlobaTech, which shouldn't be any match for the full power of North Korea's forces.

Pacing with him on the opposite side of the Oval Office was Heskith. He looked visibly calmer, but that was more for Cunningham's benefit. He knew if he looked worried, it would affect his president.

Of the two of them, he was the more grounded. While Cunningham was an idealist and a blind believer in destiny, Heskith looked at the bigger picture and focused on the realistic concerns. He thought GlobaTech's forces were a more significant threat than Cunningham gave them credit for. Despite having the advantage of knowing every tactical detail about their operations, he still appreciated the dangers of underestimating any enemy.

"What's the latest?" asked Cunningham, pausing to look at his chief of staff.

"I'm expecting an update from Atkins in a few moments," Heskith replied. "They're monitoring everything in real time down in the Situation Room."

The president sighed. "I should be down there..."

Heskith shook his head. "No, sir, you shouldn't. Your place is here, showing strength and faith in the face of a crisis. That's what anyone else in your position would do."

"Gerry, anyone else would be down there, making decisions and—"

"Mr. President, with respect, what *decisions*, exactly, would you make? You knew this was going to happen, and we have no intention of deploying any of our own armed forces overseas. Not yet, anyway. Your job right now is all PR. You need to look strong and unafraid, so the American people feel compelled to put their faith in you. That way, when the time comes, they'll see your actions as the only logical choice. We'll get you ready to address the nation within the hour."

Cunningham started to respond but refrained. He knew Heskith had a point.

A few more minutes of tense silence passed, then the

intercom buzzed on the president's desk. He moved toward it and pressed the flashing button. "Yes?"

"Sir, Director Atkins is here for you," announced his secretary.

"Send him in."

He exchanged an excited glance with Heskith as the door opened. Dennis Atkins strode purposefully into the room, a folder tucked under his arm. Cunningham was quick to note the troubled look on his face.

"What is it?" he asked him.

Atkins took the folder in his hand and passed it to the president. "This is the latest briefing on the attacks," he explained. "The Koreans have established themselves in the capital cities of most countries across Asia. Beijing, Moscow, Tokyo, New Delhi—they are all now officially under North Korean control. There are reports coming in from all over of refugees being slaughtered in the tens of thousands."

"What about the Middle East?" asked Heskith. "Is there word from Egypt or Saudi Arabia?"

Atkins shook his head. "Nothing yet. We're trying to establish a feed via Cerberus, but it's difficult to do without alerting people to the fact that we're still in control of it. The eyes of the world are everywhere. The media coverage alone could undo us if we're not careful."

Cunningham nodded. "What's wrong, Dennis?" he asked, recognizing that there was more on his mind than the invasion. "Besides the obvious..."

Atkins sighed heavily. He tried to speak a couple of times, but the words seemed to fail him.

"Director?" prompted Heskith.

"We had word last night from our asset in New Jersey regarding the Adrian Hell situation," he said finally.

Cunningham tensed. "And?"

"And... The European found them in a suite at Caesar's. He advised that he was proceeding with the hit."

"So, what happened?"

"We heard nothing, so I sent a small team to recon the area. They arrived there a few hours ago. They found The European dead on the floor. His neck was snapped. They also found..." He closed his eyes momentarily, knowing what he was about to say would not be well received. "They found General Matthews there too, sir. He was slumped on the floor, with a hole in his head and his brains all over the wall."

Cunningham put a hand over his mouth and processed the information. "So... what? The European took out Matthews and then Adrian took *him* out?"

Atkins shook his head. "No, sir. We checked surveillance footage from the hotel's security feeds. Matthews walked into the suite where Adrian Hell was staying *before* The European made his move. He was holding a briefcase..."

Cunningham looked over at Heskith, worried. He said nothing, remaining silent in order to stop the flash of anger inside him from bubbling to the surface.

Heskith stepped forward. "Dennis, was there any sign of the briefcase in the suite?"

Atkins took a deep breath, understanding the implications of his next statement. "No, Gerry. It wasn't there."

"Fuck!" yelled Cunningham, taking both men by surprise. "Fuck!"

In a fit of rage, he turned and grabbed the first thing he saw from his desk, which was a paperweight made of thick glass in the shape of a globe. He spun back around and launched it across the room. It smashed against the back wall, just to the left of a portrait of Thomas Jefferson.

Heskith stood still but held his hands out in front of him

to try calming him down. "Sir, you need to relax. This isn't—"

"This isn't what?" he challenged. "As bad as I think? The only man alive who could feasibly ruin this has in his possession every last shred of evidence that will help him do just that. You tell me how this isn't as bad as I fucking think, Gerry!"

Heskith swallowed hard. "Sir, I was going to say, this isn't worth worrying about... *yet*. We don't know for certain that he has the briefcase. Or, if he has, that he's realized exactly what it contains."

Cunningham looked at both men in turn, disbelief and fury etched on his face. "Right now, Secretary Fielding is in the Situation Room, following my orders and helping organize this nation's armed forces, preparing to launch a counterstrike against the North Koreans. That will happen tomorrow. When it does... when we officially declare war, our allies across Europe are going to rally behind us, looking to our country—to *me*—for leadership. If there's a chance, no matter how miniscule, that Adrian *fucking* Hell could jeopardize that support—jeopardize this entire country—by bringing to light what we've done here, we have to stop him. Do you understand me?"

Atkins stepped forward. "Sir, let's think about this for a moment. Let's say he has the briefcase, and he knows exactly what's inside it. What could he do with it, really?"

"The director's got a point, sir," added Heskith. "He can't go public with it. The media will easily find out who he is, and when they see he's still wanted by every government agency in the United States, anything he says will immediately be disregarded."

"Exactly," agreed Atkins. "And there's no sense giving it to GlobaTech because they're too busy fighting a war for us.

If we've learned anything about this man, it's that he's smart. He'll know these things, and he's likely frustrated because he'll feel he has a magic bullet but no gun to fire it from. I think any concern is unjustified at this point, and we shouldn't let this distract us from the mission."

Cunningham took a few deep breaths, moved around his desk, and sat heavily in his chair. He leaned forward and clasped his hands together in front of him. He stared absently at the Great Seal imprinted on the carpet.

Just then, the phone on his desk rang. He stared at it and frowned, then picked up the receiver.

"President Cunningham…"

25

ADRIAN HELL

We're standing outside Veronica's house in a tight circle at the edge of the sidewalk, next to the Mercedes. The sky has clouded over, and the wind's picking up. Our disguises are in place, and each of us looks drastically different than normal. Ruby's friend is exceptionally talented. There's no doubt about it.

I can barely feel the fake nose on my face. I've shaved my head, so my hair is back to its usual length. I quickly stroke my smooth chin, which feels strange. I had become somewhat accustomed to the coarse beard I had grown over the last couple of weeks. I looked in the mirror when Veronica finished, and it was like looking at a photo of a stranger.

The others look different too. Oscar especially. He's not a thin man—a fact he would happily admit himself—but the way she's applied makeup to his face, he looks twenty pounds lighter.

I asked Veronica to take some pictures of us with our

makeup in place. I left them attached to a blank draft e-mail for Josh. He'll use them for the ID badges we'll have as part of our disguise.

Ruby and Jonas are dressed appropriately in business attire for their journey to the State Department. Ruby can look great in just about anything, but Jonas looks uncomfortable in a suit. I suspect he feels a little restricted, especially with his bulky frame.

Veronica has kindly donated her ride to our cause—a small, two-door Mini Cooper with a barely-there back seat —which will carry them to Washington. Oscar and I will take the Mercedes to Annapolis.

We're about to split up and go our separate ways, but there's something I need to do first. I take out the cell that belonged to the former CIA director.

"Okay, listen up. I'm gonna turn this on and make a quick call. It's a safe bet that they'll be scanning for the signal, so we're about to become very visible to the bad guys."

Jonas frowns. "If that's the case, why do it?"

I smile. "Because it's time they knew what they're up against."

I switch it on, enter the code Matthews gave me, and dial a number I found in his briefcase.

"Everyone, stay quiet," I say as it starts to ring. "Let me do the talking."

I put it on speaker just as it's picked up.

"President Cunningham..."

Everyone's eyes go wide with surprise. They exchange glances that silently ask if they can really believe it's him on the other end.

I smile. "Hey, Charlie."

"Who is this?"

"I'm the ghost of Christmas future, asshole."

"Do you have any idea who you're talking to? Or how much trouble you're in? How did you even get this number? I can have this call traced and—"

"Yeah, yeah. Save it, will you? I know exactly who you are. And I got your number from a mutual friend—General Matthews."

There's a moment's silence on the line.

"Adrian Hell, I presume?"

"Guilty. So, how's your day going, Mr. President?"

"You've got some nerve, calling me. Do you have any concept how quickly I could have you killed? Have you squashed like a bug hitting a windshield? Because that's all you are, Adrian. You're an insect. An insignificant speck of crap on my shoe. You're in way over your head."

I exaggerate a yawn. Oscar hangs his head with disbelief. Ruby smiles. Jonas simply raises an eyebrow.

"Big talk for a guy hiding behind his advisors and fancy screens in the Situation Room, watching the world fall apart."

He scoffs. "I'm not hiding, you arrogant sonofabitch. I'm standing in the middle of *my* Oval Office, preparing to lead this country into war."

I smile. Now I know exactly where he is. Sucker. Seems my initial gamble paid off.

"A war that *you* started."

"I don't know what would possess you to make such outlandish claims, but I'm—"

"Charles... Charlie... Chuck... Chuckie... Chuck-a-roo... Chuck-a-reeno. Let me stop you right there before I throw up. I'm not recording this call. I'm not live on Fox News. I'm not streaming this on YouTube, all right? It's just me and you having a conversation. So, please, for the love of all that is holy, quit with the bullshit."

Another moment of silence.

"What do you want?" he asks.

"Me? I don't want anything. I just thought it was time we had a chat, that's all. You've been chasing me up and down the East Coast for days now—indirectly, of course. I wouldn't expect you to get your hands dirty because you're a fucking coward."

"*I'm* a coward? Coming from you, I'll take that as a compliment!"

I frown. "Meaning?"

"Meaning, Adrian, you're the one who's running away from everything. You're the one who's letting your friend do all the real fighting for you. And *you're* the one who left your little girlfriend back home, all alone, to embark on this foolish crusade."

I fall silent, gripping the phone so hard that I think I might actually crush it.

"What, nothing to say?" he continues. "No smart-ass comment? No, I didn't think so. We've had our eye on her since the beginning, you know—ever since you escaped back in Atlanta after witnessing General Matthews commit the most heinous, most treacherous of acts. An act I had no knowledge of or involvement in, by the way. Yes... maybe I'll send a couple of CIA agents over to that backwater town of yours in Texas and bring her in for aiding and abetting a known terrorist. That could get her life in prison, if I wanted..."

I take a deep breath. The following words won't be easy to say, but they're essential.

I crack my neck. "Do whatever you want. She doesn't mean anything to me, anyway. All that matters to me is my next hit. I'm an assassin, remember? And we both know I'm far from insignificant, so stop kidding yourself that you're in control here. You've been trying to kill me for almost two weeks, and yet here we are, talking like old friends. I imagine by now, you've found out Matthews is dead, and I have the documents that can bury both you and your entire administration."

"You're a terrible liar, Adrian. Now, if you have a point to make, I suggest you make it. I'm a busy man."

"My point, Mr. President—*Mein Führer*, or whatever you prefer to be called—is simply this: it's over. I know everything, and I'm going to make sure the rest of the world does too. You're not going to swoop down and save the day because GlobaTech is going to kick North Korea's ass all the way back to the Stone Age. And you're not going to kill me because I'm better than you and smarter than you."

"You think very highly of yourself, Adrian."

"I've never been one to fly in the face of public opinion..."

"You arrogant prick! You do realize I have the resources of the most powerful country on Earth at my disposal. Every intelligence agency is looking for you. The military will soon be patrolling the streets of every city in every state, protecting the American people from the threat of war. You are but one man. Are you honestly trying to tell me you think you can beat *me*? That you can stop what I've spent my *entire life* planning?"

I pause and look into the eyes of each person standing with me. In a short time, I've come to respect and trust and believe in them. They are prepared to fight with me. They are prepared to die for my crusade.

There's only one answer I could possibly give.

"There's an old saying, Charlie: 'It's not the size of the

dog in the fight. It's the size of the fight in the dog.' You're the worst thing to ever happen to humanity, you steaming-hot piece of shit, and there's no escaping what's heading your way. You can't hide from it. You can't stop it. Nothing in this world can save you from what's coming."

"Really? And what, *exactly,* is coming?"

"Me."

I hang up the phone, drop it on the ground, and stamp down hard with my heel, smashing it.

Ruby steps forward and puts a hand on my arm. Her eyes are soft and her expression is genuine. "Adrian, I'm so sorry..."

I smile gratefully at her. "Ruby, it's fine. *She'll* be fine. I need you to focus, okay?" I look at Jonas briefly, then back at her. "The two of you have an important and difficult job ahead of you. You *cannot* fail. Do you understand?"

They both nod in agreement. Ruby reluctantly steps back, moving next to Jonas.

I thought I could keep Tori away from all this. I guess I was kidding myself. But what Cunningham said did nothing except add more fuel to the fire. I just have to trust that I'll stop Cunningham before he finds a way to use Tori against me.

I close my eyes. I allow myself three seconds for every negative and unhelpful emotion to swirl around inside my head, screaming and tearing away at me.

I take a deep breath... hold it... and breathe out slowly, expunging all those feelings. They've had their fun. Now I'm done with them. All that's left inside me now is determination and fury. My Inner Satan is watching me. Normally, I can feel him ready to fight against logic and break free. But not this time. This time, it's different. There's nothing holding him back anymore. He's standing unrestrained, looking on with curiosity. I don't need to lock him away behind a door anymore. He's no longer the personification of unbridled primal rage. He's a weapon. A tool I've finally mastered. I'm in complete control, and it feels both liberating and terrifying at the same time.

"Okay," I say to everyone. "We ready?"

There's a silent, collective nod.

"Good." I pick up the briefcase, which has been standing beside me, and hand it to Ruby. "Do whatever you gotta do to get *this* in front of Secretary Phillips."

She takes it off me with a deep breath and nods again. "We've got this, Adrian. You focus on what you need to do, and we'll see you in Washington in a few hours."

I look at Ruby and Jonas in turn. "Good luck. Both of you."

I walk over to the Mercedes and slide in behind the wheel. A moment later, Oscar gets in beside me. I watch in the rearview as Ruby and Jonas get into Veronica's car and drive off.

"You sure you're okay, Adrian?" he asks.

I rub my tired eyes. "Yeah, I'm fine. This is the home stretch. Just need to get it done."

"I don't mind driving..."

"Oscar, I'm fine. But thanks."

I start the engine, ease away from the curb, and soon settle into an easy cruise, which should see us all the way to Annapolis.

16:39 EDT

. . .

We've taken the 301, which runs across the state line and cuts through Maryland, crosses the Chesapeake Bay Bridge, and leads us into Annapolis. Ruby and Jonas will be on I-95, heading for Washington, DC, which is a slightly longer run. We'll meet up to prepare our approach once Oscar and I have the van.

We've traveled mostly in silence, broken up by the low radio in the background. I can't even begin to explain what's going through my head right now. Tori was meant to be safe. I've kept my distance purely for that reason. Maybe I've been kidding myself this whole time. Was she really *ever* going to be safe with me out here doing what I'm doing?

Oscar looks across at me. "You okay?"

I shrug. "I guess. You?"

"Man, I'm shitting bricks over here. I'll be honest." He laughs nervously. "But I'm good. Just glad I can help out."

"Yeah, I'm sorry for dragging you into this. I know you didn't even want to give me the weapons..."

"It's fine. But seeing as you didn't give me a choice about joining the good fight, you can be expecting an invoice for the guns!"

I glance at him and see him smiling. I relax a little. "Oscar, if I'm still around at the end of this, I'll pay you double."

"You will be. I can see it in your eyes."

"Really?"

"Uh-huh. Same look I saw when I dropped you on that rooftop back in Pittsburgh a couple years back. It's the kinda look that makes me grateful to God I'm not the one who's pissed you off."

I smile to myself. "I feel it, y'know? It's pumping through my veins... that *urge* to walk in through the front door and shoot at anything that moves."

"So, why don't you? Even I know you hate all this bullshit planning and strategizing. Why not just do what you normally would? It always works out."

"Because I'm smarter than I look. So people tell me, anyway. Not giving a fuck and going in guns blazing has worked before, yeah. Many times, in fact. But it wouldn't work now, and I can't afford to fail. Too much is riding on it. I don't wanna sound like an overdramatic douche and say the fate of the world is hanging in the balance, but y'know... it kinda is."

He lets out a heavy sigh and glances out his window. We're crossing the bridge, approaching the toll booth that lets us back onto the mainland.

"Yeah, this is a doozy. I'll give you that," he says. "You ever thought about what happens if we actually pull this off?"

I frown. "How do you mean?"

"Well, let's say you kill the president, and North Korea gets its ass kicked. What then? Knowing what I know, I can't say I like Cunningham or what he's doing, but even you must be able to acknowledge the positive things he's accomplished for this country. There's little crime, and there's hardly anybody homeless or unemployed anymore. Everyone's living the American dream. And what he did for us was starting to rub off on other countries, wasn't it?"

I nod. "I agree these are prosperous times. Or at least, they were. Seems to have all gone to shit now, doesn't it? Makes you wonder... why do it? What could he possibly achieve that he couldn't have achieved carrying on as he was?"

Oscar shrugs. "That's easy. He's a lunatic who wants to rule the world. He's like a goddamn cartoon villain, Adrian. I'm not saying he doesn't want what's best for everyone because I think, on some level, he does. I'm saying his vision of how to get there differs drastically from that of any normal person."

I agree with what Oscar's saying, and he makes a valid point. What *will* happen if we succeed? Half the government is involved, and if the whole conspiracy is made public, it will crush not just this country but the entire world, setting us all back decades. There will be no faith in the White House, the stock markets will crash, the world will hate us forever, and we'll end up being no better off than anyone else. We just won't have the residual radiation poisoning.

That said, it's no excuse to let him get away with it. The way I see it, everything's going to shit no matter what happens next, so I might as well do the thing that feels right.

We pass through the booth and take the first exit off the bridge.

Shit!

I slam the brakes on as a car appears from nowhere and jumps in front of me. I sound the horn and bang my palm against the wheel.

"Asshole!"

I look ahead of us. We've just joined the end of a long queue of traffic.

I sigh. "Great…"

I hope things go smoothly for the others.

26

MEANWHILE...

Ruby insisted on driving, which left Jonas in the passenger seat, feeling tired and frustrated. They coasted along I-95 for just under two hours, maintaining an anonymous speed and hitting minimal delays. That eventually became I-495, which led them onto New Hampshire Avenue. From there, it had been a straight run into the capital, and they were closing in on their destination.

The State Department stood just a few blocks west of the White House. As they navigated the crowded streets alongside George Washington University, the gravity of the situation they now faced finally hit home. Traffic was close to a standstill. Sidewalks were crammed with people moving with a courteous urgency in every direction. Soldiers in full fatigues and armed with rifles lined the curbs. They were spread strategically thin but still provided an effective barrier between pedestrians and the street.

"Jesus…" muttered Jonas as he gazed out at the military presence. "Shit just got serious, huh?"

Ruby slowed to a stop at a red light. "I think shit's been serious for a while. This is just the first time we've seen it up close."

She got the green and set off, guiding the borrowed vehicle onto 23rd Street NW. After a few hundred yards, she pulled up opposite the main entrance to the building. It was a large block structure with beige brick and stern angles. The main doors were glass, and they could see the security checkpoints within.

Jonas glanced over his shoulder at the briefcase resting on the back seat. "Have you any idea how we're going to get inside there?"

Ruby was silent for a few moments, distracted by her own thoughts on the task ahead of them. She found herself wondering what Adrian would do in this situation. She smiled when she realized that even *he* wouldn't have a clue. He wasn't one for talking, and she knew that quick thinking and finesse would be required for this to work.

"It's going to be like playing a part," she replied finally. "We just need to get into character. Let me do the talking. You carry the briefcase."

"So, you actually *do* have a plan?"

She shrugged. "Working on it. Come on."

Jonas rolled his eyes. "You've spent far too long with *him*…"

They climbed out of the car in sync, and Jonas leaned back inside to retrieve the case. They waited for a gap in the traffic and crossed the street, then walked across the short plaza and pushed their way through the glass doors into the building's lobby.

Inside was teeming with activity, and security was everywhere. Their shoes clicked and clacked on the polished gray tiling that covered the floor as they approached the first of two visible security checkpoints. It was a semicircular desk with two men behind it, wearing matching uniforms. One was sitting down, just about visible over the counter. His unwavering gaze was focused in front of him. Ruby figured he was scanning the security feeds. The other was standing tall, professionally eyeballing everyone who moved.

Ruby nodded a terse greeting to him as she neared the desk. "Good evening. I'm here to meet with Secretary Phillips."

The guard raised a curious eyebrow. The mere mention of the name seemed to pique the interest of everyone within earshot.

"Name?" he asked.

"Ruby Andrews." She gestured at Jonas, who was standing a couple of steps behind her. "This is my colleague, Jonas Dyke. We're CIA intelligence officers from Langley. We've been sent to brief the secretary on the latest reports following North Korea's attacks."

The guard studied them for a moment with a firm, emotionless gaze, then looked down at his system. Ruby assumed he was checking a visitor's schedule.

"You're not on the list," he said after a few moments. "I'll need you to wait while we obtain the correct clearance from your super—"

Ruby held up her hand impatiently. "General Matthews himself sent us to brief Secretary Phillips. He told us he would arrange for the necessary clearance in advance, so we wouldn't have to wait."

"There's no record of your clearance, and until we have it, I can't sign you through. Now if you'll just wait—"

"What's your name?" she asked, cutting him off a second time.

He frowned. "Young."

"Okay, Mr. Young, have you seen a television in the last twelve hours or so?"

He didn't respond or react. He just stared at her, growing more uncomfortable with each second that passed.

"I'm assuming you have," she continued. "The director of the CIA sent us here to brief the secretary of state on the current situation with North Korea. This is of the highest importance, not to mention a matter of national security. I don't have time to wait around while you take your thumb out of your ass long enough to maybe do your job. If you want to check with Langley, be my guest, but can you please do it after you've allowed me to do *my* job and brief *your* boss. She's waiting for this intel, and time isn't something anyone has much of right now. So, Mr. Young, do you want to be the one who pisses off the CIA and the White House on a day like today?"

He shifted uncomfortably, exchanging sideways glances with his nearby colleagues. They tried to remain neutral, almost disowning him now that they believed he was in trouble, like they didn't want to be blamed as well.

After a few tense, silent moments, he reached down and picked up two temporary security passes attached to lanyards. He handed them to Ruby and Jonas.

"I'm sorry, ma'am," he said. "I'm just following procedure."

Ruby took the pass and placed it over her head. "I understand, and I'm sorry for snapping. It's just days like today don't happen all that often, and when they do, things tend to become a little more urgent, y'know?"

He nodded his agreement and gestured them past the

desk, to the security scanner, which was manned by three of his colleagues.

Ruby strode confidently ahead. Jonas followed, clutching the briefcase. Neither of them had any items on their person, and the case itself simply showed the papers contained within when it was X-rayed.

Beyond them was a wide corridor, which led to an elevator lobby. More corridors branched off to either side of it.

After both passed unhindered through the metal detector, they walked unprompted toward the nearest bank of elevators and stepped inside the first one that dinged open. Ruby pressed the button for the top floor, assuming that's where the important people would be.

The doors slid shut, and they began their ascent.

Jonas breathed a heavy sigh of relief. "Jesus Christ, that was intense."

Ruby took some deep breaths, silently proud of herself for pulling it off. "At least it worked. Now we just have to find Elaine Phillips before they decide to follow up on our authorization and discover we don't have any."

"Yeah, so what happens if they do that before we get out of here?"

She shrugged. "Then we probably won't get out of here. But if we can get that case to Phillips, at least Adrian will stand a chance, having the secretary of state on his side."

Jonas rubbed a sweaty palm over his head, forcing himself to calm his nerves. "Oh boy..."

17:43 EDT

.   .   .

The doors opened on the top floor, revealing another small lobby, with corridors stretching off to the sides and directly in front of them. The floor was covered with a worn, pale red carpet, and the walls and ceiling were painted the same generic off-white.

"Which way?" asked Ruby.

Jonas shrugged. "Beats me. Straight on?"

She looked along both corridors for any indication of layout but saw nothing.

"Okay, straight on it is."

The floor was quiet compared to the lobby. Only a handful of rooms lined the hallway, and only one of them was occupied. Inside, a small group of men in suits were talking animatedly while staring at an image of a spreadsheet projected onto a whiteboard.

All the real work must be done on the lower floors, thought Ruby.

They reached the opposite end of the corridor, which again branched off to either side.

Jonas stared along the left side. "Looks dead that way," he observed. "A short hall with only two rooms. No signs of life."

Ruby was looking right. "Yeah, I think it might be this way."

Jonas moved alongside her and followed her gaze to a large office at the end of another short corridor. It stretched across almost the full width of the hallway, and the vertical blinds at the window were opened enough for them to see inside. They glimpsed a woman sitting behind a desk, writing feverishly.

Elaine Phillips.

"Come on," said Ruby, walking purposefully toward the office.

Jonas followed hastily. Their muffled footfalls were the only sounds to be heard.

Eagerly, she reached the door and walked straight in without a moment's hesitation. Secretary Phillips looked up from her work and watched impassively as the new arrivals stood in front of her.

"Elaine Phillips?" Ruby asked.

Phillips sat back in her chair, staring thoughtfully at them both. She placed her pen slowly on top of a small stack of documents covering the surface of her solid, expensive-looking mahogany desk.

When she spoke, the words were clear and deliberate. Stern, without being challenging. "I'm pretty sure someone from the CIA would know to address me as Madam Secretary."

Ruby let out a small sigh. "Right. Sorry. Madam Secretary, I—"

"You are a bold and stupid young woman." She glanced over at Jonas before continuing. "Today really isn't the day to try passing yourselves off as government employees. Frankly, I'm astounded you even made it into the building. There will be some serious questions raised about the level of security at our front desk, given you talked your way in with the promise of fake credentials. But—"

"Elaine... Madam... Secretary... Phillips... if I could just—"

"*But...* that doesn't change the fact you're in a level of trouble I can assure you is beyond your comprehension." She looked past them both at the door just as it opened and four armed guards entered the room. "Get them out of here. Please."

Two of the guards stepped forward, each placing a hand on Jonas's shoulders. He quickly shrugged them off, spun around, and held the briefcase up in front of him like a weapon.

"Get your fucking hands off me!" he growled.

"Jonas!" yelled Ruby, glancing at him. "Easy. Madam Secretary, I'm sorry. I really am, but I need five minutes of your time. It's a matter of national security."

Phillips regarded her silently for a moment, flicking her gaze between the two intruders and the briefcase. Eventually, she looked back at the guards and said, "Take them away."

"No! Wait! Please... my name is Ruby DeSouza. Adrian Hell sent me here. Do you know that name?"

Phillips's eyebrow twitched, and she held her hand up to the guards. "Adrian Hell is a wanted terrorist."

Ruby shook her head. "Adrian Hell is a goddamn hero. He's being framed to cover up a massive conspiracy, which we have undeniable evidence of. Please, you *have* to give me time to explain."

Phillips leaned forward and rested her elbows on her desk, interlocking her fingers. She nodded to the briefcase. "And is this evidence in there?"

Ruby nodded. "Yes. It was given to us by General Thomas Matthews, the former CIA director."

"Former?"

She glanced respectfully down at the floor. "He's dead."

Phillips's face failed to hide the shock and emotion, which Ruby picked up on.

"You didn't know... shit. I'm sorry. But he was involved in this conspiracy."

The secretary of state recovered quickly. "Show me."

Ruby turned to Jonas and nodded. He stepped forward and placed the briefcase on the desk. Phillips opened it, and her eyes widened with surprise at the volume of content contained within.

"Care to summarize this for me?" she asked.

Jonas smirked. "Good luck with that..."

Ruby ignored him. "I'm not as familiar with it as Adrian is, but basically, President Cunningham was the brains behind the 4/17 attacks *and* this North Korean invasion. Everything that's happened and that's happening now is because of *him*. I know it sounds crazy, but the evidence is there in front of you."

Phillips stared at her with an unblinking gaze. Her heart rate began to climb slightly. She absently brushed a hand through her hair and then looked at the four guards. "You can leave us. It's okay."

"Madam Secretary, are you sure?" asked one of them. "I'm under orders to detain these people pending a formal arrest."

"I'm fairly certain any order *I* give outranks any orders given by anyone else in the building. I said *leave*."

Her tone was strong and final and prompted no further dispute. The guards filed out of the room, and the last shut the door behind him.

Ruby and Jonas watched them go, then looked back at Phillips, who had leaned back in her chair once again.

She stared at them both in turn. "Start talking."

27

ADRIAN HELL

This traffic is shit. I can see the turn I need to take coming up on the left, which will lead me to the security firm and our van, but these *assholes* in front of me aren't moving when they have a chance to.

A gap appears for me to go through, but this clueless dick in front of me isn't paying attention.

"Come on..." I say, mostly to myself.

And now the gap's gone again. Fucking great!

I let out a heavy, impatient sigh.

Next to me, Oscar chuckles. "Man, I bet your road rage is somethin' else!"

I look across at him, unable to shift the angry expression from my face. But a smile slips through after a moment.

"I don't like waiting. I called in sick the day they were handing out the patience allowance."

"We're almost there. I'll drive to Washington once we're in the van, to give you a break."

"Thanks." I glance ahead. "What's causing this hold up?"

"I can't really see. It looks like—"

An explosion sounds out, shaking the vehicle and everything around us. Ahead, a thick, dark plume of smoke rockets into the air, distributing dust and brick over the nearby area.

"What the fuck was that?" I step out of the car, stand, and lean on the open door as I look around. People on every side of me are doing the same. The bitter stench of the smoke is traveling quickly, burning my nostrils.

Oscar joins me outside the car. "What the hell?"

My spider sense is doing somersaults. "I don't like this..."

Another loud explosion sounds, this time to my left. I instinctively duck my head a little. I look over and see two military Jeeps full of soldiers speeding toward our traffic jam. Behind them, in a black pickup truck, are four guys—two in the cab, two in the back. One's standing, holding on with one hand and carrying a machine pistol in the other. His friend, whom I can just about see crouching behind him, hanging onto the side, is throwing grenades at the soldiers.

What the...

I look back up the street and see another pickup truck appear from the right. All around me, people start screaming. Some lock themselves in their cars, and others abandon them.

"Adrian, what's happening?"

"If I were to guess, I would say Cunningham's decreed martial law on account of the world being at war with North Korea. And by the looks of it, some of the locals ain't all that pleased..."

The guy on the left raises his machine pistol—which looks like a TEC-9 from here—and empties his mag into the air. A very amateurish attempt at crowd control, I think.

I turn to Oscar. "This is gonna turn real ugly real fast. We should leave. Now."

"I'm with you on that."

I move to the trunk, open it, and take out the black sport bag full of weapons. I unzip it and select a handgun—a Beretta—and some ammo. I quickly tuck it at my back, pocket the spare mags, and pass the bag to Oscar.

"You carry this, and I'll shoot anyone who comes near us. Deal?"

"Yes, sir."

People begin stampeding past, away from... whatever the hell is in front of us. Until I know exactly who's behind this and how many there are, I need to stay smart and invisible.

I crouch and signal to Oscar to do the same. "Follow my lead and stay close. Move when I do. Hide when I do. We need to make it to that security firm. Nothing else matters. Understand?"

He nods. "I hear you."

"No, Oscar, listen to what I'm saying. *Nothing else matters.* You see innocent people in trouble, you don't help. You don't look. You don't even *think* about it. We can't afford to let anything stop us from getting to that van. Everything depends on it."

He takes a sharp breath, steeling himself and tensing his jaw. "Shit... I understand, Adrian. Let's just get out of here."

"Okay, follow me."

I keep low, move around the driver's side of the car, and pause level with the hood. I hear Oscar behind me. A sea of open doors and screaming people stand between us and where we need to be. A little farther on, the pickup truck is circling in the street, and the one that was chasing the military Jeeps has joined it.

I take my gun out, make sure the mag's full, and work the slide. Safety off.

There's a small gap between the hood of one car and the trunk of another. Crouching, I move as quickly as I can down the side of the next car, then pause again by the front wheel.

"Oh my God! Help me!"

A man's crawling along the ground toward me. His face is a crimson mask as blood gushes from a head wound above his eye.

"Please!" he insists.

I close my eyes for a second, cursing my own sense of morality and justice. Ordinarily, I would be compelled to get as many people to safety as I could. But if I don't get to that van, it's game over. It won't matter how many people I save here. Millions will die elsewhere.

Sometimes the greater good is a real bitch.

I look at the man next to me and place a finger on my lips. "Hey, keep quiet. You'll attract attention to yourself."

He shakes with emotion as he tries to keep his pleading and whimpering to a minimum.

"You got a cell phone?" I ask him.

He nods, terrified.

I hold my hand out. "Gimme."

He reaches slowly into his pocket and hands it to me.

"Thanks. Now shut up, okay?"

I quickly dial Josh's number. He's probably busy, but it's worth a shot. It rings three times.

"Hello?"

A female voice? Huh?

"Hello?"

"Who's this?"

"Where's Josh?"

"He's a little busy. We all are, believe it or not. Who's this?"

"I'm Adrian Hell. Who are you? His fucking secretary?"

"Adrian? Holy shit! I'm Fisher. Julie Fisher."

"Julie... you're heading up Josh's new D.E.A.D. unit, aren't you?"

"For my sins, yeah."

"How come you're answering his phone?"

"He gave it to me. He had to duck out and sort some urgent shit."

"Yeah, there's a lot of that right now. Well, look, I need your help. You got access to satellite feeds or something?"

"I do, as it happens. What d'you need?"

"I'm in Annapolis, Maryland. Two explosions have just brought the street to a standstill. I've got eyes on two pickup trucks full of assholes shooting at civilians and soldiers. No fucking idea why, but they're in my way, and I need to know how to get rid of them."

"Jesus... sounds like a modern-day lynch mob to me. There have been reports coming in from all over about locals trying to take control of their districts. Cunningham has imposed martial law for our so-called *protection* in most major cities in the last six hours. Some of the smaller towns don't like the idea. Gimme a sec."

I look back at Oscar, whose eyes are rapidly flicking in every direction. "This shit is happening all over," I explain. "Locals don't like the Army taking over."

He frowns. "What's their problem? Better our army than Korea's, right?"

I shrug. "I don't think logic is playing a very pivotal role right now."

Julie's voice sounds in my ear. "Still there?"

"Yeah, I'm here."

"I've pinged your cell signal and triangulated your exact location, so I have eyes on you now. Where are you heading?"

"There's a security firm just off the next left turn ahead of me. Josh has arranged a van full of goodies for me, but I can't get there."

"Yeah... you've got two pickups in front of you, plus I count... six men on the ground. The Jeeps are surrounded, and the soldiers look like they've been disarmed and are being held at gunpoint. Not sure how you're—"

Loud whipcracks of rapid gunfire sound out. The burst of death and noise start and stop before I even have chance to react.

"What the fuck was that?"

I hear a sigh on the phone. "Shit. Yeah... they're not being held at gunpoint anymore."

"Jesus. How many?"

"Soldiers?"

"No, assholes..."

"I've got eyes on fourteen."

"Am I clear on all other sides?"

"To your left and behind, yeah. Nothing on your right, and once you're past the mob, you should be fine getting to the van. What are you—"

"Thanks, Julie. I'm guessing the police aren't rushing to help here. I'll handle this."

"What? You're just gonna—"

"Look after Josh for me, would you? Just in case I don't... y'know."

She sighs again. "Yeah, of course. So, listen, are you the man he says you are? Can you really stop this?"

I stare blankly at the ground for a moment. "Yeah, I can."

"Good. When you have, head over to California for some R and R. The boys and I wanna buy you a drink."

I smile. "Sounds great. Give Jericho and Ray my best."

I hang up and toss the phone. My immediate vicinity has fallen silent. I think most people have either managed to escape or have died. I glance back at Oscar. He's holding an extraordinary-looking gun.

I'm a little excited.

"Oscar, what in God's name is that?"

"This is the AX-19. It's GlobaTech's standard-issue assault rifle."

"There's nothing standard about *that*!"

The gun looks bulky but smooth, like it's been shaped and forged from a single piece of metal. The scope looks more like a cylindrical computer, and there are two magazines clipped into the underside of the barrel at mirrored forty-five-degree angles.

I take it from him and hold it, getting a feel for the weight.

"Man, this is nice!"

"Yeah, it is. Don't tell Josh I'm selling his shit illegally, okay?"

I smile. "I'm pretty sure he'll let you off."

"Go get 'em. Get it out of your system. You know you want to…"

I glance over at the pickup trucks, roughly five hundred yards ahead of me. They're not really doing anything now. They're just… sitting there. The men are milling around aimlessly, sharing jokes. Their laughter is drifting on the wind.

I look back at Oscar. "I really, really do. Wait here."

I move left, to the edge of the street, and then stop for a

moment on the sidewalk. Dust from the explosions has covered the buildings and has lined this side with a thick layer. I make my way along the side of the stationary traffic, keeping low and quiet. I find a gap that gives me a line of sight on the trucks and the rebels.

I drop to one knee and bring the rifle up, close one eye, and stare down the sight.

"Jesus..."

The view is... exquisite! There's no other word for it. It's a full-color, hi-def image with a small display down the right side, showing distance and wind.

I move the rifle around, tracking each of the fourteen men so that I can plan my assault. Normally, I wouldn't actively seek out a fourteen-on-one gunfight. Even I like at least a slim sporting chance. But these guys are amateur hour at best, and they've just killed soldiers who were just doing their job—innocent, in the grand scheme of things. Plus, they're in my way, which means we have a problem.

Safety's off. I flick the switch near the trigger with my thumb, moving to the single shot fire rate. The guys on the ground aren't an issue. I reckon I've got four good shots before they figure out what's happening and where I am. The driver of each truck is definitely going first, so they can't back away quickly to regroup. If I can get a couple out of the back as well, that's a bonus.

I take a couple of deep breaths to compose myself, slow the flow of adrenaline, and take complete control over mind and body, becoming the weapon I was born to be.

Here we go...

I fire three rounds in quick succession, accompanied by the slightest of movements in direction. The driver of the nearest pickup goes first. His head snaps away to the side as I remove half his skull with the first round. The guy standing in the back is next. He slams backward as the bullet catches him just below his ear, in the fleshy part of the neck, behind the mandible. He never knew what hit him.

The third is aimed away to the right, at the driver of the second truck. It blasts through the windshield and hits his chest. He falls forward onto the wheel.

I spring to my feet, switch the rifle to fire three-round bursts, and take aim at the startled mob. I hold the rifle steady, as if it's an extension of my body. It faces forward at all times, sees what my eyes see, and turns when my body turns. I walk slowly back into the middle of the street and depress the trigger three times. Each burst finds a target.

The yelling starts and panic sets in. They try to regroup but don't really have a clue what's happening. They're running in circles, trying to find a target. It's like they're moving in ways they've seen on TV, copying that as opposed to actually knowing what to do with their weapons.

Fucking amateurs. It's a disgrace that they were able to get the drop on those soldiers. They deserved better.

Four more bursts. Four more targets down. Every man who wasn't in a vehicle is now dead, sprawled on the ground with blood pooling around them. I count four left—both passengers in the cabs and one more on the back of each truck.

One pops up on my right and returns fire, but I don't even flinch. His aim is terrible, and he's emptied almost his entire mag into the ground five feet away to my right.

I snap to him and fire once. The burst of bullets runs up and hits him in the chest, throat, and face milliseconds apart. He flails backward out of sight. I aim for the passenger of the right pickup and give him two bursts. The windshield shatters, and he's pushed back in his seat from the impact in his chest. I can see the blood staining the seats from here.

The man in the back of the other pickup truck jumps down to the street. I have no idea why. Now he's easier to hit. What a prick! He's aiming his TEC-9 at me, holding it sideways like he's in *Boyz N the Hood*. I look him in the eye as I press the trigger—one, two, three bursts. His torso is destroyed by the impact, and he falls to the ground, twitching as the last breath leaves him.

I stare at his body for a moment, embracing the controlled anger that's pulsing through me. In the past, when my Inner Satan took over, it was almost like I went to sleep while it happened. But now I'm standing beside him, watching him at work, telling him where to shoot and what to do. It's an amazing feeling!

I drop the AX-19 where I stand and draw the Beretta, then pace hurriedly around the hood of the truck. I yank the passenger door open. The remaining asshole is cowering in his seat.

I lean in and grab him by the collar of his shirt. I haul him out and push him against the side of the vehicle.

"What the fuck are you doing?" I ask.

His eyes are wide and filled with fear. "Th-this is our t-town! It's our j-job to protect it! W-we need to—"

I stop him talking by forcing the barrel of the Beretta into his mouth. I stand up straight, using my gun to keep him in place.

"You know what? I don't care."

I pull the trigger once. His head disappears in a thick cloud of crimson steam. The window behind him shatters, painting the remaining shards with blood. I take my gun out of what's left of his mouth, and he slumps to the ground. His eyes are wide and lifeless, and his jaw is locked open in an expression of eternal surprise.

I take a quick look around, but Julie's assessment was spot-on. There's no one else here.

"Come on out, Oscar," I shout as I put the gun away. "We're good here."

I see him appear over where I had come from. Holding the bag, he makes his way through the maze of abandoned vehicles and rejoins me.

He looks around in horrified amazement. "Holy shit... this as a goddamn massacre."

"Yeah. Fuck 'em. Let's go."

We walk briskly down the street and go left. The security firm's building is the first one we see. The van, as promised, is parked just inside its lot. It's dark gray, with the company's logo emblazoned across the side. I open the rear doors. The dispersal unit, uniforms, security badges—everything is there as ordered.

"Your boy came through," says Oscar.

I nod. "Never any doubt. Now let's go. Time's a-wasting."

Oscar puts the bag in the back and slams the doors shut. As promised, he slides in behind the wheel. We reverse out of the lot and drive away from the carnage I just caused.

Next stop: Washington, DC.

28

MEANWHILE...

Ruby did a good job of explaining everything to Secretary Phillips and was surprised at how open-minded she was throughout. She flicked through the plethora of evidence in Matthews's case and listened intently, asking questions as they came to mind.

"So, what do you think?" Ruby asked finally.

Phillips sat in silent thought for a few moments. "I think you're crazy. But..."

Ruby's eyes lit up with hope. "But?"

"*But...* I have to say I've had my doubts about President Cunningham. I could never quite put my finger on it, and for the most part, he made the same decisions I believe any other president would've made. But these last six months..."

She sighed, ran her hand through her hair, and fell silent once more.

"Madam... whatever. Elaine, look... this sucks, and it's

hard to believe, but we're kinda on the clock here. Can you help us stop this?"

"I... I'm not sure. I mean, what can I really do?"

Jonas, who had been standing quietly by the door, stepped forward and spoke for the first time since Ruby began her story. "First thing you need to do is keep this quiet. From what I could tell when I looked at that stuff, you're pretty much on your own... *Elaine*. Everyone else is on Cunningham's payroll, which means we have few friends right now."

"*You* have very few friends. *I* have plenty."

"What are you thinking?" asked Ruby.

"I'm not sure yet. I'll need time. What's your friend doing? Where is he?"

"Adrian? Erm... I'm not sure you really want to know what he's doing..."

Phillips slammed her palm on the surface of her desk, then pointed her finger at Ruby. "Hey, full disclosure, lady! You came to *me*, remember? You should be grateful I even agreed to hear you out, let alone *believe* you! And I'm still not sure I do, fully. Or maybe I just don't want to... I don't know. This is an incredible situation, like nothing else in history. So, if I'm going to help, I need to know everything. By all accounts, Adrian *Hell* is a hard man to support."

"We're managing," shrugged Jonas.

"Yes, but you probably don't care that much about the twenty-plus NSA agents and the fifteen or so CIA agents he killed. If what you say is true, he might not be the terrorist we've been told he is, and he may well be trying to do the right thing, but that will count for nothing if he's apprehended. He's still a mass murderer, regardless of his intentions."

Jonas glared at Ruby, who simply smiled apologetically

as she realized Adrian clearly hadn't mentioned any of that to him when he first brought Jonas on board.

She thought for a moment. She wanted to help Adrian, not make matters worse for him. She knew she had to choose her words carefully. "You make a fair point, I admit, but those people he killed were sent to silence him, not bring him in for questioning or to arrest him. To *kill* him. It was him or them, and they were blindly following the orders of a twisted despot who—"

"I think you should stop yourself right there. I don't care what his reasoning was. And regardless of everything that's happening, I'm still a patriot, so I advise you to watch how you address the office of the U.S. president, even if you have issues with the man inside it. Am I clear?"

Ruby sighed, growing impatient. "Yeah..."

"Now the issue with your friend notwithstanding, I'm on your side. I suspect I *am* the only friend you have right now, and you have to trust me. I don't know your story—either of you—but my advice to you both is this: *leave*. Get as far away from Washington and Adrian as you can and let me handle this from here. The world is at war, and you need to keep safe."

Ruby sat on the edge of the desk, crossed her ankles, and clasped her hands on her lap. She leaned in close. "Thank you, Elaine, for your advice. And I've read that file. I *do* trust you. I know you're going to leave this room and do everything you can to help stop President Cunningham and stop this war with North Korea from escalating any further. But... there is no way I'm leaving Adrian to fend for himself. He's planning to kill Cunningham. And let me tell you, he's the best damn assassin I've ever seen."

She glanced at the clock on the wall by the door.

"I reckon you've got about three hours to do something

monumental. Otherwise, this information is going to end up on every news channel in the world, right after the report detailing how the president has been found dead. You want to stop him? Fine. But at least wait until you've fixed the bigger, more pressing issue of World War Three, okay?"

Phillips was speechless for the first time in a long time. She watched as Ruby stood and moved over to the door with Jonas behind her.

"Thank you, Madam Secretary," she said. "Please do what you can."

They left the office, striding with urgency toward the elevator. They rode it to the first floor in silence and left without incident, pausing only to hand back the lanyards they had been given on the way in.

Neither of them spoke until they got back in the car. Ruby had relinquished the driver's seat.

"Did he really kill all those G-men?" asked Jonas.

Ruby nodded. "Yeah. I even helped him with a few of the CIA spooks."

"Shit..."

"Come on. Let's head over to the rendezvous point. They should be on their way by now."

He started the engine and pulled away. They quickly dissolved into the sea of traffic moving slowly along the street.

Ruby turned on the radio, which was in the middle of a news report, and buzzed her window down to feel the cool, crisp air blow through.

They stopped at a red light.

"Can we not put some music on?" asked Jonas. He leaned forward to change the station.

Ruby put her hand on his arm, stopping him. "Wait. Turn it up."

He adjusted the volume.

"... ninth report in the last hour. The military presence in major cities across the country has been hailed as a bold and intelligent move on the part of President Cunningham, yet smaller towns and communities have been actively rejecting the support. Some stand in protest, while other, more extreme cases have seen outbreaks of violence in the streets. The latest incident was in Annapolis, Maryland, where not fifteen minutes ago, eight U.S. soldiers were executed by a group of fourteen armed locals. Yet, in a bizarre twist, all fourteen men were killed just moments afterward. Reports from eyewitnesses who fled the scene said one man fought back, killing every single member of the group before disappearing with an accomplice in a gray van. More on this situation as it develops.

"Meanwhile, North Korean forces continue to attack GlobaTech peacekeeping operatives in parts of Eastern Europe and Asia, with many refugees from the 4/17 attacks being caught in the crossfire. The death toll is estimated to be in the millions. A spokesperson for the White House said that—"

Ruby turned it off and looked at Jonas, who was staring straight ahead, wide-eyed.

"Well," she said, "at least we know they got the van."

29

ADRIAN HELL

Realizing I haven't slept much in the last—oh, I don't know —*month*, I figure it's worthwhile to try to get some sleep on the ride out of Annapolis. Traffic is heavy, and we're doing our best to stay off the main streets where we can. Consequently, what should take less than an hour is taking closer to two.

Oscar hasn't said much since we left. I've occasionally glanced over at him throughout the journey, and he was always staring straight ahead, barely blinking, functioning on autopilot and chewing his gums. I think he's trying to wrap his head around everything.

He knows what I do and what I'm capable of. He's even seen the aftermath of it, in Pittsburgh a couple years back. But he's never actually seen it happen for himself. I imagine it's a little unsettling.

I have a lot of time for Oscar. He's a good man—at least, he is to me. I guess I could even go so far as to call him a

278

friend. So, I say this with all the respect in the world, but at the end of the day, Oscar is an arms dealer. And much like a paid assassin, it's not the kind of job you can easily justify doing. If I were to guess, I would say he deals with it by detaching himself from it, kind of like I do. He sells weapons to people. He probably tries not to consider what those people actually *do* with the weapons they buy from him.

Well, he just witnessed firsthand what people do with the weapons he sells, and it's never pleasant being reminded that you're not as nice a person as you think you are.

"Look alive," he says, distracting me.

I refocus and look around. The sun is all but gone, and the low clouds are making dusk a less attractive event than it usually would be. People crowd the streets of our nation's capital in groups of varying sizes. A mixture of military and law enforcement patrol every corner. The whole place bears no resemblance to the country I've lived in and served for most of my life.

We hang a right off Madison Drive and pull into the near-deserted parking lot of the Smithsonian. Oscar guides the van slowly into a spot and kills the engine. I jump out and see Ruby and Jonas climbing out of Veronica's Mini Cooper next to us.

We stand in a close circle, huddled together and partially lit by a nearby streetlight, tense in the evening chill.

Ruby playfully punches me in my arm. "You made it."

I smile, somewhat forced. "Piece of cake."

Jonas scoffs. "Yeah, we heard about your *cake* on the fucking radio."

"Ah…"

"What the fuck, man?"

"What was I supposed to do, Jonas? Ask them real nice

to stop and let me pass? Pretty please with a cherry on top? They were killing soldiers. They were firing at civilians. And most importantly, they were standing between me and this van." I gesture to it behind me with my thumb. "I did what I had to, all right?"

He holds his hands up in reluctant defeat and falls silent.

I look at Ruby. "How are you holding up? Did you manage to speak to Secretary Phillips?"

She nods. "We did. And we walked out of there without handcuffs, so I think it went okay. She advised us to get away from you. She said even though you're not a terrorist, you're still a murderer."

I shrug. "Yeah, well, she *does* have a point. I figured out a while back that I'm probably not walking away from this one."

"Hey, you can stall that shit, okay? We're *all* walking away from this one. And we'll walk away legends."

"And rich," Jonas adds.

I smile, more genuine this time, and pat her right shoulder. "Yeah, maybe you're right. Thanks."

She winces and tries to hide it with a smile. I notice and frown for a second, wondering what's wrong, but I quickly remember she was shot about thirty-six hours ago.

"Shit. Sorry. How're you doing?"

She waves me away. "I'm fine. It's nothing a couple of painkillers won't fix. So, are we doing this, or what?"

For a moment, I can't help but think how much Josh would like her. Aside from the fact that she has no shame whatsoever—which is one of the first things he tends to look for in women—her attitude and abilities are exemplary in our field. I might introduce them when this is over. He could do with some company.

I move over to the van, open the rear doors, and step to the side so that everyone can see. Running along one side is a rail attached to the roof, with four sets of dark gray coveralls hanging from it. Each one has a personalized security badge sticking out of the breast pocket.

In the middle, on the plywood-lined floor, is a large square box. Jonas moves toward it and looks inside.

"Sweet Jesus... it's beautiful!" he says.

He reaches in and takes out a smaller square container made of thick, clear plastic. Inside it are two gas canisters, each about eighteen inches long. The nozzles are sticking out through holes at the top, with wires leading from them to another square affixed to the back of the container.

Jonas flips it around and turns to show us. "This is the interface. We'll link this up to the main airflow unit that leads to the West Wing. Once it's in place, we'll be able to remotely release the gas in these." He points to the canisters. "It will then flow through the AC and out through the vents."

He glances over his shoulder at the original box again.

"Yeah... the remote is in there, along with masks for us all." He turns the plastic box in his hands once more, then looks at me. "This is top of the line stuff, Adrian. I'm impressed."

I shrug. "When you get out of here, thank my friend at GlobaTech. This is their tech."

Oscar points to the black sport bag resting behind the box. "We've got plenty of hardware in there. Maybe a couple dozen less bullets than yesterday..." He glances at me. "There's not much in there for non-lethal attacks, but I threw in a flashbang or two, which might come in handy."

"We're not going to get in there with any weapons," I say. "We'll never get them through security. We'll need to relieve some people of their firearms once we're inside and they're out cold from the gas. Jonas, put the dispersal unit in the sport bag. Empty the guns into the box."

He nods. "On it."

I look at Ruby, who smiles and nods silently back at me.

"Okay, guys and girls, this is it. We've got the plan and the equipment. Once we're inside, we'll head for the maintenance area, so Jonas can do his thing. Once it's in place, we mask up, and I'll set it off. Unless they're shooting at you, assume anyone outside the Oval Office you come into contact with is innocent. They should be out from the gas, but if it misses them, put them down and leave them with nothing more than a headache. Clear?"

The three of them murmur their understanding.

I look at Oscar. "You're driving, so you're the one who's got to sweet-talk our way through security. Our details are in the system, so they're expecting us. No need to act suspicious. There's nothing out of the ordinary in what we're doing, okay? If they ask, we're there to run a preliminary assessment of their internal security. We'll be checking server rooms and maintenance access points. It's protocol, so they shouldn't think twice about it."

"I have a question," says Ruby. "We'll be passing through... what—two or three checkpoints?"

"Two, I think."

"Okay. They'll do the mirror under the vehicle thing, shine a light in the cab... the usual, right? What happens when they inevitably look in the back? The weapons and gas bomb might prompt some questions, y'know?"

I smile. "Good point. Well made." I move to the back of the van and lean inside. I reach up, unhook the coveralls from the railing, and pass them behind me. "Someone grab these a sec..."

I feel them be taken from my hand and lean back inside. The paneled sides of the van are made from the same plywood as the floor. There's also a casing over the wheel arches. I pull each side down in turn, guiding the panel so that it's resting flat on the floor. Both sides slot together to form a false surface that is raised enough to conceal everything underneath perfectly.

I look back at the group. "Voilà! There are two pull-down seats attached to the back of the main seat in the cab. Ruby and I will be on them, out of the way, seeing as we're the most recognizable of us all. The makeup and disguises look great, but I don't want to risk any added visibility if it can be avoided. If someone opens the rear doors, all they'll see are two people and an empty floor, save for a tool kit."

Ruby shakes her head and laughs to herself. "Y'know, this is actually starting to sound like a brilliant plan. Be careful, Adrian. You have a reputation to think of."

I roll my eyes. "Well, don't tell anyone I actually know what I'm doing, all right?"

I look at Jonas, who is holding the coveralls. "Hand them out, would you? We'd best get this party started..."

Everyone gets their uniform. Ruby changes in the back of the van, while Oscar and Jonas simply step into their coveralls outside.

I pace away absently, taking in the evening noise and bustle of a city living on the edge. A world away—and getting closer with each hour that passes—there's a war raging, masterminded by a maniacal asshat sitting less than a mile from me, in a fancy chair in the most powerful office in the land. And at the risk of sounding melodramatic, only I can stop him. I'm one of the few who have knowledge of what's really happening. And along with the three people behind me, I'm the only one not currently being scrutinized by a global audience.

I turn and watch my colleagues getting ready. I know twenty million dollars is a good incentive, but under the circumstances, even the most morally ambiguous among us would think twice about doing what we're about to. No—these guys might not admit it, but I think they're motivated now by a sense of duty, not a large payday. You can tell just by how they act and how passionate they are.

I've been lucky to find this team. A little unlucky that it's two intended members short, but shit happens. Mostly to me.

"Your turn," says Ruby, climbing out of the back.

The three of them are standing in a line, wearing their matching gray coveralls. They look like the Ghostbusters! I smile to myself, walk back over to them, and take my uniform from Jonas. I climb in the back and quickly change. A couple of minutes later, I step out and stand with the rest of them. I look at each one in turn. They stare back at me with determined expressions on their faces.

They're ready.

Even Oscar, bless him.

"What?" I ask. "Are you waiting for some big motivational speech now? Well, you're not getting one. You don't need to be reminded what's at stake here. You know what we need to do. You heard me on the phone to that sorry sonofabitch. It's the size of the fight in the dog that matters. And right now, between the four of us, I can guaran-fucking-tee we've got more fight than North Korea's entire army. We stay smart and do our job. If we see tomorrow, chances are it'll be a slightly better world than it was today. So, let's go."

Jonas and Oscar nod to me, then walk away and climb inside the cab of the van. I hold the rear door open for Ruby.

She climbs inside, and I follow her, pulling it shut behind me.

We sit in our makeshift seats. A moment later, the engine starts and we drive off.

Next to me, she nudges my arm. "Y'know, considering we weren't getting one, that was a pretty kick-ass motivational speech."

I remain silent. I stare ahead with a small smile on my face, focusing on what comes next.

30

ADRIAN HELL

Pennsylvania Avenue is busy. Despite only having to travel a few blocks, we've been traveling nearly twenty minutes, and we're still not there yet. I glance over my shoulder, between the headrests of the front seats and out through the windshield. There's nothing but crowded sidewalks and nose-to-tail traffic ahead of us.

We crawl forward slowly. After another few minutes, Oscar's finally able to turn left and pull into the first security checkpoint, to the right of the north lawn. There's a guard hut on either side of the driveway, and large automatic metal gates block the path. I hear Oscar buzz his window down. I can't see how many guards there are. Ruby and I exchange a tense glance.

"There are no deliveries," says a man, whom I'm assuming is one of the guards. "State your business."

Oscar clears his throat. "We're from Tyger Security. They called us in to run an assessment and install some upgrades.

286

Said it was an emergency. Heh... with everything going on, I bet you've got a lot of *them*, huh?"

Nice, Oscar... nice.

There's a moment's silence.

"You could say that..." replies the guard. "Got your ID?"

"Sure."

Another moment's silence. I'm guessing he's checking the picture and running it through their system to make sure we're on it.

This is where Josh earns his money.

I know... he *wishes* he got paid for this shit, right?

"Is it just you two?" asks the guard. "Our paperwork says a team of four was dispatched?"

"Yeah, the others are in the back."

"Okay, turn off your engine while we check the vehicle."

"Sure thing."

The engine stops. A heartbeat later, the rear doors open. A flashlight beam floods in, burning our eyes. The internal lighting is poor in the back, and we've had to rely solely on what shines through the windshield. We both hold up a hand to shield us while we adjust to the sudden brightness.

"Can I see your IDs, please?" asks one of the two men standing in front of us.

Squinting, I reach into my pocket and hand him my badge. Ruby does the same. I watch as they move their lights over them. Outside, behind the guards, a cacophony of horns ripples along the street, and people hurry along the sidewalks, a visible urgency in their collective body language.

The guards hand the badges back with no fuss and slam the doors. Ruby and I look at each other again, and we both raise a relieved eyebrow.

"Okay," says the first guard. "Drive through to the second

checkpoint. Head right up ahead, and make sure you keep to the right of the drive. You'll be issued with passes giving you the required security clearance."

"No problem," replies Oscar calmly. "Thanks, guys."

"Just do what you have to do, all right? Today isn't the day to be racking up your overtime."

Oscar chuckles. "Overtime? We should be so lucky!"

There are a few seconds of awkward silence...

"Yeah, I hear that, man," says the guard. "Go on through."

"Thanks, my friend."

Oscar restarts the engine as the gates squeak and grind open. We drive through, and I look over my shoulder again to stare ahead through the windshield. The driveway up ahead splits. Left would take us in a wide, shallow semi-circle along the north lawn and eventually lead us back to the street. We head right, toward the second checkpoint and the entrance to the West Wing.

Another guard appears, walking toward the van with his hand held up. Oscar slows to a stop, and the guard heads to the driver's door.

"Tyger Security?" he asks.

"That's us."

"Just pull in on the left. We need to check the vehicle before we can issue your badges."

"No problem."

Oscar moves forward and turns a moment later, once again killing the engine.

This is the part I've been dreading. The fake floor is the only thing they could find, and if they do, it's game over before the opening bell sounds. I just hope they don't make us get out of the van.

"You okay?" Ruby whispers next to me.

"Yeah, just nervous. I want my plan to work."

She pats my hand with hers. "We'll be fine."

Everything goes quiet outside. We're far enough into the White House grounds that the noise from the street is less audible. I hear Jonas shifting in his seat. Oscar is drumming his fingers on the wheel.

I wish I could see what's happening. I hate flying blind like this.

"You're good," says the guard through the open window. "Drive past the checkpoint and pull in anywhere on the right. Your passes are being printed, and you can pick them up when you enter the building."

"Thanks," replies Oscar.

He reverses, then drives on and turns right again a moment later. As soon as he turns the engine off, I climb out of the back and stretch, cracking my neck and shoulders.

I take a brief look around, familiarizing myself with the surroundings and layout. There are two rows of parking spaces, one running along each side of the drive. We're on the right, nose-in. A wall easily eight feet tall, partially obscured by bushes and greenery, runs along the perimeter in front of us, separating us from West Executive Avenue.

On the other side, the White House looms over us, lit from beneath by floodlights. It's a remarkable building. I can't deny it. Like the name suggests, it's a brilliant white brick, which seems to shine, even at night. All the windows are bulletproof. I can't see any from where I'm standing, but I know there's a team of Secret Service snipers on the roof—all of whom will be a damn good shot.

Basically, if we try leaving here in any way other than normal, we've got no chance...

We gather at the rear doors of the van. I pass Oscar the tool bag and then lift up the floor panels, revealing the other bag and the pile of weapons. Jonas grabs his bag without needing to be asked.

"Everyone get your ID badges visible," I say. "Clip them to your pockets or something. We'll be getting our security access once we're inside, and from there, we need to head straight for the maintenance room, so Jonas can do his thing. We need to move like we belong. Understand? This is our job. This is who we are. No need to feel out of place or self-conscious."

"There are gonna be security cameras everywhere in there," says Ruby. "Shouldn't we have baseball caps on or something?"

I shake my head. "Looks too conspicuous. That's why we got the strategic makeovers. A normal team of security experts wouldn't wear a cap inside, so why should we? We'll be visible, but thanks to Veronica, we look different enough that people won't look twice at us. Worst case is they have facial recognition software running on their security system, but even then, it would take a lot longer to determine who we really are based on how we look now. It'll be fine. We just have to play it cool."

I look at each member of the team in turn. Oscar and Jonas are holding their respective bags and look impatient, like they just want to get it over with. Ruby looks different. She seems impatient as well, but her eyes are sparkling, alive with the rush and thrill of a job. Instinctively, I pat myself down to make sure everything I need is in the right pocket, then I fold the fake floor back into place and slam the rear doors.

"Here we go..." I say to myself.

I start walking toward the main doors and hear the footsteps of my team behind me. We stride confidently into the lobby. Inside is immaculate and wonderfully designed. The floor is a dark marble, complemented by mahogany high-lights and accessories. In the corners are pillars that stretch to the ceiling. I think they're more for decoration than necessity. There's a half-moon desk with a gateway scanner beside it in the middle of the large entrance hall. Three guards are behind the counter. I step to the side to allow Oscar through first.

"Tyger Security," he announces as he approaches the desk.

The man behind the desk is Caucasian, probably late forties. Judging by what I can see of his torso—his shoulders and chest—I suspect his stomach is preventing him from seeing his shoes. His muscles seem to sag inside his uniform.

He glances down, then back at Oscar. "Four of you?" He points to the scanner. "Place your bags on the side and step through."

We move to the left and form a line in front of the metal detector. Another low counter runs along one side of the central desk, with the scanner level with it, roughly halfway along. Oscar places the tool bag down carefully, along with his ID badge. He walks through the scanner, which remains silent, and collects his things on the other side.

Ruby's next up. She places her badge on the counter and steps forward. The machine beeps loudly, and all three guards stare at her. She steps back, slowly, and passes through the scanner again.

The first guard looks at her. "Can you remove any metallic objects on your person please, ma'am?"

She shrugs. "I have."

Another guard moves around the desk and walks toward her, holding a wand scanner. He's much younger than the first—younger than me, certainly. He seems in good shape and moves with confidence.

"Place your arms out to the sides," he says to her.

She does, and he moves the wand thoroughly and efficiently over her body. It beeps as he moves it over her crotch. He looks at her questioningly.

Ruby chuckles nervously, which I'm sure is part of the act, as opposed to actual nerves. "Heh... well, *this* is embarrassing."

"Ma'am, I'm gonna need you to—"

"I... can't. It's a piercing. It's not coming out. I'm sorry."

The guard flicks a quick glance at his colleague, who nods. He finishes his scan of Ruby and stands up straight. "Okay, go on through."

Ruby nods and walks through again. The machine beeps, but the guard behind the desk does something to override it. She collects her ID and waits beside Oscar on the other side.

Jonas steps forward and heaves the large bag onto the counter. The equipment inside will likely show up, but it's been designed not to look like what it is. To the casual observer, it looks like a couple of aerosol canisters in a box, which isn't uncommon for a security team to have. Could be WD-40 or compressed air for cleaning the inside of server cabinets.

Or a nitrous oxide dispersal unit for knocking out everyone in the White House...

He moves through the scanner with no problems, retrieves the bag and his ID, and stands with the others.

I'm last up to bat. I take a deep, discreet breath and step toward the scanner, placing my ID on the side. I move through.

The scanner beeps loudly.

Shit.

I look innocently at the guards, who urge me back through. The guy with the wand walks back around the desk and meets me.

"Arms out to the sides," he says.

I comply, and he searches me with the same level of thoroughness and efficiency as he had Ruby. The wand remains silent.

I smile. "No piercings on me."

He regards me with an impassive look and stands up straight. He nods toward the scanner. I take the hint and walk through it a second time.

It sounds off again.

Are you fucking kidding me?

I sigh and step backward through it, glancing at the guards impatiently.

"Sir, do you have any metallic objects on—or in—your person?" asks the first guard.

I look him up and down. From this angle, I can see more of him since the side counter is much lower than the front of the desk. I was right. He *is* a fat bastard...

I shake my head. "I've got nothing. You just gave me the wand to prove it."

The guard frowns, turns to his computer terminal, and presses a few buttons.

"Try again," he says to me.

I roll my eyes and step through the scanner for the third time.

Silence.

Phew!

I retrieve my ID and nod to the guards. "Thanks, guys."

I join the others, and we walk across the rest of the lobby and head left at the end, into the West Wing.

The corridor is wide, with curved arches at even intervals along the ceiling and a bright red carpet with gold trim along both edges. The walls are off-white, plastered to a smooth finish, and adorned with works of art—some landscapes, some portraits of former presidents and notable politicians. To the right of every doorway is a Marine standing at attention in full uniform, armed with a standard-issue Glock 19. There's normally just one in the West Wing, but given the world is at war, I'm guessing they've stepped up security.

We're walking two by two, with Oscar and Ruby in front. We pass a thick wooden door on the left. I casually glance inside through the glass and see a large mahogany table with people sitting around it and military officers standing around the edges of the room.

Wonder what they're discussing—North Korea or me?

I pat Oscar on the shoulder, and he glances around. "Should be up here on the right. Play the part."

We stop in front of another Marine outside a door that says MAINTENANCE on a small black sign. Josh kindly sent me a floor plan of the building—just a general one you can find on the internet—so I have a rough idea of where we're going.

We all turn to face one another.

"Okay," says Oscar, loud enough to be heard. "We'll do a preliminary check of equipment in here—ventilation, alarms, the works. We're looking for any potential breaches, as well as opportunities for breaches. We fix what we need to and log it for the guys back at the office. Then—" He points at Jonas and me. "You two head over to the server room and install what patches you need to. We work fast and thorough. Questions?"

Beautiful. Oscar's a natural!

We all shake our heads.

Oscar looks at the Marine outside the door. "Excuse me, buddy? We're about to test the equipment in here. Do we need to tell anyone if we're testing the alarms? I don't want them to go off and make everyone panic." He chuckles. "Probably not the time for that. Am I right?"

The Marine glances up and down the corridor as if he's checking before he responds because he's not allowed to.

"Yeah, you need to let the Secret Service Agent-in-Charge know," he says.

Oscar nods. "Okay, we'll do the alarms last. Thanks."

He opens the door and walks inside without another word. We all follow, and I close the door behind me.

The room isn't huge, but there's enough space for us to stand comfortably. The floor is plain white tiling, and the walls are gray cinder block. There's a large unit on the left, easily seven feet high, with a large silver cylinder sticking out of the top, running into the ceiling.

"This is it," says Jonas quietly. "Gimme some room to work."

We step back, and he moves next to the unit and opens the main hatch on the front. Inside is a network of wires and pipes, but he assesses them with a professional eye. You would think he was an electrician, not an assassin.

He unzips the sport bag, lifts the dispersal unit out carefully, and sets it down at his feet. He crouches in front of the open hatch.

"Hand me a screwdriver, would you?" he calls over his shoulder.

Oscar rummages inside the tool bag and hands one to him. Jonas promptly sets to work attaching the gas canisters to the ventilation system.

Beside me, Ruby is taking some deep breaths. She sounds like she's giving birth.

"You okay?" I ask her.

She nods quickly. "Calm before the storm. Just getting myself ready."

"Well, try not to pass out beforehand."

She pulls a face, and we continue watching Jonas do his thing. He's technical. I knew he specialized in poisons, which I've always considered a niche part of our business, but his knowledge clearly stretches beyond that.

He connects the dispersal unit and attaches the wires to the ventilation pipes. Then he starts pressing buttons on the small console, presumably configuring it. After a minute or so, he stands and briefly stretches his arms and legs.

"Okay, we're good."

He bends down, takes out the gas masks, and hands them to each of us. I place mine over my head and adjust the straps and clasps at the back. It covers my entire face, though my field of vision is pretty wide. Attached to the bottom is a thick, round filter, maybe three inches in diameter.

I look around the room, getting used to the feel and the weight.

Jonas moves toward me and hands me the remote. "All yours, Adrian. When you activate it, it should take no more than two or three minutes for the nitrous oxide to vent out. Allow maybe another minute as a safety net to make sure everyone's dropped off, then a final minute for it to clear enough that we can remove the masks."

I take it and nod, trying not to laugh at the fact he sounds like Darth Vader when he talks with his mask on. "Thanks."

The device is a simple design. It's black and narrow with two buttons: On/Off and Activate.

I reckon even I can figure this out...

"Everyone ready?" I ask.

They all nod.

I press the button.

20:43 EDT

We wait exactly five minutes. There was some commotion outside the door at first, but it seems to have gone quiet now. I check the time again and look at the rest of the team. "Shall we?"

I move toward the door, grab the handle, and turn it slowly. I ease it open and create a gap just a couple inches wide. I look through it down the corridor. I can just about see the leg of one of the Marines on the floor.

That's encouraging...

I open the door wider and step out. The guy we spoke to earlier is leaning against the wall, still upright, using his shirttails to cover his nose and mouth. I can hear him coughing into them, and his eyes are blurry with tears.

I don't hesitate. I whip my hand up and back, hitting him hard in the throat with the outside edge. His eyes bulge momentarily, and he drops to the floor, landing heavily at my feet. I crouch beside him and take his gun, which I tuck into the belt around the waist of my coveralls.

The rest of the team appears from inside the maintenance room.

"Jonas, you think it's safe to remove the masks?"

He nods. "Should be all right."

He rips his off quickly, like a Band-Aid, and takes a deep breath. We wait ten seconds to see if he falls over. He doesn't. The rest of us follow suit.

"Okay." I point to the right. "The Oval should be that way. Keep your eyes open, everyone. Remember what I said —anyone this side of that office not holding a gun is innocent."

I set off walking, keeping my pace purposeful but cautious. Outside and in the other parts of the building, I suspect all hell is breaking loose. But I reckon we have at least five minutes before the doors are kicked in by masked SWAT teams armed to the teeth.

Plenty of time.

The corridor doglegs slightly to the right. Every room we pass is the same. People are out cold, either on the floor or slumped over a desk or chair. About halfway along, a double door leading into a waiting area stands open. I stop to look into the room. There's a desk facing me, with a woman still in her chair, face-down, sprawled across the surface. There's another desk to the immediate right, which is empty. In the corner is a single white door, closed.

The Oval Office.

I close my eyes for a moment, taking some calming breaths. From my bedroom above my bar in a small Texan town to the doors of the president's office in Washington, DC. It's been a little over three weeks since I found myself involved in this shit, and in that time, the entire world has changed. The terrorist attack that wiped out almost five percent of the world's population... the conspiracy behind it that began with the U.S. president... me and the people I care about being branded terrorists and hunted by the CIA... North Korea declaring war on everyone...

It's all led to this moment, right here, right now.

And this is where it ends.

I look back at Jonas, at Ruby, at Oscar. I wouldn't be here without them. Ruby, especially, has saved my ass more than once along the way. She's... well, she's a character. There's no doubt about that. But she's proven herself as someone deserving of my friendship. And she's definitely earned her twenty million.

I walk back and stand beside Oscar. "Okay, this is it, everyone. We've finally made it. Let's finish this."

I gesture everyone forward, and they turn to walk inside the first room. I put my hand in my pocket and retrieve two hypodermic needles, each enclosed in a thin tube. I quickly remove the tubes and step forward, jamming the needles into the necks of both Ruby and Jonas. They both let out a shocked yell, clasp a hand to the point of injection, and spin around.

I look at each of them regretfully. "I'm sorry. But I'm not having you go down with me."

Ruby reaches out to me. "Adrian..."

They both drop to the floor, landing awkwardly on each other.

Oscar moves next to me. "They're gonna be pissed when they wake up. Y'know that, don't you?"

I nod. "Yeah, I know. But this started with me, and I'm gonna make sure it ends with me. Thanks for helping with this, Oscar. They've both done me a great service. Make sure you tell them their money is already in their accounts and that I'm sorry."

"I will. Don't worry."

"You gonna be okay getting them out of here?"

"Yeah. Like you said back in Veronica's kitchen, I'll drag them to the lobby and claim ignorance. It'll be fine. No one's looking for us dressed like this."

I extend my hand, which he shakes. "Thank you, Oscar. You're a good friend."

"Just make sure I don't lose my best customer in there, all right?"

We both smile. "I'll do my best."

He bends down and grabs their collars, one in each hand, and slowly starts to drag them away.

I watch him for a moment, then I take off my coveralls. Underneath, I'm in a simple, inconspicuous outfit of jeans and a T-shirt. I tuck the borrowed gun into my waistband at the back, then pick up my discarded disguise and gas mask, placing them on the desk just inside the room. I peel off the makeup Ruby's friend expertly applied as best I can, revealing my true features once again.

I glance around the room. Nice furniture, deep blue carpet... even a paperweight with the presidential seal on it on the desk in front of me. I remember a time when seeing this in person would've impressed me. I would've considered it an honor. Now I feel disgusted by it. The magic is forever tainted by the corruption and greed of the man sitting a few feet away behind this white door.

I take the gun from my back, gripping it tightly in my hand. I crack my neck, welcoming the new and improved, disciplined Inner Satan to stand beside me. Not in front of me. Not behind the wheel. By my side. Working with me to make me a better killer. A better weapon. A better man.

I stride toward the door and thrust my leg forward, connecting just next to the handle. It flies open, nearly off its hinges. I step inside the Oval Office and—

Oh.

I drop the gun to the floor.

Sonofabitch.

In front of me on the left, President Cunningham is

sitting calmly behind his fancy-looking desk, wearing a nice suit. There's a smug look spread across his annoying fucking face. On the right, following the curve of the room, standing in a spacious line are six—no, *seven* Secret Service agents, all wearing their standard-issue black suits and holding their standard-issue firearms. In the middle of the room, sitting across two brown leather sofas are three men, also wearing suits. Two of them have their backs to me. The other is facing me, but I don't recognize him.

I feel the barrel of a gun touch my temple. I flick my gaze to my left.

Oh, my mistake—*eight* Secret Service agents.

Cunningham stands, walks around his desk, and rests casually on the edge. He crosses his arms across his chest.

"Good evening, Adrian. We've been waiting for you."

I close my eyes and feel my shoulders involuntarily sag forward with defeat.

Fuck.

31

ADRIAN HELL

"Please, come in," says Cunningham, gesturing to the middle of the room.

Words fail me. I silently ask my Inner Satan for help, but he's backed down, as confused as I am.

I don't understand. I did everything right. We all did. It might have looked a little straightforward, considering what we were actually doing, but the planning was meticulous, and everything was put in place by Josh and his team at GlobaTech. There's no way they messed up their side of things, and we did everything correctly our side. I just don't get it. I mean, how is...

Cunningham's still smiling at me. He still has that smug look on his face. "Adrian, you look perturbed."

I shrug. "I don't know about that, but I'm really fucking confused. How are you not... y'know... unconscious?"

"That's easy. The air conditioning system isn't linked to this office. Too much of a security risk."

"Huh... makes sense."

Cunningham moves back around his desk but remains standing. "You see, Adrian, despite proving to be a world-class pain in the ass, you're still predictable and insignificant. I've done the impossible. I've set in motion things that will change the course of history. Did you really think I wouldn't be able to handle a lowlife, two-bit assassin like you?"

My jaw muscles tense involuntarily. I glance around the room. The guy on my immediate left is pissing me off because he keeps pressing his gun against my head, forcing me to lean away slightly. The agents lining the opposite wall are like statues. They haven't moved an inch. They're simply keeping their guns trained on me.

The men on the sofas have stood. I'm pretty sure one of them is the chief of staff. Something Heskith, I think his name is. No idea about the other two.

Cunningham's staring at me, challenging me, acting like he's already won. And I have to admit, from the outside looking in, I understand his thinking. I mean, I'm pretty screwed, right?

Well, yeah... I am. Sorry. I've got no secret plan. I didn't see this coming. I'm frozen, and my mind hasn't reengaged yet. I just feel... sorry. Like I've failed and let everyone down in the process. Like it's all been for nothing.

I go to speak, but words fail me.

I know, I know... it's not like me at all.

Cunningham continues to smile at me. "Cat got your tongue, Adrian? You were never going to stop this. Just because you figured it out doesn't mean you could ever really do anything about it. You didn't stop 4/17 from happening, did you? You got right to the end... right to the final hurdle... and you just didn't have it in you. And now here you are, at that last hurdle yet again. And look what's happened. You've stumbled for a second time. You know, if the situation were different, I'd offer you a job. A man like you—resourceful, talented, intelligent—would've made one hell of an ally in all this."

I close my eyes. Not the *wish you were on my side* speech —please!

My teeth are aching from clenching my jaw so hard. Angry? No, anger doesn't come close to what I'm feeling now. There's a rage coursing through my body that no human has any business understanding. It's a primordial fury that I honestly don't know how to express. My fists tighten, and every muscle in my body tenses. I breathe slowly, doing everything I can to remain in control. It's not the time.

Not yet.

I open my eyes slowly and fix Cunningham with a stare reserved only for the most horrific of bastards. "Stop."

He frowns. "Excuse me?"

"I said stop. Stop talking. Stop acting like what's happening was inevitable. We all know it wasn't. You think you've won. You think this is over because you have a gun to my head. But you're wrong. I came here pretty much certain I wasn't leaving, so killing me in your fancy little office means precisely fuck all. I'm prepared to die for this. But you... you're not. I think *you're* a coward. You're smart, but you're a pussy. You want to change the world so that you can rule it like some modern-day Caesar, but ultimately, you don't want to die for the cause, do you? And that's the difference between us. I'm prepared to do what's necessary, whereas you're only prepared to do what's safe. That's why you won't win."

He sits down and leans back in his chair. "Nice speech.

Really. Great speech, Adrian. But... before you get too high and mighty, I want you to see something."

He opens up a laptop that's resting on his desk and spins it around to face the room. He nods to the agent beside me, who gestures me forward with another prod of his gun. I move into the middle of the room and stand just to the left of the sofas.

Cunningham points at the screen. "Take a look at this. Recognize it?"

I frown as I stare at the laptop. It's showing a grayscale image of a town, presumably viewed from a satellite. It might even be a real-time feed. I'm not sure. He reaches over and presses a button. The picture zooms down to a street-level view. It shows a quiet, dusty road. An empty sidewalk. A restaurant facing a companion club and...

The Ferryman.

My eyes react, going wide with a mixture of anger and fear. "What is this?"

"This is your bar, is it not? Your little slice of happiness. The only evidence you ever existed, bought and built using a stolen fortune."

"Why are you showing me this?"

"I'm glad you asked. You see, this laptop is showing a live feed from the Cerberus satellite. We might as well dispense with the courtesies. I think that ship has sailed. You know I still have control of Cerberus, and what you're seeing is me targeting your bar with a missile that belongs to North Korea."

"You piece of shit! You're insane!"

I step forward, but the gun at my head prevents me from moving farther.

"Insane? Not at all. This exercise serves multiple purposes—the most important of which is to bring the invasion home, so to speak. The thing that will allow me to unleash an unprecedented military response that no one will dare question—that people will *thank* me for—won't be GlobaTech's systematic destruction across the world. It'll be North Korea reaching American soil. I've publicly held off joining the fight. I've told the people that GlobaTech is handling it, that they can protect us overseas, and that I want to protect us on our homeland. But when that security disappears, the people will cry out for me to send forth the full might of our military and wipe out North Korea with a swift, decisive strike."

Focus, Adrian. You're no good to the residents of Devil's Spring if you lose it now.

"That's a good plan. But what makes you so sure Globa-Tech will fail? My best friend and your former secretary of defense are running that place. They know what they're doing, and North Korea only outnumbers them six to one."

He scoffs. "Only?"

"Please... I could take out ten on my own, easily. And every single one of those GlobaTech peacekeepers are well trained, so six each should be a walk in the park."

"I know everything there is to know about GlobaTech Industries, Adrian. They will fail. Trust me."

"Okay, what about North Korea? Do they have any idea you've asked them to publicly poke a bear purely so they can get bitten?"

Cunningham smiles but says nothing.

"No, of course you haven't. It's El-Zurak all over again, isn't it? They think this is a partnership, but you're using them to show the world that *you're* the only logical choice moving forward. You want to be handed this planet on a silver platter, to mold it as you see fit. You're a fucking psychopath! And coming from me, that's saying something."

"You have it all worked out, it seems."

"Yeah, you can thank your old friend, General Matthews, for that."

"Yes, his involvement was unfortunate but ultimately irrelevant. It won't change anything."

I smile. "You seem pretty sure about that..."

"Oh, I am. You see, you wouldn't have walked in here without some contingency in place. Credit where it's due, Adrian. You're a smart man. You would have made sure the evidence Matthews gave you was made public if you don't get out of here. But obviously, I can't allow that. So, here's the thing—you make the call right now to stop that evidence going wherever you intend it to go, and I won't use Cerberus to destroy your bar, your town, and the woman you love." He picks up the desk phone receiver and holds it out to me. "Sound fair?"

I need a minute.

It's funny, isn't it, how sometimes the scale of something can be so big, it becomes lost on you. Like, the size of it is simply too massive to comprehend. Take the speed of light, for example. It's something ridiculous, like nine hundred and eighty *million* feet per second. I think it's the equivalent of traveling the entire circumference of the planet seven times. But when you think light travels that distance every second, it suddenly becomes just a number, with all meaning and scale lost because you can't wrap your head around how something could possibly move that fast.

That's how I feel right now.

I'm face-to-face with the man who is literally trying to take over the planet, but that's a meaningless statement. All I can think about is two people in a small town in Texas. I can't help myself. Despite knowing the fates of billions are hanging in the balance, resting solely on the outcome of this conversation, I'm standing here thinking only about Tori Watson and John Raynor—my girlfriend and the sheriff of the town I call home.

She's only the second woman I've ever loved. And he was a good friend who put his ass on the line for me and trusted me when he had no reason to. I owe them both.

Tori... I can't lose her.

But I've already lost her, haven't I? Because I know I'm not walking away from this. I'll never see her again.

Besides, the priority is stopping Cunningham. If he succeeds, the world will be nothing more than a dictatorship.

Though, while that world would suck, at least she would be alive to see it.

But is that a life worth living? Is it a life worth sacrificing?

I feel my Inner Satan stand next to me and put a friendly arm around my shoulder. I glance to my right, as if seeing a person no one else can see.

Adrian, my man. You know what you gotta do, right?

I nod to myself.

Yeah, I know.

You and me... we're a team now. You hear me? I'm not the Hulk to your Bruce Banner anymore. Together, we're what King Kong is to the Empire fucking State Building! You understand? He didn't just tear through the lobby. He scaled the side... focused on taking out the whole thing. See what I'm saying here?

I smile. I bet I sound crazy, right? Well... sometimes sanity just doesn't cut it.

"Everything all right, Adrian?"

I take a deep breath, treasuring every ounce of oxygen that flows into my lungs as if it's my last. "Yes, sir, Mr. President. Everything's peachy."

"So, what'll it be?"

I stroke my chin thoughtfully. "It's a no-brainer, Charlie..."

He smiles.

I smile back.

After a moment, I'm still smiling, but his starts to fade, giving way to uncertainty. He won't understand why I seem so calm and relaxed. But I'm that way because I know what I need to do, and smiling while I do it will stop me from screaming.

"Go fuck yourself, Mr. President. Fuck you and the horse you rode in on. That evidence is staying right where it is." I nod at the laptop. "So, go ahead. Fire that missile. I fucking dare you."

He hesitates, his brow furrowing with indecisiveness. He doesn't believe me. I can see it in his eyes. It's the look a poker player has when he believes his cards are better than the guy who's just raised the stakes. He doesn't think I would sacrifice someone I care about so quickly. And usually, he would be right. But these circumstances are far from usual, and I'm trying my best to remain objective, to keep my focus on the bigger picture.

Plus, I have a plan. I think.

"You do realize I'm not bluffing, don't you?" he asks me after a moment. "This isn't an empty threat. This *needs* to be done. And yes, while I could theoretically target anywhere in the United States, it makes more sense to use this situation to its full potential and break *you* at the same time."

This gun hasn't left my temple since I kicked down the door. The seven pairs of eyes along the right wall remain fixed on me. The two assholes near the sofas look relaxed, comfortable... confident. Cunningham looks like he believes he's in control.

I don't know how I look to everyone else, but I know how I feel inside.

I feel like... Adrian Hell!

I whip my left arm up and back, ducking slightly as I deflect the gun away from my head. I step around the agent next to me, putting my left arm under his chin and around his throat. I grab his wrist with my right, controlling the gun. I'm a little taller than he is, so I crouch slightly, hiding as best I can behind him.

No one's reacted yet. I reckon I have maybe three more seconds before they do.

I drag this guy backward by his throat, moving as fast as possible around the desk to stand next to the president.

Three seconds. They know what I'm doing. They're taking aim...

I squeeze tightly with my left arm. I feel him loosen his grip on the gun. That's what I was waiting for. I slide it from his hand in a swift, practiced motion and let go of him. Then I throw a quick, short elbow to the back of his head as I arc the gun clockwise. I'm close enough now that I hold my arm out and place the barrel against Cunningham's temple at the exact moment he spins the laptop around, sits down, and places his finger over the Enter key.

I'm standing at an angle, looking at him and most of the room. I can see the open door and the right corner in my peripheral vision.

"If anyone moves, he dies before I do. We clear?" I shout.

The agents hesitate and glance at their commander-in-chief, who gives the slightest of nods, ordering them to stand down.

I gesture to the laptop. "Now I can only assume that pressing that button launches the missile. Am I right?"

Cunningham nods, leaning slightly away from me under the pressure of the gun.

"Okay, if you press that button, you'll be dead a second later. That's not a bluff or an empty threat. I don't do those things, either. I will blow your fucking head off if you so much as think about that laptop again. You understand me?"

He nods again. His eyes appear calm and collected. "Surely, your intention is to kill me anyway?"

"I thought about it. I'll be honest. I've thought about shooting you pretty much exclusively for the last two weeks. But Matthews told me it wouldn't make a difference. Not now. And believe it or not, my priority is to prevent North Korea from doing any more damage, not to settle the score with someone who isn't fit to breathe the same air as me."

Out of the corner of my eye, I see the agent on the far right shuffle to his left. A very subtle movement, but I saw it. He'll be trying to widen their coverage of the room and make it harder for me to defend myself.

Uh-uh.

I bring the gun around and fire once, shooting from the hip, not bothering to aim. At this range, I'm never going to miss. The bullet catches the agent in the middle of his chest. He falls backward from the impact, and I snap the gun back against Cunningham's head. He winces as the heat from the barrel hisses on his face.

The other agents react slowly, taking a collective step forward and raising their weapons a few seconds after their colleague hits the floor. The men by the sofas gasp and take a step back, looking less comfortable than they did when I got here.

"Hey, hey, hey! Back off!" I press the gun hard against Cunningham's temple. "Tell them!"

He looks over at them, silently instructing the remaining agents to stand down again.

"That's right. Do as your master says, boys. Now, Charlie, I gotta ask... why are you doing this? I get that you wanna change the world, make it a better place, blah blah blah. But you did that in your first six months in office. Crime was down, drug crime was nonexistent. There were more jobs, better health care—hell, you could get high or laid and no one would give a shit. You were doing everything right, and it was working. Why go to all this trouble to tear it all down?"

He looks across at the men standing by the sofas, whom I notice are now standing up straight like they're proud fathers. He strokes a hand across his chin, as if choosing his words carefully. Ever the politician.

I notice his other hand stays hovering over the laptop.

"Adrian, quite frankly, you lack the mental capacity to understand why this is happening. You don't see things the way I do. You don't appreciate the scope of a situation. All you see is the end of your gun, whereas I look miles beyond the target."

"Do yourself a favor and try not to patronize me, all right? You think you're safe in this room right now? You think you can relax because you've got six armed Secret Service agents with you?"

He shrugs and smiles.

I don't like how confident he is. Let's do something about that...

In the same fluid, expert movement as before, I aim the gun and fire once, hitting the agent on the far left of the room in the face. The bullet strikes just above the right side of the jaw, shattering his mandible in two. His head snaps back violently as one half flies away, spraying a thin trail of blood in the air. It hits the far wall beneath the portrait of a former president. The other half is still attached but hanging loose. The agent is dead before he hits the floor.

Straight away, the gun's back against Cunningham's forehead. "Sorry, *five* agents. Are you starting to see where this is going?"

The rest of the agents are getting twitchy. I can understand how hard it must be for them to ignore their instincts and obey an order they don't agree with.

"Okay... okay. I'll tell you, Adrian. I'd like you to understand why I've done this. I really would. But before I do, I need you to know that you've got me all wrong. You see, I'm not a coward. I'm the president of the United States. I've dedicated my life to making sure these events unfold exactly as they are. Years and years of meticulous planning and strategy have been poured into this."

"What do you want? A fucking medal?"

"Not at all. I'm not doing this for recognition, despite what you might think. I'm doing this because it's what the people *need*."

"And who are you to decide what's best for everyone?"

"Adrian, I'm the president. It's why I was elected."

"Yeah, you're the president of *this* country... not the entire world! You can't just enforce your ideals on everyone because you think you're right. Did you not pay attention in history class? It never works. And the people who try it end up dead."

He smiles. "History simply teaches us that if you start with nothing, that's exactly what you'll end up with. Hitler... Stalin... even Bin Laden. The problem they had was that they started trying to—how did you put it—*enforce their ideals* at the same time they were rising to power. That never works because the people who would object to a leader's beliefs can see him growing. They can simply monitor him and step in when they need to. There is no surprise, no shock. They just prepare for the day when they would inevitably have to stop him. But me... I rose to power first. Only then did I start to implement my plan for a new, better world. I started when I was already in charge, so the things I'm trying to do are more easily accepted. See, it's easy to stop someone from running for the throne when you're running alongside them, Adrian. But it's much harder to approach that throne when they're already sitting on it, surrounded by their kingdom."

I raise an eyebrow. My arm and shoulder are starting to ache a little from holding this gun to his head for so long. But I'm not moving it.

"Huh... did you, like, write that little speech beforehand? Have you been rehearsing it every day in case you get a chance to reel off your bullshit to someone? You're a whole other level of crazy, Chuck. You'd be better off in Stonebanks."

"Actually, I think we're a lot alike, you and me. We're both smart and driven. We're also instinctual. I'm a gambling man. I go with my gut when I need to, just like you. Like now, for example. You've shot two members of my security detail. Rather impressively, I might add. But I don't think you'll shoot me. In the same way you thought that flash drive around your neck would keep you alive this whole time, I think you're banking on staying safe while you have a gun to my head. But you're wrong because I *am* prepared to die for my cause. I will not let anything or anyone stop me. Not now. And I will not be threatened by the likes of you. So, tell me, Adrian Hell... what do you intend to do *now!*"

He holds my gaze and smiles as he presses the Enter key.

32

ADRIAN HELL

No... he can't have. He's... Tori is... I have to...

"No!" I yell out, watching the screen in horror.

My arm drops to my side, and everything around me fades away. The gray image in front of me still shows the quiet, dusty road running through the center of the town I've called home for the last two-and-a-bit years.

The small shape of a person walks into view from the north and turns into my bar a moment later.

Huh... she must've gotten the place reopened. Way to go, babe!

I smile, thinking about—

Sweet Jesus!

A long, thin line flickers into view from the east. A split-second later, a bright flash covers the entire display.

Is that... was that it? I don't understand. Did I just see...

The glare fades, revealing...

My eyes go wide. "Holy mother of God..."

There's... nothing! It's a goddamn wasteland—just fire and debris for miles.

I turn to look at Cunningham. He's still in his seat, but any visible tension is gone. I stare into his eyes. There's a glint in them... pride, I think. He's relaxed, leaning back in his chair like it's a Sunday afternoon and the family is around. He thinks he's won. He thinks I'm beaten, and he viewed me as the last remaining obstacle in his path.

The room slowly fades back into view. The desk, the carpet, the men by the sofas, the Secret Service agents...

Oh, shit. The agents!

I look up as they advance toward me, guns raised but fingers outside the trigger guards. I'm too close to their boss to risk a shot. But if they get close and surround me, I'm finished.

Tori...

Anger and sadness fill up inside me in equal measure. Every fiber of my being is screaming at me to simply drop to my knees in grief. Let them take me. I don't care anymore. I've lost. At the press of a button, Cunningham took away everything I had. Everything I worked to get since starting my new life.

There's nothing left for me now.

There's just—

Hey, Adrian. It's me. Satan. Your Satan. Have you finished? Because I can come back if you're still wallowing...

I frown to myself.

Are you... are you good? Okay, listen up. You see that gun in your hand? Well, when you've finished being a dick, take a moment to think what Adrian Hell would do with it. Not winning isn't the same as losing, man. Tell you what... I'll make you a deal. You get us out of this, and I'll leave you alone to grieve. Sound fair?

316

I smile to myself. I think I've finally been tipped over the edge. There's a voice in my head actually insulting me!

Boy, I swear, if you drop to your knees now, you and I are through! These pussies can't take you. No one can. Now wipe that dumbass smile off your face and start shooting people. They haven't won yet!

I look down at my hand and examine the weapon. It's a Sig Sauer P229R. Two shots have been fired, which leaves me nine in the mag and one in the chamber. I count nine people in the room, not including me.

It's like it was meant to be...

I take a breath and stand tall as my lungs fill with air. Time slows down. I move backward, stepping around Cunningham as I open fire. No need for me to keep track of ammo. I won't be wasting any.

I fire the first two rounds one-handed, taking out the two agents on the right of the group. Both catch a bullet in the chest—a nice, big target for quick aiming and lethal pretty much wherever you hit, so it's the obvious choice.

I quicken my pace, moving around the desk and putting Cunningham on my right, between me and the remaining agents.

Keeping my gun focused to the right of the group, I fire two more rounds in quick succession, this time with both hands on the gun. With the steadier aim, I put each bullet in an agent's head. The two were moving fast, so they slide forward a little as they drop to the floor. Their momentum carries them to Cunningham's feet.

One agent left. He's had plenty of time to figure out what's happening, which his colleagues didn't have since I started shooting with zero warning. But he won't fire at me. Cunningham's still in his chair, shocked and subsequently unresponsive at this stage. I'm directly behind him, with a gap no larger than two yards between us. The three stooges over by the sofas have fallen back into their seats, looking scared for their lives.

As they should.

I pause and allow the scene to resume normal speed. The sole remaining agent is shaking, his body is that tense. His gun is wavering in front of him, and the sweat is glistening on his brow.

I fire once, hitting him in the center of his forehead. His eyes turn blank almost instantly, and he drops back, lifeless before he lands.

I place the barrel on the back of Cunningham's head. "Any last words, asshole?"

He turns, glancing at the others by the sofa. I look over at them. "I'll deal with you three in a minute."

The one I vaguely recognize steps forward. "You're not going to get away with this. I'll make sure—"

"I'm sorry. Who are you?"

"I'm Gerald Hes—"

"I don't care. Shut your fucking mouth. I have no intention of trying to get away with anything. But I will make damn sure you don't, either." I look at the others. "So, who are you two shit-stains?"

"I'm Dennis Atkins, the Director of National Intelligence," says the man to Heskith's immediate right.

I shake my head. "Whatever. And you?"

"I'm... I'm Bruce Fielding, the United States Secretary of Defense. And you are a terrorist, who will be brought to justice. I'll see to it personally that you—"

I fire once, hitting him in the clavicle, just left of center. He spins counterclockwise and falls, crashing through the small table between the two sofas. Cunningham jumps in his chair from the shock. Heskith and Atkins stand rigid, like statues, terrified to move.

"I liked the old secretary of defense better." I place the gun against Cunningham's head once more. "Now you— stand up nice and slow."

He does.

"Turn around and face me."

He does.

I look into his eyes. I see the belief and the passion within them. He *knows* through and through that what he's doing is right. And that's the scary thing.

He's about my height, and he's wearing a dark blue suit. He's a handsome, clean-cut politician. He looks... normal. It's hard to believe he's the greatest terrorist and mass murderer the world has ever seen.

And now he's going to die.

I walk toward him, stop an arm's length away, raise the gun, and level it right between his eyes.

"You're done, Charlie. It's over. And these are the last few seconds of your life. Believe that or don't—I don't care. These two retards aren't gonna stop me, I can promise you that. Any last words?"

The door behind me, in the opposite corner to the one I kicked in, bursts open, and bodies pour into the room. I don't move an inch, but out of the corner of my eye, I can see the SWAT lettering on their uniforms. They form a wide semicircle around the room and aim their M4 carbines in my direction.

Jesus, there must be twenty of them, at least!

"Adrian, stop!"

Now I move. I look over and see two people, a man and a woman, standing side by side across the desk from me. The man I recognize immediately—Ryan Schultz. He looks out of breath and stressed. His cheeks are flushed crimson and he's frowning.

The woman I've never seen before, but I can hazard a guess who she is. In front of me, Cunningham visibly relaxes as he turns away from me and my gun.

"Secretary Phillips. Thank God you're here!" he says. "This man has launched an attack on—"

"Hey! Asshole! I'm still here. Don't turn away from me!" I step toward him and reattach the barrel to his temple. "How many times—stop acting like you're safe and you've won!"

He smiles. "Adrian, you're done. This is Elaine Phillips, my secretary of state. And these gentlemen are a well-trained SWAT team, clearly here to apprehend you. I *am* safe. You, however, are in a lot of trouble."

"You know what makes what's about to happen even sweeter, Charles? That smug, arrogant look on your irritating fucking face."

He frowns. "What are you talking about?"

"All that evidence Matthews gave me? I read it all. You know that, right?"

"So?"

I gesture at Secretary Phillips, who's standing patient and authoritative. "Where do you think I sent it?"

He stares at me blankly for a few seconds and then I see it. The exact moment when he realizes the SWAT team isn't here for me. Then he realizes that the CEO of GlobaTech Industries is standing beside her.

"How are you doing, Ryan?" I ask, not taking my eyes off Cunningham.

He sighs a heavy breath. "I'm tired, son, but I'm damn sure glad this is over."

"Is Josh all right?"

"Heh... ain't he always?"

I smile. "Yeah. How's that whole North Korea thing going?"

"I can tell you that GlobaTech peacekeepers have pushed them back in almost all major areas of conflict. We're still taking casualties but not as many as they are. They came in angry and well-armed but underprepared. Hell, they never stood a chance!"

I wink at Cunningham. "You hear that, you piece of shit?"

Secretary Phillips steps forward and places a piece of paper on the desk, facing us. "President Cunningham, I've just come from an emergency session of Congress." She points to the paper. "This is a declaration, agreed to by an overwhelming majority of people *not* involved in your conspiracy, giving me authority to invoke the Twenty-Fifth Amendment, removing you from office with immediate effect. You will be taken into custody and tried for war crimes. You will answer for what you've done."

He shakes his head. "No... you can't do this to me! I'm your *president*! I order you to—"

I flick the butt of the gun forward, cracking him hard on his nose. "Shut the fuck up, Charlie."

A man walks in the room wearing a suit and tie and looking nervous.

Secretary Phillips gestures to him. "This is a judge, here to swear in the next president of these United States."

"You're not fit for this office, Elaine! You won't be able to handle the backlash of what I've done!"

She holds her hand up. "I agree with you completely, Mr. President."

He falls silent and frowns. I admit, I'm a little intrigued as to where this is going...

"I have no wish to be your successor, despite the chain of

command dictating that I am. Under these exceptional, unique circumstances, I put it to Congress that they approve someone outside of that chain, independent from the government, as the next acting president."

Ryan Schultz steps forward.

My eyes go wide, and I laugh with disbelief. "Ryan? Holy shit! Good for you, man."

He nods but stays silent.

Phillips looks at me. "Adrian, I need you to stand down, put the gun away, and come with us. Your efforts in trying to stop this conspiracy have been noted, but you're wanted for the murder of over twenty government agents."

Oh, yeah... them.

It's probably closer to forty. I think she was being generous.

I look at all the SWAT guys, aiming at me quietly and professionally. A couple of them have secured Atkins and Heskith, sitting them down on the sofas and keeping a gun on them.

Phillips is staring at me expectantly. Schultz looks a little more worried, but then, he's met me before, so that's understandable.

Finally, I look at Cunningham. He's distraught at the fact his grand plan has fallen at the final hurdle. Ironic, given the speech he gave me before. For all the atrocities this man has committed, it's his most recent that I can't move past. He launched a missile at U.S. soil, destroying my bar—my *life*—and killing the woman I love in the process.

He doesn't deserve to stand trial for war crimes. He doesn't deserve the justice of the world born in the wake of his endeavors.

My finger tightens on the trigger.

He deserves my justice.

"Adrian, stand down," urges Phillips. "This doesn't have to be the end for you. But I need you to be smart here. I need you to do the right thing. Stand... down!"

I can't look away from him. I'm relishing every second I spend looking into his eyes and seeing fear.

"I can't. Not now. Charlie, you made this personal. Even after everything *you've* done... all I can think about is what *I've* lost. My girlfriend, my bar, my dog—everything. Does that make me selfish? Does that make me crazy?" I shake my head to myself. "No, that makes me human. That makes me who I am. This is the only way I can think of to stop myself from eating a goddamn bullet somewhere down the line. I blame you, Charlie. Everything that's happened to me—to everyone—is on *you*. And making you stand in front of a grand jury before letting you rot in a cell is not justice. It's not what you deserve. All these SWAT guys can't protect you now. I want you to know... I want you to understand, to *believe* that you've lost. It's over. Finally. And I want you to use these last seconds to think about all the great things this world is gonna do to get back on its feet after you fucked it up."

In the corner of my eye, I see Schultz reach out to me. "Adrian, don't do this..."

I ignore him. "Can you see it, Charlie? Can you see how great we'll become?"

"No!" he screams. "No! This is my world! My dream! You have no right to take this away from me! You can't—"

I pull the trigger.

A crimson cloud bursts into the air as the body of the president—sorry, *former* president—drops to the floor with a loud thud.

I stare down at his corpse, watching the blood pool and stain the carpet. "Fuck you."

The silence that follows lasts only a few seconds. The SWAT team swarms the desk, grabs me, and forces the gun from my hand. They press my head down against the surface of the Resolute desk and secure my hands behind me with plastic ties.

With a gloved hand on my face holding me still, I look up at Schultz. He's staring at me in shock, his jaw hanging loose.

I look him in the eye. "I acted alone, Ryan. Do you hear me? I did this all on my own, and the fucker deserved it."

33

ADRIAN HELL

I'm sitting on the floor of my eight-by-eight holding cell, resting against the back wall and staring blankly ahead of me, through the bars. There's a fold-down bed attached to the wall on my right. Overhead, a single light bulb flickers dimly.

It's been a long twenty-four hours. No one else is around. I haven't seen anyone in a while. I doubt they'll put any regular prisoners in here with me. Not after what I've done.

The way I see it, in the end, I had no choice. Cunningham had to pay for what he had done. On top of all the atrocities he masterminded, he killed Tori. He blew up the entire town of Devil's Spring and most of Texas to do it. I just know he would've found some way of beating the system, so killing him was the only way I could guarantee justice.

I have to admit, speaking as a professional, I'm a little proud of the fact I managed to carry out what many in this game would class as the impossible kill. I had a lot of help, I know, but still... I pulled it off.

That said, look where it's gotten me. They don't put people like me in prison for long. They put people like me in a chair. Any feeling of victory will be short-lived. *Very* short-lived, I suspect.

The people who know the truth have already made their apologies, which were gestures that offered little comfort, although I appreciated them all the same. But regardless of the circumstances, which I know they'll do their best to keep out of the public record, the bottom line is that I shot and killed the president. In the Oval Office. In front of almost thirty witnesses.

I'm not expecting any favors from the new president, either. Schultz will have to show the world that America has its house in order. I understand that, and I don't hold what he'll have to do against him.

I'm just glad I was able to keep Josh away from it all. I've left him my fortune. Dollars won't be worth much where I'm going.

There's a rattling of keys outside. I look up and see a security guard fumbling hurriedly to unlock the door. Behind him, eight of his friends are standing in line, alert and armed, staring at me like I've taken a shit on their front lawns.

Maybe this is it? No trial, no fuss, no wait—straight to the executioner. Can't say I blame them. They can do away with me quietly and then spin whatever story they want afterward.

The guard pulls the door open and takes a step inside. "On your feet. You've got a visitor."

A visitor, eh?

I stand casually and lean against the back wall. A man `

strides into view, his steps patient and deliberate. He's wearing a brilliant white suit with a black shirt and white tie. He's got the shiniest pair of black shoes I've ever seen. He looks like a walking negative.

His heels click as he stops and turns to look at me. He glances at the guard. "You can leave us. I'll be fine."

His voice is like a whisper, yet I can hear every word with frightening clarity.

The guard shuts the door and steps a respectful distance away. The guy is standing silently, staring impassively at me.

I look him up and down. "So, Colonel Sanders, what can I do for you? Bit snazzy for a state-appointed lawyer, aren't you?"

He must know who I am, yet he's standing here almost like *I* should be afraid of *him*. The man's face shows no emotion whatsoever. His green eyes are dead, and the coarse, loose skin around his cheeks is the only thing giving any indication of his age.

Silence.

"Adrian. It's an honor to meet you."

"I'm sure it is."

"I have waited... many years for the moment to arrive when I could stand before you."

Say what now?

I fight the urge to respond, despite being confused.

"We've been watching you, monitoring how you progress. How you... *evolve*."

Okay, I'll bite.

"Who are you? And what do you mean you've been watching me?"

"Killing the president of the United States... that's an impressive feat."

I wave my hand dismissively. "Well, I'm not one to blow my own trumpet or anything, but... y'know... *toot*."

I smile, but he says nothing. His eyebrow rises with an almost imperceptible twitch, but that's all he gives me.

"Adrian, are you aware of what will happen to you now?"

I stare at the ceiling and exhale slowly, like I'm giving it some real thought. "Oh, I dunno... a cold beer and floor seats to a Lakers game?"

The man sighs, which I take as a sign he's growing impatient. "Not quite. In approximately eighteen hours, you will be sentenced to death via lethal injection."

"Huh. Well, *that's* gonna suck. Hang on—how do you know?"

"I know lots of things, Adrian. I represent an organization who hires people with certain... skill sets. My employers then invest considerable amounts of money to help those individuals perfect those skill sets. Tell me, have you ever heard of the Order of Sabbah?"

My eyes widen involuntarily. I'm trying to hide that I've been caught off guard and am shocked, but I can't.

The Order...

They're like an urban legend among assassins. They're an organization that allegedly stretches back thousands of years and is made up of the greatest killers the world has ever seen. It's a load of bullshit if you ask me, but every now and then, I hear a rumor about someone disappearing or turning up to a job to find it's mysteriously been taken care of. No one reads too much into it, as those examples can usually be explained. But in the same way devout Catholics use God as the answer to almost any scientific question that doesn't have a logical explanation, many of my fellow assassins like to use the Order of Sabbah as the explanation for anything out of the ordinary.

"Is this a joke?" I ask finally. "You turn up and tell me I have less than a day to live and then expect me to believe you work for some silly ghost story?"

The man smiles humorlessly, like he's seen the same reaction a thousand times before. "I assure you, Adrian, the Order is no ghost story. We are very real, and we believe you are ready to join the elite of your profession."

I shake my head. "I hate to burst your bubble, but I already am the *elite of my profession*. I'm—"

"You're good. There's no denying that. But you could be so much more... with the right guidance. I am here to present you with the opportunity to join our ranks. To become that ghost story, as you put it."

"You've got to be fucking kidding me. You just told me I'm gonna die tomorrow."

"If you remain here... yes, you will."

"Ah, I see. But if I just walk out the front door holding your hand, you'll take me some place far, far away, right?"

"I can save you, if that's what you're implying."

This guy's a basket case. But for no other reason besides having nothing better to do on the last day of my life, I'll humor him.

I shrug. "Okay, lay it on me, then. What's the catch?"

The guy looks at me thoughtfully. He slightly curls the corner of his mouth the way people do when they're trying to hold back a smug smile because they've just proved someone wrong or won a bet.

"The catch, if you wish to call it that, is that we'll kill you."

"Hmm... I'm failing to see the benefits. I'll be honest."

He shakes his head. "You will be pronounced dead as a result of your not-so-public execution. You will officially cease to be, leaving you free to do whatever you want. Or, more specifically, whatever *we* want. No one can track you because all they would ever find are records of your death."

"And how, exactly, do I trust you to do this?"

"You don't. And Adrian, if you honestly thought you could, then I'm afraid we've made a mistake, and I'll leave you to the last day of your—"

I hold my hands up. "All right, all right. So, what—you fake my death and then I'm part of the team?"

The man nods. "It's along those lines, yes. But I need your decision right now. And you need to realize you will be *dead*, Adrian. Officially. Which means you will no longer be able to contact anyone in your life. The world must believe you no longer exist."

I let out a heavy sigh and move over to the pull-down bed, which I lower and sit on.

This is crazy!

I'll be dead. Josh will think I'm dead. Can I really put him through that just to save my own ass?

The man checks his watch. "Tick tock, Adrian."

I look up at him. "Hey, don't rush me! This is a lot to think about, all right?"

"Big choices are never easy to make."

I shake my head and resume staring at the floor.

Fake my own death and join the Order of Sabbah? That's insane. And I'm still not even sure I believe this guy. I can only compare it to someone turning up at your front door and telling you that they're an angel. To have something that has been forever shrouded in mystery and myth suddenly proven to you is... well, it's a lot to get your head around.

The Order.

Fuck.

I sigh and look across at the man in white, who's staring at me, watching me struggle to decide.

I would never see or speak to Josh again. I'm sure he's working his ass off to get me out of here. But what if he can't? I'm not afraid to die, but that doesn't mean I'm ready to.

The Order is an assassin's fairy tale, right? I mean, no one *actually* believes an organization comprised of the best killers in history really exists. What did those stories say? That they shape humanity's future by removing people they think will have a negative impact on the world, or something like that.

Sounds like bullshit.

But then, what have I got to lose? I say no, I'm dead. I say yes and I'm wrong, I'm dead. I say yes and this guy's on the level, then I stay alive, but the world will *think* I'm dead.

And how the hell is he going to do that, anyway? I know you can get pills and things to make you ill. Is that his plan? Make me sick, get me to a hospital, and then—I don't know —switch my body with a fresh corpse, maybe? Fake a car crash on the way there? What? I have no idea...

Christ.

And I don't know what's worse—dying, or allowing Josh to *believe* I'm dead when I'm not. I don't think I can do that to him. He's like my brother. He's been there—

"Time's up," says the man, moving toward the door. "What's your decision? Become a legend or greet death?"

I stare into his blank green eyes. Outside my cell, I hear the rattling of keys again as the guard approaches.

He places a hand on the bars of the door. "Last chance, Adrian..."

I tense my jaw muscles and stand. I take a deep breath, hold it for a moment, and then let it out in a slow sigh. I close my eyes.

I must be crazy...

He turns to leave.

"Okay, wait. I'll—"

He stops and looks at me. "I'm sorry, Adrian. But you were too slow. My offer has expired. If you're so unsure about the decision, the Order probably isn't right for you. And vice versa."

"What? Hey, wait a goddamn minute. You said—"

"I said your time was up." He turns to face the door again. "Guard?"

The security guard from before reappears and opens the door. The man in white steps out and to the side so that the door can be closed again behind him.

He looks at me through the bars. "I'm sorry, Adrian. It's a real waste of potential. But you should've been more committed to the idea. You know what they say: hesitation can get you killed."

He smiles and walks away, disappearing from view. I'm left standing, lost for words and a little confused, facing the row of armed security personnel assigned to watch me in my final hours.

I shake my head. "Sonofabitch."

34

ADRIAN HELL

I haven't slept. I'm about to sleep forever, so I didn't want to waste my final hours of life with my eyes closed. I'm just sitting on my fold-down bed, staring at the floor.

I sigh heavily. This is really, *really* shit. I always figured I would go out in the proverbial blaze of glory. A gunfight or a fistfight—something with a bit of dignity. But instead, I'm about to be strapped to a chair and killed by a three-inch needle.

It's actually a little humiliating.

I've been playing in my mind over and over again what that walking negative said to me yesterday, about how I was good but could be better with training. What's he talking about? I don't mean to sound... Y'know what? Screw it. I don't care if I *do* sound bigheaded. I'm about to die. I am the *best* fucking assassin on this planet. I know that. I *believe* that. I don't need the approval of some prick with poor taste in clothing.

But it would've been nice if he had given me ten more seconds to mull over the biggest decision I've ever had to make. And I was going to take him up on his offer too. I know that probably makes me look like a dick—choosing to put Josh through the grief of believing I'm dead. As it turns out, I'm going to do that anyway. I just won't be around to feel bad about it.

I hear a door opening somewhere outside my holding cell, away to the left, out of sight. The sound of multiple footsteps gradually gets louder on the tiled floor. After a few moments, ten armed security personnel appear. They're wearing ski masks and holding assault rifles, safeties off, fingers hovering over the trigger.

"On your feet," says one of them, taking a step forward.

I stand begrudgingly. "Don't I get, like, a last meal or something?"

The door opens and he steps inside. The men behind him arrange themselves into a trained formation.

"Let's go," he says. "Nice and easy."

I hold my hands to the sides and shrug. "Not much point putting up a fight now, is there?"

I step out, and the other guards swarm around me, their weapons trained on me from all angles. The first guy follows me and moves to the front of the pack. He starts walking and we follow.

I have no idea which facility I've been taken to. It won't exist, anyway. It'll be some off-the-books CIA black site somewhere obscure. There are no windows—certainly not in the parts of the building I've seen. It's all artificially lit and has a fresh smell, like it's recently been opened or renovated.

We're walking along a seemingly endless network of narrow corridors. There are rooms periodically on both sides, but I've seen no one else here. After a few minutes, we stop outside two large swinging doors, like those in an operating room.

The guard turns to me. "Wait here." He disappears inside.

I look around casually, examining the building with a professional eye, searching for a weak spot or something I can use. Maybe I *can* try to escape. I reckon I could take out at least half of these assholes around me before they realize what's happening. Steal a gun, shoot them all, make a break for it. I get lucky, maybe I get away. I don't, I die from a thousand bullets. A blaze of glory.

I smile to myself. Who am I kidding? I can't be bothered. Not anymore. I've done a lot of bad things in my time. And I like to think I've done some good too. Question my methods all you want, but by killing President Cunningham, I did this world a massive service.

I guess I'm exactly where I should be. Where I deserve to be. I don't like it, but I'm coming to terms with the finality of the situation. I've passed the point of no return here. Whatever I do from this moment on, I know I'm going to die. Apart from Josh, there's no one left for me in this world. Not anymore.

I've tried not to think about Tori. Or the sheriff. Or anyone else I knew back in Devil's Spring. That place was my home. This might sound heartless and selfish, but I don't want to spend my last hours wallowing and thinking about loss and death. If I allowed the emotions to run free in my mind, I'd be crushed... distraught with grief. I don't want to die feeling that way.

The guard reappears. "They're ready."

The huddle disperses, forming a loose U-shape around the doors.

I crack my neck, stretch my arms and back, and take a long, deep breath. I look around the formation. "Thanks, fellas. Good job all around. No hard feelings, okay?"

No one responds. That's fine. I didn't expect them to, really. Just wanted to be polite.

I push open the doors and step inside a white, clean, air-conditioned room. I hear one of the guards follow me through, but I don't bother looking around at him. In front of me is one horrible-looking chair. My God! It looks like it belongs to a dental surgeon with a bondage fetish. There's a stand on either side, one of which has tubing that leads into a hole in the wall. The room next-door will be where the drugs are, I guess.

One wall is covered by a large, floor-to-ceiling curtain, which is currently drawn. I wonder if there's much of an audience on the other side...

There are three people present in the room. One looks like a doctor, and the other two look like guards. All three are wearing plain, white uniforms and disinterested expressions.

One of the guards, a youngish guy with ginger hair and a scraggly beard, looks at me. "Step forward."

I move over to the chair.

"Sit."

I do, shifting in the seat until I'm reasonably comfortable. I place my arms in the rests on either side. The second man in white moves to my side. Along with the first guy, they secure me to the chair.

I instinctively try to pull my arms free, testing the restraints.

Yeah... I'm not going anywhere.

They step aside, and the doctor moves next to me. He runs an alcohol swab over my arm. Courteous but slightly irrelevant at this stage, I think. They're about to kill me, yet they're making sure I don't get any last-minute infections...

Fuck me.

He inserts an IV line into my arm, then connects it to an adapter linked to a second line, which disappears into the wall. The doctor nods once, somewhat regretfully, then moves over to the back of the room. The ginger guard walks toward the curtain and pulls a cord, drawing it back to reveal a large glass window. On the other side is a small viewing area.

My eyes widen a little in surprise. I didn't expect to see anyone, but it appears this little event is a sellout. President Schultz is sitting front and center, with Elaine Phillips by his side. He looks genuinely reluctant to be here, and when we lock eyes, his expression portrays an apology.

I don't recognize anyone else, but I'm sure they're all important.

The guard next to me takes a step forward. "Adrian Hughes, you have been sentenced to death by lethal injection for the crimes of murder in the first degree and treason."

The doctor moves next to me again on the other side and clears his throat. I turn to look at him. "You will receive three injections," he says. "The first will be sodium thiopental. This will act as an anesthetic, making this as painless as possible for you. The second will be pancuronium bromide, which is a muscle relaxant to induce paralysis. And finally, potassium chloride, which will overload your heart, speeding it up until it simply stops beating altogether. Do you... have any questions?"

That was technical.

I'll be honest. Hearing exactly what is going to happen to me like that made it all real. I have no issue admitting that at this precise moment, I'm scared. I can count on one hand the number of times in my life I've known genuine fear. This is definitely one of them. I close my eyes and take a deep breath, trying to calm myself.

I look back at the doctor. "No questions. Hell, I don't even have a sarcastic comment, and that's really not like me."

He smiles briefly and places a hand on my shoulder. "Go with the grace of God, sir."

He leaves the room without another word.

The guard nearest to me turns. "Do you have any last words?"

I think about it for a moment. I gaze at the room full of onlookers. I meet Schultz's gaze again. He looks a little worried. But I won't embarrass him. I've never really liked the guy, but he's always had my back in his own way.

I smile to myself. "Last words? I didn't really have time to prepare a big speech or anything..." I take another deep breath and survey the crowd. "Okay, here's the thing. I was a soldier. I served my country well. Then I worked for the government, and I did that pretty well too. I did questionable things for a greater good and did so willingly. Then I retired and turned my hand to contract killing. Now that... *that* I was really good at. I was the best. I guess that makes me a bad person. So be it. I'm not looking for forgiveness. I'm not trying to justify my actions to anyone. But when you look at the people I took out over the years, each and every one of them was a certified piece of shit. Every... single... one. I know people have to do what they have to do. For my part, I'm sorry I couldn't do more. I just hope... I hope the world recovers. Genuinely, I do. And for the record... Cunningham? I'm just sorry I didn't kill the bastard sooner."

I glance up at the guy next to me. "Do what you gotta do, kid. I'm done talking."

He exchanges a glance with his colleague and nods. They both leave the room. The door slams shut, echoing in the remaining emptiness. A few moments later, my chair starts to rise. It tilts forward a little, giving everyone a nice view.

I take a couple of deep breaths, tensing my jaw muscles repeatedly as I fight to suppress the fear inside me. It's a strange yet somewhat liberating sensation, knowing this is it. I'm about to die.

I think about everything I've done and accomplished. If there *is* an afterlife, I suspect I'll be heading down, not up. But at least I can hold my head high. I have no regrets. I feel sorry for Josh. He's the only thing that meant something to me that I never lost. It sucks that I'm going to cause him grief.

I let out a heavy sigh. Not much I can do about that now, is there?

A few moments pass.

Things are flowing down the IV into my arm.

Whoa, I'm starting to feel a little drowsy already...

Must be the anesthetic...

My eyes are...

Damn, they're getting... heavier by the... second...

I look around... the room...

Schultz looks like he's... about to hurl...

Heh... pussy! He'll be a... a good president...

There's movement... on my... on my right...

Holy shit... the second needle... must be kick... kicking in...

I can... barely... lift... my head.

More movement...

Is that...
Looks like...
Ah!
Third... needle...
Oh... my... God! It hurts!
Crushing me... inside...
Tastes... like... shit! Tastes... bitter...
Bright light... moving to... the right... window...
No... not a... light...
A man... bright... white suit...
Are... the guards... back?
No... it's...
Looks like... Colonel... Sanders...
Come to... watch...
The sick... bastard...
I gasp...
I... breathe in...
The pain... it's... too much!
Head... heavy...
He's... staring... at me...
Ah!
Shit!
Oh... my... God!
Feels like... I'm running...
My heart... it's going so... fast... *too* fast...
Man in white... smiling...
Oh... shit! My heart... it's...
I'm going to...
I can't—

THE END

Dear Reader,

Thank you for purchasing my book. I hope you enjoyed reading it as much as I enjoyed writing it!

If you did, it would mean a lot to me if you could spare thirty seconds to leave an honest review on your preferred online store. For independent authors like me, one review makes a world of difference.

If you want to get in touch, please visit my website, where you can contact me directly, either via e-mail or social media.

Until next time...

James P. Sumner

CLAIM YOUR FREE GIFT!

By subscribing to James P. Sumner's mailing list, you can get your hands on a free and exclusive reading companion, not available anywhere else.

It contains an extended preview of Book 1 in each thriller series from the author, as well as character bios, and official reading orders that will enhance your overall experience.

If you wish to claim your free gift, just visit the website below:

linktr.ee/jamespsumner

You will receive infrequent, spam-free emails from the author, containing exclusive news about his books. You can unsubscribe at any time.

Made in the USA
Columbia, SC
08 August 2023